LOKI

WHERE MISCHIEF LIES

MACKENZI LEE

D1078337

AUTUMN
PUBLISHING

Published in 2021
First published in the UK by Autumn Publishing
An imprint of Igloo Books Ltd
Cottage Farm, NN6 0BJ, UK
Owned by Bonnier Books
Sveavägen 56, Stockholm, Sweden
www.igloobooks.com

© 2019 MARVEL

0921 005
6 8 10 12 11 9 7 5
ISBN 978-1-78905-621-1

Printed and manufactured in Italy

For Becca, an unstoppable force
for good in my universe

Part One

Chapter One

*T*he Royal Feast of Gullveig, like all Asgardian feast days, was enjoyable for those who were fond of listening to overly long speeches, exchanging inane niceties and getting their feet stepped on, because the Great Hall was always too crowded and no one knew how to walk in heels.

Loki was convinced everyone loathed the feasts but no one dared say so for fear of appearing small-minded. Being quite confident of the size of his mind – large – *and* his ability to walk in heels, he was comfortable saying it.

"I hate feast days."

In the royal receiving line beside him, Thor didn't drop the politician's smile he had been practising for state occasions like this. It had only faltered when Loki had suggested showing that much teeth made it very obvious there was something stuck in them, and he had fumbled with his tongue for several minutes – lips bulging in a grotesque way that made several approaching courtiers change course – before realising there was nothing there.

"The feasts are important days," Thor said. "They instil competence in Asgard's leaders among our court."

"Confidence," Loki corrected.

The smile didn't slip, but Thor's eyebrows crept together. "What?"

"I memorised the same quote," Loki replied. "It's *confidence.*"

"What did I say?"

"You— Never mind." Loki fixed his own overly large smile, raising his voice so Thor could hear him over the musicians playing a lively folk song. "You did it perfectly."

Thor adjusted the circlet resting on his forehead. Beads of sweat were beginning to gather around it, and it was slipping over his brows. Loki had been offered a circlet as well – his mother had selected a silver braid inlaid with small gemstones for him. But while Loki loved few things as much as a bit of sparkle, he had opted instead for a more sophisticated, understated look that the circlet would have ruined entirely. He didn't have to enjoy feast days, but he could look good for them. The boots made him feel like doing a strut down the middle of the hall – black, over the knee and with heels as long and thin as the knives he kept up his sleeves. His coat had a high collar and green ribbing on the shoulders, and he wore loose trousers of the same colour. Amora had told him green made his eyes look like jewels, but he had been careful not to wear it too often. Best not to let Amora think he was taking her advice too seriously. She might have always been right, but she didn't have to know that.

Loki glanced down the line of dignitaries, past Thor and Frigga in her flowing silver robes, hands tucked beneath the sleeves as she smiled and nodded to the Asgardian woman fumbling a compliment about how lovely the queen's hair looked with its streaks of grey. On her other side were the ambassadors from Varinheim and Ringsfjord, talking with their heads bent towards Queen Jolena, who kept asking loudly if they could speak up. Past them, Karnilla, the Queen of Norns and Odin's royal sorceress, stood like a soldier, the plaits of her dark hair wound together and wrapped round a gold headpiece with a purple stone set upon her brow. Her face was blank – in the time she'd been at court, Loki had never seen her wear any expression beyond a dutiful grimace of acknowledgment. One of her long-fingered hands rested on Amora's shoulder, like she was certain her apprentice would slip away if a hold wasn't kept on her.

It wasn't outside the realms of possibility.

Amora was looking far more obviously bored than Loki felt she should. Far more bored than he was sure he could get away with without a lecture from his father. She may get one from Karnilla too, but Amora seemed to care so much less about what her teacher thought than Loki did about Odin's opinions. He wished he could afford not to care, not to feel like everything he did right or wrong was ticked off in a corresponding column and kept on file for the day Odin would name either him or Thor as the heir to the Asgardian crown. It would be so much easier if there were only one of him – Amora was the only student Karnilla had ever taken on and the only magic wielder in Asgard powerful enough to take up the mantle of royal sorceress and Queen of the Norns. Amora's power made her desired; Loki's power made him feel the need to keep it hidden.

No one wanted a sorcerer for a king. The kings of Asgard were warriors. They wore their golden hair long and their armour polished and their scars from battle casually

on display like ostentatious accessories. *Oh, this old thing?*
Merely a token from a rogue Sakaaran who was foolish enough
to test his strength against mine.

Amora managed to wriggle away from Karnilla's side
long enough to snatch a goblet off the tray of a passing
kitchen servant, and Loki watched as she touched one finger
to the surface and levitated a small drop from it. It hung in
mid-air, a few inches from her palm, until Karnilla reached
over without looking and clamped a hand over Amora's,
squashing the spell. Amora rolled her eyes, then, perhaps
sensing the inappropriate duration of Loki's gaze, glanced
around. She caught his eye, and offered her crooked finger
of a smile. Loki felt his ears go red, and he almost looked
away, like that would negate the fact that she'd caught him
staring. Instead he offered her an exasperated eye-widening,
to which she responded by pantomiming hanging herself.

He snorted. Thor frowned at him, then followed his
gaze, but Amora had straightened herself out again, smiling
alongside Karnilla at the courtier who had come to speak
to them. She seemed to be putting a great deal of effort into
making her smile look as forced as possible – as much as
Thor had been putting into making his look sincere – but
she was smiling, so no one could accuse her of a contrary
disposition.

Thor's frown went deeper, burying his circlet farther into his brow, and he pushed it up before turning forwards with a huff that sounded like an imitation of their father.

When Loki caught Amora's eye again, she made a subtle gesture down at the tiles and raised her eyebrows.

Loki hesitated. Carrying out the small spells she taught him at a dinner or in their classroom was one thing, but doing it at a state function was quite another. It would be harmless – turning the tiles of the Great Hall pink had been his idea, after all. But he had suggested it half in jest, hoping he would impress her with the boldness of the idea and creative use of spell weaving without actually having to execute it.

But Amora had to see everything through to the end. Everything that could be tried had to be, no matter the consequences. And there were always consequences, whether a whack on the back of the head from a wearied tutor or a private summons to Karnilla's chambers.

Amora did it all anyway.

Loki felt the burn of jealousy at her fearlessness – the way she didn't seem to feel any shame when Odin or Karnilla scolded her. His own heart always twisted no matter how high he raised his chin in defiance. No matter how blameless he thought himself. Once, as a boy, Loki had used his magic to extinguish all the lights in the palace simultaneously. He was baffled when Odin had not been delighted and proud as he expected, but rather so enraged Loki had feared his father might strike him. Instead, Loki was sent to his chambers to sit in isolation, and he was wriggled with a shame he didn't understand. His mother finally came and explained that it would be best if he did not use the magic he could feel vibrating through his bones, but instead dedicated himself to becoming a warrior like his brother. It would be best, she had said, for his future. She had spoken gently – it was the only way his mother ever spoke – but the humiliation of that moment had never managed to detach itself from every spell he cast.

Though he had done very little spell-casting until Amora arrived in court. He had tried to make himself a warrior, tried to run faster and train harder, learn to take a blow without buckling. All the things Thor seemed to do without trying, the skills they had been told were most becoming of a future king of Asgard, while Loki's only skill seemed to be turning the mead in his brother's goblet into slugs once he began to drink, and then back into wine when he spat it out.

It wasn't the best strategy for dealing with emotions, but it was *his* strategy.

Chapter One

The slug trick was what first caught Amora's attention. When Thor had spluttered his mead across the table, Odin had berated him for his poor manners in front of their guests, the Norn Queen, Karnilla, and her apprentice, Amora, on their first night in the Asgardian palace. As Thor had insisted over and over that there were slugs, there had been slugs, he was certain there had been slugs, Loki's gaze had drifted across the table to Amora without knowing why, only to find she was already watching him. The corners of her mouth had turned up around her fork. But then she looked away, and he had gone back to staring at his stew.

He had told himself the slugs were to get his brother back for knocking him flat in the sparring ring that morning in spite of promising not to – a promise that had been quickly forgotten once he realised Sif was watching. It wasn't because Amora was a magician – the first other magic-wielder he'd ever met besides his mother, whose uses of magic were always small and controlled. *Tea party magic*, as Loki had begun to think of it. Frigga had always worked to keep her powers out of sight, and encouraged Loki to do the same. But Amora was allowed to wear *her* powers on her sleeve and flaunt them as part of her training for her future position in court. It wasn't because her long hair was the colour of honey and she wore it wrapped round her head in an endless loop that looked like snakes winding together. It wasn't because of those slanted features or that crooked smile.

What did you expect? He chided himself as he poked at a chunk of meat, watching it bounce back to the thick, oily surface. *For her to be thrilled about finding another magic-wielder in Asgard?* A magician who had never been taught to control his powers, which meant they usually escaped in inelegant, clumsy stunts he was struggling to teach himself?

The slugs had been good, though.

His gaze drifted again to Amora, but her dark eyes – black but for a few thin veins of emerald that forked through them like an acidic lightning storm – were on Karnilla. As she listened to Karnilla and Odin discuss the upcoming tutelage Amora would be given at court before the Feast of Gullveig and how it would prepare her for her future role as right hand to one of Odin's sons, Loki felt small and strange again, not worthy of notice by someone he had thought might resemble himself.

But at the end of the meal, when he finished his wine, he'd found a small snail at the bottom, writhing lethargically in the dregs. He'd looked up, but Amora was already gone, leaving him with that single disgusting calling card.

Chapter One

"The slug trick is clever," she told him later, when he found her in the palace library, curled into the bench of one of the circular windows that overlooked the gardens. She had a stack of books at her feet that he was certain she had selected only for aesthetic effect. "But what if you waited to change them until just as he was swallowing? It's far more horrifying to swallow a mouthful of slugs than to spit one out all over the table, don't you think?"

Loki hadn't thought of that. He also wasn't certain he had enough control of his own magical powers to time a spell so perfectly.

When he didn't say anything, Amora's eyes flicked up from the page of the book she had open on her lap, and he was certain she knew how good aloofness looked on her. She had let her braids loose, and the tilt of her chin sent her hair cascading perfectly down her shoulders, like a carpet unfurled before the feet of a visiting king. "Who taught you how to do that?" she asked.

"No one," he replied. He had honed any skills he had alone, making his grasp of his own powers rough and rudimentary and frustratingly tenuous. He could feel the well inside him, how deep and strong it ran, but could find no way to tap it.

"I didn't know Odin's son was a sorcerer," she said.

"There's a reason for that." He wanted to sit beside her, but somehow that felt too presumptuous, a bold assumption that he was interesting enough for her to want around. Instead he went for a casual lean against one of the shelves, which he realised mid-tilt was much farther away than he had thought. "Asgardians don't want their princes to be magicians. It's not the sort of power they value."

Amora stared at him for a moment, then folded the corner of the page before shutting the book, a gesture that felt like such destruction in miniature that it made Loki want to crease the pages of every book in his father's library.

"Hasn't Odin hired someone to teach you?" she asked. "Or your mother? She's a sorceress."

"No," he said, certain he sank a few inches deeper into the carpet. "I mean, yes, she is. But my father doesn't want me to study magic."

"Because he's afraid of you."

Loki laughed before he could stop himself at the thought of Odin, built like a boulder and with a rough, smashing demeanour to match, being frightened of his own son, particularly the smaller, skinnier one. "He's not afraid of me. He just wants me to be the best contender for the throne that I can be, so he has me train with the soldiers."

Now it was Amora's turn to laugh. "That's like keeping

a warship in shallow waters. What a waste." She stroked the spine of the book, appraising him. She seemed to be made of smoke the way her body spiralled and swooped with the shape of the window sill. She had kicked off her shoes, and her bare toes curled against the stone. "You're not a soldier," she said. "You're a magician. And someone ought to teach you how to be one."

"Someone ought to," he replied.

She offered him a smile, one that felt like a dagger drawn slowly from its sheath, that dangerous hum of scraping metal in the moment of stillness that preluded a strike. Then she flipped open the book on her lap again, and his heart dropped, thinking he had been too opaque, too unreadable, too cold, all the things his brother wasn't, the things his tutors had told him not to be, the things the other trainees in the warrior camp had teased him for.

But then she slung her feet off the seat beside her and said, "Are you going to sit down?"

And he did.

That had been months ago. Months over which Loki and Amora had knit themselves into an inseparable duo that the servants whispered about and the courtiers disapproved of. Even now, in the Great Hall on a feast day, Loki felt their eyes glancing at him, trying to determine whether his partnership with Karnilla's headstrong apprentice had altered him in a way they could see.

Above him, the candles in the boat-shaped chandeliers that lined the Great Hall flickered, their light dancing along the golden leaf that blanketed the wainscoting. The shape of the ceilings had always reminded him of the inside of an instrument, bowed and curved in places designed to amplify sound and make every gathering feel bigger and more impressive. Loki peeked down at the tiles under his feet, black with streaks of gold shooting through them, carving out the elaborate intricate roots that joined to form Yggdrasil at the bottom of the grand stairway. When he met Amora's gaze again, she did an exaggerated eyelash flutter and pressed her hands together in pleading, and he knew he would set the hall on fire and then run naked through it if she asked.

"What are you plotting?" Thor muttered beside him.

"Plotting?" Loki repeated, pinning on his best smile to scare an approaching courtier away from them. "I never plot."

Thor snorted. "Please."

"Please what? Please plot?" Thor ground his foot into Loki's, and Loki bit his tongue to stifle a squeak of pain. "Careful, I love these boots more than I love you."

Thor glanced down the row again, to where Amora had put on another exaggeratedly innocent face. Thor had not taken to her the way Loki had. He had joined them on a few escapades around the palace, but always with his feet dragging, checking over his shoulder to be certain they wouldn't be caught, and repeating "I don't think we should be doing this" so often that Amora had suggested they start charging him for every repetition. Eventually he had stopped coming along, which suited Loki fine. He didn't want to share Amora with his brother. He didn't want to share her with anyone. She was all his in a way no one had ever been. No one had ever wanted to be. And it was nice to see Thor left out of conversations for once.

Thor had never offered a direct opinion on Amora. No one had – they just whispered about her behind her back the way everyone always had about Loki. Too unpredictable, too strong, shouldn't be allowed out of Nornheim, even if the king and his sorceress thought the structure and rigidity of the royal court would temper her strong will.

Suddenly, three thundering *booms* cut through the chatter ringing around the hall. The musicians silenced and the courtiers hushed, rotating towards the top of the grand stairway. Loki pivoted along with the rest of the royal officials in their receiving line and turned his face upwards, to where Odin stood, dressed in his feast day robes of claret-deep red, his spear, Gungnir, in his fist. His beard was woven with golden thread, and on his brow was a circlet in the same style as Thor's. Loki felt a twinge of regret. Perhaps he should have worn his after all, no matter that it clashed with the rest of his ensemble.

"Asgardians!" Odin boomed, his voice echoing off the curved ceiling and carrying easily through the hall. "Friends, visitors, distinguished guests from across the Nine Realms, you honour us with your presence at this, our holy Feast of Gullveig."

Loki had heard some variation on this speech at every feast day since he was a boy. It was remarkable how many heroic warriors Asgard had decided to commemorate with their own feast days, and while the food was always good, it was never worth having to stand in an awkward receiving line, getting pats on the head from courtiers, and then enduring his father's dull speech about whatever blond man with rippling biceps and an insatiable thirst for the blood of Asgardian enemies was being honoured that particular day.

But the Feast of Gullveig was different in one substantial way.

"Today," Odin continued, touching one finger to the

patch that covered his empty right eye socket as he looked around, "we celebrate the day of the warrior king who, one hundred centuries ago, harnessed the rime flows of Niflheim in the Siege of Muspelheim and from it forged the Godseye Mirror. That same Mirror has been brought up from the palace vault and, with the strength and power of our royal sorceress from Nornheim, shall grant a vision of the decade to come and the threats Asgard shall need to arm ourselves against. This is the way we keep our kingdom safe from threats from across the Nine Realms, and from Ragnarok itself. The Godseye Mirror gives no answers, and no certainty. Its eye is open for only this one day each decade, but it is the visions it reveals that have helped keep Asgard fortified and strong for centuries. At the end of this feast day, I will confer with my generals and advisors, and we will devise the best strategies for the future prosperity of our people."

Loki had learnt all of this from his history teachers in preparation for the feast – the first in his memory that the Godseye Mirror had been brought out and Karnilla had come to wield its powers – but he still pushed himself up on his toes for a better look as the curtain behind his father was drawn back by the two Einherjar soldiers.

The Godseye Mirror was a wall of shimmering black

obsidian – a perfect square set in a thin gold frame with carved gold staves curling round each corner. He had seen it before, when Odin had taken both him and Thor down to the vault below the palace and explained to them the power of each object kept there and the lengths to which he had gone to keep his people safe from it, but here, away from the dark walls and dim light of the vault and no longer surrounded by the host of artefacts Odin had captured to prevent the end of the world, it felt more imposing. More powerful. The Mirror stood straight on its own, with no feet or supports. The already silent hall seemed to sink into an even more absolute stillness.

Karnilla had ascended the stairs, and when Odin extended a hand to her, they walked together to the Mirror. He took his place on one side, she on the other, her palms pressed flat against the surface. Odin handed Gungnir to one of the Einherjar, then turned to his people again, arms extended. "To another decade of peace and prosperity in our great realm!"

Loki felt something brush his elbow, and then Amora's voice was in his ear. "So do we change the tile now, while your father is occupied, or do we want to be certain everyone sees how poorly fuchsia clashes with his robes?"

Loki's response was cut off by a crackle of energy from

the top of the stairs. He felt the hairs on his neck rise, the air suddenly feeling hot and heavy like the prelude to a lightning storm. A fork of white light erratically split the ceiling of the Great Hall. The assembled courtiers gasped, but from her spot across the Mirror from Odin, Karnilla raised a hand and the light flew to her fist, gathering around it in a cyclone. Loki felt his mouth hang open, marvelling at the elegance, the control, the way the magic moved through the air and answered her call.

He felt Amora poke him in the back. "Loki."

Karnilla opened her hand and pressed it to the obsidian surface. The staves at each corner of the Mirror glowed, the lines of each rune flaring so bright it seemed for a moment they might ignite. The surface rippled like a pond struck by a stone, and Odin's eye turned white, the images of Asgard's future flashing across the Mirror's surface unseen by anyone but him.

"I have a feeling you're not listening to me," Amora said, this time her lips so close to Loki's ear that he felt her breath.

"Quiet," Thor hissed at them from Loki's other side.

Amora pivoted to him. "Oh, I'm sorry, am I interrupting something important?"

Another crackle of light dancing across the ceiling flew to Karnilla's hand.

"Show some respect," Thor hissed through his teeth.

"Is something about my speaking disrespectful?" Amora replied.

"Yes – the fact that you are speaking at all."

Loki felt a sudden hand on his shoulder, and turned as his mother stepped between him and Amora, her gaze still fixed on Odin at the top of the grand staircase and her grip very gentle. "That's enough," she said quietly. Loki wanted to protest that he had been the only one *not* speaking over this important ceremony. But Frigga squeezed his shoulder, and he swallowed his words.

Another bolt of lightning leapt from Karnilla's hand to the surface of the Mirror, but this one was different. Loki felt a change in the air, a shift in the magic that made him shudder. His mother must have felt it too – her hand spasmed on his shoulder. Odin took an abrupt step back from the Mirror, one hand rising like he was trying to push something away. Then an audible cry escaped his lips. On the other side, Karnilla paused, hand still in the air with the threads of white light whirring in a hive around it.

Then Odin tore himself away from the Mirror, breaking the spell. The magic drained from his eye, leaving behind his dark iris flooded with panic. He stumbled, catching himself on the rail. There was a gasp from the assembled court. One of the Einherjar reached out to Odin, but the king pushed him away, snatching back his staff and heading down the stairs at a tripping gait. He may have been trying to pull himself together, but he looked frayed. Karnilla let the spell die on her fingers, the light extinguished, before she stepped out from behind the Mirror and walked down the opposite side of the stairs after Odin.

"Continue with the feast," Odin instructed the captain standing in salute at the bottom of the stairs. "I'll return shortly." He paused, and his eye swivelled, first to Thor, then to Loki, the gaze heavy and meaningful in a way that made Loki's skin crawl. Whatever vision his father had seen, Loki was suddenly certain in a way he couldn't explain that they had been a part of it.

Odin ran a hand over his beard, then flicked his fingers at Frigga, motioning for her to follow. "My queen." Loki felt his mother's hand leave his shoulder as she followed Odin from the hall, Karnilla and his sentries on his heels. The doors of the Great Hall banged behind him, and noise flooded back into the room, this time pitched and anxious.

On either side of Loki, Amora and Thor were silent, staring after Odin. All thoughts of pink tiles that shifted colours beneath the feet of the court evaporated. Instead,

Loki felt a cold pit settle in his stomach that he could not explain or banish. He had never seen fear like that on his father's face. If it even had been fear. That look had been so foreign it was impossible to recognise.

"What happened?" Thor asked at last.

"I think the question is," Amora replied, "what did he see?"

Chapter Two

*A*t the urging of the Einherjar captain whom Odin had flung leadership upon as he stumbled out, the feast was served in spite of the king's absence. The musicians began to play again, now in a minor key – or perhaps that was Loki's imagination. The energy in the hall had shifted into hushed whispers of speculation. Rumours were flying down the table before the first course had been cleared – Odin had seen his own death, he had seen Asgard surrender in battle, he had seen Ragnarok, the end of the world unfurling before him on that dark glass.

"Is Father coming back?" Thor asked for the fifth time.

He hadn't touched his meal but was using a knife to hack his vegetables into precise squares.

"When I find out, you'll be the first one I tell," Loki replied dryly.

"I'm sure it's taking him a while to devise a lie to cover up whatever it was he actually saw," Amora remarked across from him.

Thor glared at her. "Don't speak ill of my father."

"Really? That's your first concern?"

"My father does not lie."

"To be clear, was it him who told you that little tiara looked pretty on you?"

Thor's hand flew reflexively to his circlet. "No. I chose it myself."

"Well, then." Amora's lips skimmed the rim of her goblet. "Perhaps his record is clean."

"He will not lie to his people," Thor protested, thumbing the edge of his circlet. Loki could tell he was debating whether or not to remove it. "If what he saw concerns all of Asgard, he will tell the court."

"And everyone knows the first step to telling your assembled court something important is to flee the room in which they're all assembled, waiting for you to speak."

Thor's jaw set, and he turned his glare to Loki. "Do you always tolerate her speaking like this? It's nearly treasonous."

"Aw." Amora frowned in mock disappointment. "Only *nearly*?"

Loki wanted to clap his hands over his ears and shut them both out. He couldn't stop thinking about the look on his father's face, his stumble down the stairs, the way he had surveyed his sons.

"Loki," Thor said again, and Loki couldn't stand it a moment longer.

He threw his napkin onto the table and pushed his chair back. "I need some air."

Amora stood. "I'll come with you."

"I need some air *alone*," he said, and she froze, half standing. It may have been the first time he had denied her anything.

Loki slipped unnoticed from the hall using the servants' entrance he and Thor had discovered as children, hidden behind a tapestry of Valkyries extending their hands to the Asgardian warriors they were shepherding off the battlefield to Valhalla. Both the long-necked Valkyries and the broad-shouldered warriors had been the source of rather critical stirrings in his youth, but tonight Loki ignored the images as he ducked behind the tapestry and down the passageway it hid.

Amora had taught him more magic in the months she'd

been at court than he had learnt in his entire lifetime. Part of her tutelage had been lessons in what she knew about using magic to shift his form. He was still learning to mimic the finer details of Asgardian features, but this disguise did not need to be precise to be effective. The uniform of the kitchen staff would be the most critical thing to get correct, and as soon as he had the dress on his form, made in imitation of two kitchen girls who scuttled by him with their eyes downcast, his body shifted to fit it. He snagged a tray of empty goblets from a table in the passageway and ran them hastily under a keg at the end of the hall.

The form of a servant girl bringing the king and queen refreshments made him invisible in the hallways as he edged towards his father's chambers. He was almost certain that's where Odin would have fled with Karnilla and Frigga. Once he was in the room, the servant girl would likely go unnoticed enough to eavesdrop – certainly less noticed than a snake, which had been his initial plan, and which was easier to imitate than an Asgardian. But snakes tended to garner attention – Thor would pick up any serpent to admire it.

Loki opened the door to his father's chambers, only to find the staffs of the two Einherjar guarding the door crossed before him, barring his way. He pulled up short, nearly spilling his drinks in surprise. Behind the Einherjar, Loki could see his father perched on a couch in the antechamber, his back to the door, Frigga at his side. "Leave us!" he barked without turning around.

"I was sent from the kitchens, Your Majesty," Loki said, trying to pitch his voice into something girlish. His vocals still needed work. "To bring you refreshment."

"We require nothing from the kitchen," Odin snapped.

Frigga glanced over her shoulder at Loki, and he felt his face heat, though if she recognised her son, she gave no indication. "Return to the feast," she said gently. "You'll be summoned if we require anything."

Loki bowed, the long, loose tresses that all the servant girls wore immediately falling over his shoulder and dunking into the goblets he had brought. "I'll just leave them."

He could feel the eyes of the two Einherjar sentries as he slid the tray onto a table beside the door, metal scraping metal with a cringing shriek that somehow made the silence that had fallen the moment he entered even more apparent.

Loki offered the guards a shy smile, then, as though he had just noticed, said, "Oh, I brought too many."

As he reached for the fourth glass, he cast the spell.

He had never been especially proficient at two-way communication charms, though he had read they came in many varieties. The only version he knew was the one he had devised when he was young – he used a charm to connect a pot of rouge on his mother's dressing table to an inkwell in his own chambers so that he could listen to her discuss the gifts she'd be giving for that year's Solstice. For some reason he could no longer recall, it had felt absolutely essential to know what she was giving him. The spell had unravelled quickly, partly because he still had a tenuous grip on his own power, and because his and Frigga's chambers were on opposite sides of the castle, and any spell was hard to sustain over a distance. And partly because the spell ran both ways, and Frigga had noticed the talking rouge pot right away.

But now he had a slightly less tenuous grip on his own magic, and when his fingers met the stem of the goblet, he felt the spell stick. It felt so good to feel a spell land that way, like the teeth of two gears locking together and moving each other. From the couch, he thought he saw his mother stiffen, like she had felt the prickle in the air, but before she could turn, he picked up the fourth goblet, dipped a quick curtsey to the Einherjar then fled the room.

As soon as the door shut behind him, he ducked round the corner. He chugged the contents of the goblet – it made him light-headed, but he was determined to empty it as quickly as possible – before pressing it to his ear. It took a moment – the speech crackled, dipping in and out. The mug he had enchanted to connect to was still full, so it sounded as if he were underwater, listening to someone above the surface. He could barely make out his mother's words: "You don't know that."

"I saw him," he heard Odin reply. "Leading an army."

"That does not mean Ragnarok."

"Then what does it mean? What other cause—"

Someone grabbed Loki's shoulder and he nearly dropped the goblet. He whipped round, the hilt of the dagger he kept up his sleeve sliding into his free hand.

Thor was standing behind him, arms crossed. "What are you doing?"

Loki, still in the servant girl's form, bowed, attempting to subtly tuck the knife into the folds of his skirt. "Apologies, my lord, I was simply bringing the king—"

"You can cease with the theatrics, brother," Thor interrupted. "I know it's you."

"Brother?" Loki repeated, letting his bow sink so low

he could have licked the floor. "What brother is this that you speak of?"

Thor grabbed him round the wrist and held up his hand in between them, still clutching the knife. Loki scowled, then let the disguise drop. He pressed the goblet against his side, muffling any of their conversation that might leak through into his father's chambers.

"Are you spying?" Thor demanded.

"Doesn't *spying* imply some sort of visual component?"

"Then you're dropping eaves."

"Yes, that sounds much more refined." When Thor continued to glare at him, Loki sighed. "I want to know what Father saw."

"If it is our concern, he will enlighten us in time."

"If it's our concern, I'm almost certain he won't. You saw his face. The way he fled. He was expecting to see a threat to Asgard in that Mirror – what must it have been to rattle him like that?" Thor bit his lip, glancing down at the goblet. "I don't want to hear the rosy version he will present to the court. I want the truth."

"I trust he will give it to us," Thor replied.

"Fine. I hope your trust keeps you warm." He twisted his wrist out of Thor's grasp, pulling down his sleeve to cover the red streaks even his brother's mild grip had left on his pale skin, and started to lift the goblet to his ear, but Thor tugged at the back of his tunic.

"Loki. Don't."

"If you don't want to stay, begone," Loki replied, wiggling his fingers at Thor like he was flicking a piece of dust from his lapel. "No one's forcing you to stoop so low as dropping eaves."

He pressed the goblet to his ear, but before he could catch the conversation again, Thor leant next to him, pulling the goblet so that it cupped both of their ears. Loki resisted a smirk. They pressed their foreheads together, straining to hear, and Loki thought how ridiculous they would look to anyone who happened to pass this way, the two Asgardian princes, huddled and intent over an empty feast goblet.

A third voice – Karnilla's – had joined those of their parents. "—not weapons. They are amplifiers of strength. You can't think his power, even amplified, would be enough to end your realm."

"I do not know what he is capable of," Odin replied. "That is what frightens me."

"Stop breathing so loud," Loki hissed to Thor. His brother was huffing like he was trying to put out a fire.

"This is how I breathe," Thor replied.

"Then stop breathing," Loki said through gritted teeth. "They can hear us too, you know."

"Then stop talking," Thor scolded, loud enough that Loki threw a hand over the mouth of the goblet. He glanced behind him to his father's chamber door, waiting to see if it would open, if one of the Einherjar would be sent to investigate the source of the mysterious goblet arguing with itself.

Nothing happened.

Loki raised the goblet again, and Thor made a show of taking a deep breath without making a sound, and they both leant in.

"Perhaps the Mirror was wrong," Frigga was saying. "You said it yourself in the Great Hall – there is no certainty in any vision of the future, even one offered by powerful magic."

"It has never been wrong, in the history of our people," Odin replied. "Perhaps it could be, or perhaps that is simply something the kings have always said to protect their choices, but it never has been wrong. Everything a king of Asgard has seen in the Godseye Mirror has come to pass. It alerted me to the impending war with the Frost Giants. We survived that conflict only because of the increased fortifications we built in preparation. It's a tool of warning, not of flighty predictions that might perhaps come to pass. If the Mirror shows him leading an army of the living dead against our people, then that is the threat we must prepare for."

"You do not need to raise your voice to me," Frigga said, and Loki realised his father must have been shouting. It was hard to tell through the mead. "How do you propose we prepare for this threat? Would you have him punished because of something he may do wrong in the future? You'd have to lock up your whole court if that were the standard for imprisonment."

There was a pause, so long that Loki was concerned his spell had fallen apart, but then he heard Karnilla say, "We will increase the protections around the Norn Stones."

"That's not enough," Odin replied.

"The loss of the Stones would not—" Frigga began, but his father interrupted.

"The Norn Stones in the wrong hands could mean the end of Asgard."

"And you think those wrong hands belong to our son?" Frigga asked.

Silence. Loki felt his pulse throbbing, so loud he wasn't sure he'd be able to hear his father over it when he spoke again. His chest suddenly felt corked and impossible to breathe through. Beside him, Thor stiffened, his shoulders rising into a stance that Loki knew from facing him in the sparring ring. Thor was ready to fight, though what for, he wasn't sure yet.

Say it, Loki thought. *Say which of your sons will lead an army against Asgard. Which of us will be the one on the wrong side of Ragnarok.*

"We should return to the feast," Frigga said at last. "Your people will be looking to their king for guidance. And an explanation for your abrupt exit. Not for news of the end of the world."

Loki felt Thor grab him by the back of the tunic and tug him down the hallway, away from their father's chambers and through an open doorway, out of sight. The goblet fell from his hand, clattering to the tiled floor.

Thor had dragged them into a chapel dedicated to the All-Mothers, the one Odin used to offer prayers alone before battle. It was small, and the golden light spilling through the windows made the wooden vaults look syrupy and warm. Along the beams were carved scenes of the serpent's rampage and the All-Mothers ascending to their thrones, the varnish old and seeping so that the edges looked dewy.

Thor sank down on one of the carved benches, in

front of a mural of Gaea the Compassionate with her arms at her sides, hands turned out. Loki took the spot across the aisle from him, the hard angle of the bench making his back ache almost instantly. Thor sank into a slump, hands pressed into his forehead, but Loki sat rigid, staring at Gaea, the tip of her chin, the lowered eyes, her thin lips parted in supplication.

Thor spoke first. "Father saw one of us leading an army against Asgard."

"Yes, I remember," Loki replied, still staring at Gaea. "I was there, you know."

"One of *us*—"

"I believe the phrase was one of his *sons*, so perhaps the real question is does Odin have a secret family hidden in a palace tower plotting to slit our throats?"

Thor sat up, crossing his arms as he swivelled to face Loki across the aisle. "You wish to argue semantics with me, brother?"

"Only if you can spell *semantics*."

"Don't mock me."

"I wouldn't dare," Loki replied, still staring at Gaea's hands. Penitent. Submissive. Weak. "It might bring on the end of the world."

Thor slammed his fist against the back of the bench in

front of him, and it jumped, clattering against the stone floor. "Is this all a jest to you?"

Loki flicked his eyes across the aisle to Thor. "I think the very fact that you're so concerned proves that you're not the one who will be leading the army."

"What do you mean?" Thor asked.

"I think that if you were to take a poll of random Asgardians and ask them which of us was more likely to rebel against his father, I'd win with flying colours." Loki laughed hollowly, brushing a splinter from the pew off his trousers. "Perhaps the first contest I'll ever best you in."

"And that doesn't concern you?" Thor asked.

Loki shrugged. "Well, now that I know what father's seen, if I ever find myself standing at the head of an army, I will stop, reconsider and, oh, you know, not do that."

"But what if in trying to stop it you make it come to pass?" Thor asked.

Loki frowned. "You think what father saw is inevitable?"

"The Godseye Mirror has never been wrong in the history of Asgard," Thor replied. "It warns of dangers to come. They always come." He turned abruptly forwards again, pressing his fist to his forehead, then pivoted back to Loki. "Perhaps father doesn't know which of us it is."

"We *are* so very easy to mistake for each other," Loki said. "Perhaps I'm wrong – leading an army does sound much more like you. I prefer to be on the sidelines with a snack." He tapped his heel against the floor of the aisle. "And I would never risk these boots in battle."

Thor pressed his elbows to his knees, his head dropping against his clenched hands. "Does this truly matter so little to you?" His voice was softer than Loki was accustomed to hearing it, and it stilled him.

"Nothing is little to me," Loki replied, then stood, his heel catching in a rut between two stones.

"Where are you going?" Thor called after him as he righted himself and headed down the aisle.

"I need to talk to Amora."

"Do you think that's a good idea right now?" Thor asked.

Loki paused, nearly at the door, and considered pretending he hadn't heard. Thor was trying to provoke him. To get him to turn back. And he always tried his best not to give his brother what he wanted.

But he turned. Thor had stood too, one hand resting on the end of the pew.

"What do you mean by that?" Loki demanded.

Thor's gaze flicked down to the stone, then back to Loki. "I don't think she's a good influence upon you."

"Say that again, but this time cover one eye, and I'd swear you were Father."

"I'm not jesting."

"No, I'm sure you're not." He tried to keep his voice even, but the sting gave his words a hard edge. It wasn't like he had many options for friends. Thor and his fellow warriors-in-training had made it clear they didn't want anything to do with Loki, like his lack of muscle mass might be catching if they stood too close. "You're just jealous," he countered, though even as the words left his mouth, he knew how silly they sounded. How desperate.

"Jealous of what?" Thor asked.

"I don't know, but I'll think of something." He should have left then, but instead he took a step back into the chapel, towards Thor. "It's none of your concern whom I pass my days with."

"Of course it is," Thor replied. "You're my brother."

"Then should I be concerned about all your long nights in the sparring ring with Sif?" Loki challenged.

Thor's cheeks coloured. "That's different. She's helping me with my..."

"Your what?" Loki cocked one eyebrow, a gesture he would never admit to Thor that he had practised in front of the mirror in his chambers for hours to ensure he could execute it perfectly when needed. "Flexibility?"

"And what is Amora helping you with?" Thor snapped. "Teaching you how to be a witch like she is?"

"She's not a witch," Loki snapped. "She's a sorceress. She'll be the royal sorceress some day."

Thor snorted. "When I'm king, she'll never be allowed anywhere near the court."

Loki crossed his arms. "*When* you're king, is it?"

"That's not what I meant."

"But it's what you said."

"Fine, perhaps I did mean it," Thor said, his voice taking on a growl. "If you continue to keep company with her, perhaps there won't be a spot for you either."

"Is that meant to be a threat?" Loki asked. "If so, you might try and make it a little less tantalising. Who says I want a place in the court of a king who hits himself in the face with his own hammer?"

"That was one time!"

"And yet it's burnt in our hearts forever."

"At least I'll be on the right side when Ragnarok comes!" Thor burst out. "At least I'll fight for Asgard and not against it."

Loki sucked in his cheeks, trying not to let his sinking

heart make itself known upon his face. They had both suspected it was him, but he hadn't thought Thor would say it. He felt himself darken when he looked at Thor, like something cooking on a high heat. His brother's face was angry, but his eyes brimmed with regret.

"Perhaps the Mirror was wrong," Loki said quietly.

"It's never wrong," Thor replied.

"You say that like the future is an inevitable, unchangeable thing. What if you stabbed me right now and killed me before the end of the world? Couldn't fulfil my traitorous destiny then, could I?"

"Please don't be angry at me."

"I'm not angry."

"You're shouting."

"I'm not—" Loki stopped, realising suddenly that his voice had echoed off the vaulted ceilings of the chapel. He turned back to the door, fumbling for the latch. "Happy feast day, brother."

"Loki, wait—"

He heard Thor's heavy footsteps, felt him reach for his arm, but Loki twisted from his grasp. His heart was pounding, but he managed to keep his voice steady and less biting than he wanted it to be. "Best stay away from me. We're going to be enemies at the end of the world."

He had expected Thor to protest. Make the same excuses he always did. But Thor stayed silent, and Loki felt something dark and cold begin to curl inside him.

Of course Thor assumed he would be the one on the right side at the end of the world. Of course he would lead the forces of good for Asgard. Loki's brother was born to be a king – the whole court knew it. Anyone who looked at him knew it. The gods could not have handcrafted a more obvious model of kingship than Thor – blond and broad and fast and strong without trying. Loki was the scraps of his silhouette, the part that was discarded on the workshop floor to be swept up and thrown into the fire – thin and pale, with a hooked nose and black hair that hung flat to the nape of his neck, where it flipped into an unflattering curl. While Thor's skin bronzed in the sun so that he seemed to be made of armour, Loki was as pale as milk, and soured just as easily.

And whoever wasn't king was the traitor – wasn't that how it would work? Spurned and rejected by his father, the disfavoured son would rise up at the end of Asgard.

But he was a son of Asgard. A prince. He wasn't a traitor. He wouldn't lead an army against his own brother. His own people.

Would he?

Chapter Three

*A*mora had already left the feast by the time Loki returned to look for her, and he managed to slip in and out of the Great Hall without attracting the attention of his father, who was now seated dutifully at the head of the feast table like nothing was amiss.

Loki found Amora in the palace orangery, the plants from each of the Nine Realms pressing their leaves up against glass panes the size of playing cards as they curled their vines round each other. A bitter violet from Alfheim shied from Loki's shadow as he passed it, its petals the pure blue of the inside of a glacier. Amora was sitting under the wide leaves of a Midgardian fern at the edge of the small pond that bubbled up from the ground. She was brushing her fingers through the grass at the edge of the water like she was petting an animal, and Loki watched as, with each pass, her fingers raised sparks from the reeds.

"Is that a new spell?" he asked her, and she looked up.

"No. It's Svartalfheim fire grass." She ruffled her fingers through the blades and small sparks puffed around her hand the way most plants would shed their seeds. Amora smiled. "Not magic. Just nature."

"Does that make us unnatural?" Loki asked.

Her eyes flicked up to his, their thin veins of green seeming to take over her whole irises for a moment so that they looked as though they were fashioned from the jungle around her. Then she looked back to the grass, letting a spark linger and bloom into a small flame along her fingertips before she snuffed it out. Loki sank down beside her, close enough that their knees pressed together. Even through the hazy gloom lingering from his conversation with Thor, an electric shiver went through him when she didn't pull away from his touch. No matter how small that touch was.

"Will you answer me something?" he asked.

"Depends on the question," she replied.

He had already felt fragile and self-conscious, and the

flippancy he usually enjoyed in her instead tipped him over the edge. "Never mind."

He stood up to go, but Amora caught him by the wrist, pulling him back down beside her. "Sit down, Trickster, and don't be so dramatic. Of course I'll answer your question."

Trickster. The nickname used to make him blush. Now every time she called him that, it felt intimate and secret, a name only she used for him. *If I'm a trickster, you're an enchantress*, he had said the first time, and he was delighted by how caught off guard she looked. Amora was almost never undone, or if she was, she didn't show it.

Enchantress, she had said, and he could hear the pleasure in her voice. *So much prettier than 'witch', don't you think?*

She paused, eyeing him. "Ask me your question," she said, her hand not on his, but lingering near it. "I'll answer it as best I can."

He did not know exactly what he wanted to ask her. *Do I seem the sort of person who would help end the world? Am I destined to turn against Asgard? If I know it, can I stop it, or will trying to stop it make it happen?*

So instead, he asked, "Do you think my father will ever make me king?"

"Not if you remain devoted to your current haircare regime," she replied.

Loki rolled his eyes. "Amora."

"Really, one decent haircut and a bit of oil daily would work wonders on this mop." She reached out, flicking a lock of dark hair out from behind his ear. "You think your father would have got where he is without that lustrous beard?"

"Please don't refer to anything about my father as 'lustrous', it's very upsetting."

Her smirk didn't fade, but her face softened around it. When she looked at him, he could feel her gaze caress his face. He wished she would touch him again, even just another strand of hair tugged from its place. Let her ruffle him.

"I think your father would be a fool to name anyone but you his heir," she said.

"Do you think my father is a fool?"

Amora laughed, her lips pursed together so it came out breathily through her nose. "You're very clever."

"I have my moments."

"Many of them. You are made of moments."

A leaf had stuck to the knee of his trousers, and he attempted to brush it away, only to find it so sticky with some kind of sap that it wouldn't be parted from the fabric. He flicked his fingers, sending a small gust of wind to blow it off, but it ended up stronger than he intended, pushing both his and Amora's hair back off their faces. Loki wrinkled his nose. Control was still an elusive thing, and a skill he was certain Odin had denied him to keep his use of magic to a minimum. "You don't think much of my father," he said.

"I don't think of him at all, if I can help it," Amora replied, tugging her hair over her shoulder and running her fingers through it. "What's brought on these questions?"

"Nothing." Loki slumped backwards against the stone behind him. "I'm just brooding."

"I know, and it's adorable. You get this little crease between your eyebrows."

"Stop it." He batted her hand away as she pressed her finger into the space between his eyes. She laughed. "Have you seen Karnilla since the ceremony?"

"Not yet. Isn't she still with your father?"

"They've returned to the feast."

She ran a hand over her knees, smoothing her trousers. "Why do you ask? Do you think she has something she wants to say to me?"

"I know what my father saw in the Godseye Mirror."

She raised her head, eyes hungry. "Tell me." Loki ground his feet into the dirt, watching it halo around his heels until Amora pushed her toe against his. "Tell meeee."

"He saw one of his sons leading an army against Asgard," Loki blurted out. He had intended to say it, but not in such an inelegant tumble. "He thinks it means Ragnarok."

He expected a reaction, but her face didn't change. "Which son?" Amora asked, her voice flat.

"He didn't say."

"But you think you know."

"Thor does," Loki replied. "He thinks it's me."

She picked a strand of the fire grass, and it fizzled into ashes between her fingers. "Why does it matter what Thunderhead says?"

"Don't call him that." Loki wasn't sure why he was defending his brother after what he'd said, but only he was allowed to mock Thor. Not that anyone else ever had. "Do you think I'd do that?" he asked her. "Fight against Asgard? Against my father and my family and my people?"

"I think we are all capable of things we'd never imagine." Her tone was light but layered as pastry. She knew what it was like, to live with a birthright that felt precarious and fragile. Amora was an orphan, adopted by Karnilla from an Asgardian orphanage when her natural talent manifested in her levitating the other children across the dormitories. But Amora was fearless. She was brash. She was off-putting, a word Loki had heard applied to him, too. Yet they felt like opposite sides of that coin. Amora said too much; he stayed silent. But both of them were strange and other-worldly, disliked by most for nothing but a skill they hadn't asked for.

Amora brushed her hands off on her trousers, a few lingering strands of grass flaring against the material. "Short of asking your father, there's nothing that can be done about his vision," she said at last. "The only thing to do is live your life and wait and see if one day you find yourself standing before an army against your father."

"Or I could look in the Mirror," he said.

She raised an eyebrow, regarding him. "The Godseye Mirror?"

His mind was racing, the ideas leaving him before he even realised they had formed. "It will have been taken back to the vault by now," he said. "No one would notice if we sneaked in. And today is the only day for the next decade its powers can be accessed. If Odin can know my future, so should I."

"If you're going to look into the Godseye Mirror," she replied, "you need someone to channel magic into it."

"If Karnilla can, so can you."

"Who says I'm helping?"

"Oh." He felt himself go red. "I thought that—"

"Calm down, of course I'm helping." She dug her elbow into his side. "You don't think I'd let you sneak off into a forbidden wing of the palace to use dangerous magic by yourself, do you? That's what I live for."

He could feel his heart racing but tried not to betray it on his face. Amora didn't like fear. She said she didn't have time for it. He hadn't even considered that he could look in the Godseye Mirror until he sat across from her. Perhaps because he wouldn't be able to do it without her – whoever looked into the Mirror couldn't channel magic into it as well. The Mirror was guarded. It was protected. It was only for the eyes of the king.

But he had also never thought about turning the flowers to dragons or painting his nails black or learning how to shift his form until Amora came along.

She was staring at him, her face absent of any of its usual mocking mirth. "Do you really want to know?"

He swallowed, the word stuck in his throat. "Yes."

"Then let's find out." He started to stand, but she grabbed his wrist, stopping him. "One more thing." Suddenly he was looking down at her, at the spot her hand wrapped round his. Her nails were green, his were black. He liked the way they looked together, like the scales of a serpent. He liked the way her fingers felt against his skin, the way his hand felt in hers. But all at once, he worried that she could feel at his pulse point the way his heart beat faster when she touched him. She was staring down, and he was sure she sensed the flush running across his skin and was about to say something about it.

But then she asked, "Are those my boots?"

"Oh. Um..." They both stared at his boots. "I saw you wearing them yesterday and thought they looked nice."

Amora let out an exaggerated sigh. "Well, if you're going to be looting someone's clothes, I'm glad they're mine. It's like this entire city never discovered tailoring. All your draping and cloaks and swaths; you might as well be swaddling yourselves in window dressings."

"Well, not everyone can pull off tight-fitting clothes," Loki said. "We aren't all blessed with a figure like yours."

He wasn't sure if he imagined it or if her cheeks coloured a little when he said that. If they did, she covered it up with a sly half smile and a wink that sent him blushing. "I am rather divine, aren't I?"

Chapter Four

*T*he Einherjar sentries patrolling the entrance to the palace vault snapped to attention as Odin strode down the stairway past them, his scarlet feast robes fluttering round his ankles. They clapped their heels together and pulled their shields in tight to their sides as they bowed their heads.

Which was lucky, because in spite of Amora's tutoring, Loki was still only moderately competent at mimicking the exact appearance of another person, and had anyone looked too long, he was sure the illusion would not have held up. He hadn't got his father's nose quite right, or the shape of his shoulders, and the eyepatch was wreaking havoc upon his depth perception. He had twice nearly walked into a column and had only been spared a broken nose because Amora, glamoured as one of Odin's personal Einherjar guards, had yanked him out of the way by one of his voluminous sleeves.

But he was halfway down the stairs and the only thing he could do was walk tall, pray they didn't cross paths with the real Odin and silently thank the All-Father that the Einherjar were taught to stare at their boots when the king passed them.

At the bottom of the stairs, one of the soldiers, the plumage on his helmet proclaiming him a captain, saluted. "My king, you were not expected—"

"Don't talk to me," Loki blurted.

The guard froze. "Your Majesty?"

Loki stared at him, his heart hammering. "I'm Odin," he said quickly.

"Yes, Your Majesty," the guard replied, his brow creasing.

"Smoothly done," he heard Amora hiss almost inaudibly in his ear.

Pull yourself together. Loki tugged on the front of his robes, tried to think of what his father would say, but then announced just as inelegantly, "Just… visiting my treasures." When the soldier didn't say anything, he raised one hand and gestured stiffly down the hall, to the vault door.

The guard looked confused but did his best to paper

it over with a dutiful nod. "Of course, Your Majesty. Is there anything we can do to be of service?"

"His Majesty wishes to be alone," Amora interjected.

"Of course." The captain dipped his head. "If you require myself or my men—"

"I won't," Loki replied. "But I'll let you know if I do. But I won't. But. So. Thank you." He nodded. The captain, more confused than ever, also nodded. Then Loki swept down the stairs towards the vault door, trying to salvage that shipwreck of a conversation with his posture alone.

Beside him, Amora ran a hand over the beard of the sentry face she had taken on. "A few notes," she murmured.

Loki resisted the urge to roll his eyes – it would be less dramatic than he wanted it to be with only one visible. "Of course you have notes."

"Everything is a teaching opportunity. First, red really isn't for you," she said, kicking at the train of his robe. "You're far too pale. Greens and golds would bring out the complexion much better."

"What does that have to do with my illusion?"

"Nothing, just a general observation. Second, you forgot to change your fingernails."

Loki glanced down at his black nails. They looked

opalescent in the dark hallway, like he was capped in jewels. "No one noticed."

"I did."

"Yes, well. No one looks at me quite like you do."

She shoved her shoulder against his, her armour clanking softly. "Stop it, you're making me blush. Third, *I'm Odin?* Really? How are you so bad at this?"

"I panicked!"

"I should hope so. If that was you operating with a level head, I'd be concerned."

They reached the door to the vault, and Loki slid on his father's riding gloves, lifted from the stables with very little effort while Amora was chatting up one of the groundsmen. The doors were protected against magic, and could be opened only by his father's touch. He wiggled his fingers, letting his skin absorb the memory of his father's palm prints that rested in the leather of the glove. It was a trick Amora had taught him – small details could be picked up from items of clothing: the shape of one's shoulders written in the tailoring of a coat or the way someone's knees bent remembered by the creases in their trousers.

"And here's your moment, Trickster," Amora said.

Loki tugged the glove from his hand, his fingers now carrying his father's prints like he had been born with them, and pressed his hand to the door. With a soft click, the doors unbolted themselves before swinging open.

Beside him, Amora said, "I'm impressed."

"Didn't you think I could do it?" he asked.

"Oh, I was almost sure you couldn't."

"Well, you were wrong."

"There's a first time for everything."

The walls of the vault slanted to high ceilings, and the path forwards was lined with dark, polished stone that splintered into short walkways. Each led to an alcove holding one of the treasures of the Asgardian king, some hunted down with the aid of the Godseye Mirror.

Loki looked over at Amora as her guard face slimmed, the beefy skin suctioning so that the cheekbones popped and the chin turned smooth and pointed. The shoulder-length hair stretched like a snake uncoiling, spilling into a long plait. The clothes didn't change at first, but the body beneath them did. Slowly, the garments adjusted to match, the armour vanishing as the tunic and trousers fit to size.

Amora slicked a hand over her face – her real face – leaving behind the light dusting of freckles that sugared her nose and cheeks. She did many things well, and perhaps chief among them was knowing how to look good while doing all those things. Every movement seemed orchestrated so that if it were to be immortalised in a mural upon a palace wall, the viewer wouldn't be able to look away. And she was never prettier than when she returned to herself, as shimmering and changeable as a flame for those few seconds before she settled into her own skin, an eagle landing with its wings unfurled.

In response, Loki's return to his form was more like the flight of an awkward pigeon. Odin's silhouette fell away, turning in a manner that always felt liquid, like it might flow into any mould and fit any shape it chose. It could. But, instead, he let it fall into himself, his resting appearance, trying not to shy at the way his own body felt so small and brittle.

Amora, who had been watching his transformation with a critical eye, grinned. "There's that smile."

Loki scowled at her.

She headed off down the walkway, peering into each alcove as they passed. "Have you ever been down here?"

Loki chased after her, tugging up one of those magnificent boots that had slipped down past his knee. "Never without my father. He brought Thor and me when we were young."

"What a lovely father-son outing. There's nothing quite like showing your children all the ways the world could end that you have stored in the basement."

"I enjoyed it only slightly more than our trip to the killing fields on Svartalfheim."

Amora paused in front of the path leading down to the Tuning Fork, its surface reflecting a thin band of light across her face. "So. About the boots. I'm not mad, I'm just disappointed that they look better on you. You can have them, by the way. My treat." He glanced over just in time to catch her casting an appraising gaze up his legs. His spine prickled.

At the end of the walkway before them was the Godseye Mirror, its shimmering surface blending into the darkness. This close, it was the bluish black of a raven's wing, but when Loki stepped up to it, it gave no hint of a reflection. He looked over at Amora as she touched a hand to the gold stave and traced one of its whorls.

"You don't have to look," she said quietly.

But he did. He had to know what his father had seen.

"Stand there," he said, pointing her to the side of the Mirror Karnilla had stood on. As she stepped out of sight, even knowing she was still there, Loki felt his skin crawl with the sudden fear of being alone. Alone and staring into the end of the world.

"Do you know how to activate it?" he called, his voice higher than he would have liked.

Amora poked her head round from behind the Mirror, her braid tumbling over her shoulder. "I channel power and the staves direct it. It's basic runic magic."

"Right," Loki said, like he knew anything about runic magic. He'd never even heard of it. Yet another gap in his shoddy magical education.

She ducked back to her side of the Mirror, calling, "Runes and staves direct a spell. All the sorcerer has to do is channel power through them."

"I know that."

He couldn't see her, but he could practically hear the smirk. "Of course you do, princeling. Are you ready?"

Over their heads, he heard a crack like thunder. A flash of white light that he felt sear his skin.

"I'm ready," he said.

Amora's grasp of the energy was not as elegant as Karnilla's had been. The lightning forked and danced around the room before finding its way to her. Loki saw the tremble in the glass as she pressed her hands to the black Mirror, then suddenly his side began to sputter with light, like a firework that could not catch. An image flickered, then died, then flickered again, too blurred to be seen clearly.

"It needs more power!" Loki called to Amora, and he

heard her draw a deep, ragged breath. The air around them shimmered again.

The image began to sharpen into rows of soldiers. Not soldiers of Asgard – they had no armour, no banners and they looked instead like feral creatures, pale and foaming and bloated. They were pouring from the observatory that connected Asgard to the Bifrost, along the rainbow bridge towards the capital. A lone figure stood out among the masses of soldiers, planted at the door to the observatory, the glint of a blade in his hand. But the image was too smoky to make out much detail.

Loki balled his hands into fists at his side. He wanted to reach into the scene, wanted to grab this unknown person by the shoulders and demand to know who he was, even if it meant looking into his own face.

"It's not enough!" he called to Amora as the image flickered again.

"This is all the energy I can summon!" she shouted in return.

Loki leant forwards, pressing his fingers against the glass. *Show me*, he thought. *Show me who it is.*

The image flickered, flushed with a clarity that didn't last long enough for him to make sense of what he was seeing. It was there, right at his fingertips, his future.

He hadn't realised his own power was gathering in his hands until it burst free. The surface of the Mirror burnt with white light, and Loki tumbled backwards, his hands searing. He heard Amora cry out on the other side of the Mirror, and he threw his arm up against the impossible light radiating from their combined power, washing out the vision entirely.

The Mirror shattered. The cracks seemed to begin at a point in the centre, and then it collapsed upon itself, caving into a slick dust studded with shards as long and sharp as his knives. Several buried themselves in the walls. Loki threw his hands over his face, but Amora cast a spell, some kind of barrier, so that the shards flying towards them bounced off. One flew sideways to the alcove across from them, striking the Tuning Fork. A single crystalline note echoed through the room, so high and clear Loki felt it more than heard it, even over the sound of the breaking Mirror. It rattled his teeth. All the lights in the alcove flared, then winked out, casting them into darkness.

Loki sat up, a fine layer of black dust blossoming from his clothes. He felt coated in it. Across from him, Amora was doubled over, coughing, her blonde hair darkened from the dust. He crawled forwards to her, his palms burning. "Are you all right?"

She rubbed a hand over her face, smearing the dust into black streaks. "What did you do?"

"I think we overpowered it."

"*We* didn't do anything," she snapped, tossing her hair over her shoulder. "*You* cast a spell."

"It was an accident. I was trying to help you."

"I don't think your father will care about your intentions."

He followed her gaze over his shoulder to the remains of the Mirror – black dust and the charred, curled outline of the staves. Panic made his stomach clench, and he thought for a moment he was about to vomit. They had destroyed the Godseye Mirror, one of the most powerful magical items in Odin's treasure room.

I was powerful enough to destroy the Godseye Mirror.

The thought flickered through him before he could stop it. It should have horrified him. It didn't. It thrilled him.

I am powerful.

From the darkness, Loki heard something rumble. The floor beneath them trembled.

Amora raised her head. "What was that?"

Loki climbed to his feet, one of his knives sliding into his hand as he surveyed the damage. He could feel something stirring in the darkness, some power beyond what they had funnelled into the Mirror. "Stay here," he said, turning back to Amora. "I'll see if—"

Something grabbed him round the waist and yanked him off his feet. His knife flew from his hand, clattering somewhere into the shadows as he was thrown to the ground, landing on his back. His head slapped the stone floor and for a moment, his vision spotted.

When his eyes cleared, he heard a roar, and above him loomed a massive creature, purple skinned and six feet tall, with a shining bald head and a grotesque face, blunt teeth poking from beneath its thick lips. Its shoulders were built like boulders, and its barrel chest swelled. The monster's mouth gaped open in a roar, its skin ropey with veins and muscles as it brought down a fist towards Loki. The Trickster rolled out of the way, his heartbeat spiking with panic. The creature roared again, its torso bulging, and suddenly a third arm sprang from its side. Loki scrambled backwards, watching in horror as it seemed to grow a foot taller. Its next steps towards him smashed craters in the stone walkway.

But it reeled backwards unexpectedly, letting out a roar of pain. Amora was somehow no longer sprawled on the floor of the alcove, but behind the beast, plunging a shard from the Mirror into its back. It swiped at her with a six-fingered hand the size of her head, but she ducked, rolling under its legs to Loki's side.

"What is that?" she cried, her voice almost lost in the roar of the creature.

"The Lurking Unknown." The struck Tuning Fork must have summoned it. He had seen it before in the arena where the warriors were tested before they joined the ranks of the Einherjar. It was summoned by a note from the Tuning Fork, able to form and wither away and then form again and again, whenever called. The Lurking Unknown was the final test for the Einherjar, meant to show off both their skills in combat and their ability to face their enemies with stoic calm. "It feeds off fear," he shouted to Amora as she gathered a charge of energy between her hands. "The more afraid you are, the more it grows."

The third arm the creature had sprouted looked more shrivelled than it had a moment before, as though calling it by name had weakened the creature's hold on them, but Loki still felt a strong *whoosh* of air as the Lurking Unknown swiped at them with it. Amora sent a blast of hot blue energy towards it in return, but the flame was extinguished against its skin. Loki scrambled for his second dagger. His hands were shaking; the monster was growing, and it was his fault – his fear's fault. All the power he had felt flooding him moments before suddenly wilted.

You are not powerful. You are weak. You are afraid. You are beyond your own control.

"How do we defeat it?" Amora called to him, fumbling to pry out another one of the Mirror shards buried in the wall.

"You fight it without fear," Loki replied, though the words felt impossible. "Until it fades away."

But the Lurking Unknown was not fading. It was growing. A fourth arm sprung from its side, windmilling through the air and catching Amora across the face, sending her flying into the wall. Then it rounded on Loki and seized him by the throat. He choked, struggling to get his own hand up to the creature's neck. As soon as he felt his fingers brush the ropy cords of muscle in its throat, he conjured his knife and stuck it hard. The monster reeled backwards with a scream of pain, dropping Loki as thick black blood coursed down its neck.

Loki landed in a crouch, gasping for air, but he hardly had time to collect himself.

The Lurking Unknown had already yanked the dagger from its neck and flung it at Loki, who dodged, but not fast enough. The knife clipped his cheek before it struck the wall and clattered to the stone.

The creature raised a hand to strike again, but Amora leapt high enough to wrap her legs round its neck and use the momentum of her jump to throw it to the ground. The whole vault seemed to shake as it landed on its back. Amora stood tall on top of it, her heels digging into its chest hard enough to draw more of that dark blood. She conjured another shock of energy between her hands and sent it barrelling towards the creature's face. It screamed again. Its body seemed to shrink and grow at the same time, Amora's calm battling Loki's fear.

But once again, the energy from her blast seemed to absorb into its skin. It grabbed Amora by the legs and whipped her off her feet, sending her across the room like she weighed nothing. She struck one of the columns along the wall with a crack, collapsed at the bottom and lay still.

Suddenly Loki felt a different kind of fear entirely – his fear for Amora greater than his fear for himself ever could be. And the creature was growing, the dull bricks of its teeth becoming sharper and another arm sprouting from its back. It made a hulking lurch towards Loki. He stepped backwards, his foot catching the edge of the walkway, and he slipped down into the space between the path and the wall. The stone crumbled beneath the creature's foot as it took a few lumbering steps towards the door.

Loki heaved himself back up onto the walkway, the turned-up stones tearing his clothes. If there was a spell to stop the Lurking Unknown, he didn't know it. The creature let out a howl, then threw its shoulder into the door at the end of the vault, splintering it. A second hard shove burst it open. Loki heard the shouts of the surprised soldiers beyond it.

Amora was suddenly at his side, her face spattered with blood from a gash in her forehead. "You're bleeding," he said.

"So are you." She threw out a hand to him and dragged him along. He felt the pull in his ribcage. "Come on."

Outside the vault, the creature had continued its rampage, and with each shocked soldier that it met, it grew, feeding off their fear until its shoulders were straining against the ceiling, knocking chandeliers from their hooks. Fighting the Lurking Unknown in the sparring ring was one thing – it was another entirely to fight it without warning. It snapped the tops of the Einherjar's spears as they jabbed at it, their calls to each other feathered with panic as they tried to step into an attack formation, only to find themselves cut off by the stone-crushing footfalls of the Lurking Unknown. One of the soldiers must have managed to break away, for the gong warning of an attack began to bellow through the hall, drowning out the scream of the monster.

From the doorway to the vault, Loki watched, frozen, as

the creature smashed an Einherjar – one of Loki's sparring teachers, the man who had taught him to hold a sword properly and to keep his knees bent when he parried – into the wall, and he slumped, lifeless. Loki didn't know what to do.

Then the creature let out a scream of a different sort than its hulking battle cries. The sound bore the same crystalline resonance of the struck Tuning Fork. Its body began to shrink, shrivelling and curling in on itself. Loki stared at the writhing creature as it shrank to the floor – Loki's size, then half his size, then small enough to fit in his hand, and then... nothing.

Loki looked up.

Karnilla and Odin were standing at the top of the stairway, Karnilla with a hand still extended from the spell she had cast to stop the Lurking Unknown. She moved towards them, her skirt reshaping into trousers so that the train didn't drag through the blood of one of the Einherjar that was dribbling down the steps. Odin stayed where he was, his arms folded and his face still, his anger betrayed only by his reddening cheeks. Behind him, his personal guard of Einherjar stood, their spears extended. The two in front looked as though they were trying very hard not to let the horror show on their faces. Behind them was Thor, his eyes fixed on Loki.

Odin signalled to his men, and they trotted down the stairs, joining Karnilla as she examined the fallen soldiers, checking for injuries that would require a healer, and those already beyond help.

"Loki," Odin called, and his tone was like the misplaced step that cracks the surface of an icy pond. Loki raised his head and met his father's cold stare. He felt a trickle of blood run down his cheek and resisted the urge to wipe it away. "Explain this," Odin demanded.

Loki glanced over at Amora. She was staring at Odin with the sort of unapologetic ferocity that Loki wished he could turn on his father. But under Odin's stare, he crumpled. "I'm sorry, Father."

"Why did you come here?" Odin demanded, his eye still on his son, and Loki knew that whatever he said next would feel trivial and feeble. Odin had the power to make anything seem stupid just by hearing it.

"We came to look into the Godseye Mirror," Loki mumbled, trying to keep his chin raised, though he was sure everyone could sense the hollowness of the gesture.

"And what happened when you looked into it?" Odin asked coolly.

Loki swallowed. "We destroyed it."

Whatever Odin had been expecting, it was clearly not this. The stony set of his face slipped for a moment, and raw shock coursed over his features. Shock and fear. "You did what?"

"It was an accident."

"You destroyed the Mirror?"

His father didn't sound angry – he sounded afraid. Loki felt his own heart, still slowing itself after their fight, pick up speed again. His father was afraid of him. Afraid of his power. Afraid of anyone who was strong enough to destroy an artefact like the Godseye Mirror. The same realisation – *I am powerful* – this time left him cold. Now Odin knew the truth, knew the extent of his son's gifts, knew he was too powerful to be unleashed. Powerful enough to lead an army against Asgard.

Perhaps Amora sensed it too. Perhaps that fear chilled her. Perhaps she knew Loki would never be a contender for the throne if the court understood how deep his power ran. Whatever it was that made her act, she stepped forwards, her shoulder brushing against his, and faced Odin. "It wasn't Loki who destroyed the Mirror," she said. "It was me. I channelled energy into the Mirror, and I was too strong, and I destroyed it."

At the bottom of the stairs, Karnilla froze. Amora glanced at the sorceress, and Loki thought she looked proud of herself, like the power that had shattered the Mirror had been hers alone, and she relished it. Odin's face changed, shifting back into its set of anger, though Loki caught a flicker of relief that made him sick. Odin sighed, running a hand over his face, then nodded to the Einherjar soldiers at his back. "Arrest her."

The colour drained from Amora's face. "What?"

"No—" Loki called, but the Einherjar were already upon them. One of them, in an attempt to seize Amora, crashed into Loki and knocked him to the ground. They grabbed Amora by the elbows, and when she fought, they wrestled her arms behind her back and forced her to her knees. Amora shrieked in surprise and pain, trying to squirm out of their grip, but before she could conjure a spell to free herself, the Einherjar had her bound with a set of the chains they used in the dungeons to suppress magic in foreign prisoners.

"Father, please!" Loki cried, struggling to his knees, hating the look of supplication but unable to stand fast enough without tipping over. "I'm complicit as well."

Odin did not look at him. "Stay back, my son."

"Then arrest me too!" Loki cried, his voice breaking. "I was trespassing; it was my idea!"

"I said stay back!" Odin roared, then shouted to the soldiers, "She'll await judgement in the dungeons."

The Einherjar began to drag Amora away, but she dug in her heels, trying to fight their grip. When her legs gave out, they kept dragging her so that the raw stones torn up by the Lurking Unknown slashed her trousers until blood ran down her legs. "Let go of me! Karnilla, please! Karnilla, don't let them do this to me!"

Karnilla turned away.

Loki wanted to follow Amora. He wanted to chase down the soldiers, demand her release or throw himself into the cell after her, surrendering the protection she had just granted him. But he couldn't move. He was pinned like an insect to a board, caught in his father's gaze as Odin moved down the stairs, taking in the wreckage with a weary expression. "Thor," he called behind him. "Take your brother to your chambers and wait for my instructions."

Thor edged forwards, skirting the banister like the Lurking Unknown might spring to life again from wherever it had vanished. He extended a hand to Loki, but Loki didn't take it. He stood on his own. It was a halting stagger more than an actual 'stand'. Not the defiant gesture he'd hoped for.

As they left the vault, Thor tried to pull Loki's arm over his shoulder, but Loki jerked away. "What are you doing?"

"You're hurt."

"Yes, but I've not lost a leg." Loki touched a hand to his face before wiping away the thin trail of blood. It had dripped all the way down his chin and stained the collar of his tunic. He walked ahead of Thor, his stride wobblier than he would have liked.

"Loki." Thor easily stepped in front of him, blocking his path. "I'm sorry."

"What are you sorry for?" Loki asked, folding his arms even though the gesture sent a sharp burst of pain across his ribs. "That you missed out on all the fun?"

"I'm sorry for what I said."

"Good, I'm glad you're so worried about my impressionable heart."

"I didn't mean it. What I said about…" Thor rubbed a hand over the back of his neck. "You'd make a fine king."

"I would, wouldn't I?"

"And you'd never betray Asgard. No matter what Father saw." Thor's gaze darted from Loki's, glancing across the hallway and the ceiling, and then he said quietly, "What did you see?"

Loki swiped the back of his hand over his cheek again, though the cut had stopped bleeding. "You and me and mother and father all together at the end of the world. One big happy un-treasonous family."

"Please tell me." A note of desperation punctured Thor's voice.

"Worry not, brother," Loki said, pushing past Thor. "It wasn't you."

Chapter Five

"Am I dangerous?"

Frigga's fingers stilled upon the small bag of herbs she was packing. She stared down at them for a moment in silence before she looked up at Loki, folded in the window seat of her chambers with his legs pulled up to his chest. His bruised ribcage burnt, but he didn't move. It felt safer to stay this way, tucked into himself.

"Why do you ask me that?" Frigga said.

Loki looked out over Asgard. The smoky dusk sat low over the spires, and at this hour, the whole city seemed to emanate light. Everything gold and shining. He rested his chin on his knees.

Amora had been arrested because of power that was his. If she was thought dangerous for that strength, then *he* was dangerous. But that same power, before his father had condemned it, had made him feel strong in a way he had never felt among the other warriors, or standing beside Thor.

Loki pressed his forehead into his knees. "Everyone is afraid of me."

"They're not afraid of you," Frigga replied.

"They're afraid of magic. Of people like me."

"And me?" she asked, pulling tight the drawstring on the pack of herbs.

Loki opened his mouth, then closed it again as Frigga raised the bag to her lips and mumbled a small spell into it. The scent blossomed in the air, flowery and medicinal. There was no one in Asgard as beloved as his mother. So it wasn't magic. It was him.

"Here." She crossed the room towards Loki, and he pulled up his tunic so she could press the bag against his bruised ribs. The pain eased, and he took a deep breath. It was the first time his lungs had felt full since he and Amora had faced the Lurking Unknown in the vault. "Keep that in place," Frigga said, crossing back to her dressing table to retrieve the cloth and bowl of water resting there. "It won't take long to heal."

Loki shifted his grip, pressing the herbs in place with his elbow and leaning backwards against the window sill.

Frigga dipped the cloth into the water and wrung it out between her hands. Loki watched the water fall and tried to take another breath, but this one was a struggle in a way that had nothing to do with his sore ribs. "Come here." Loki melted off the window seat and moved to where she stood and took a seat on the stool next to her before she asked him to. She dabbed the cloth against his neck, mopping up the blood that had dried below his ear.

"What did Father see in the Mirror?" Loki asked, trying to keep his tone innocent. "He fled the feast like the hall was on fire."

She pressed the cloth against his face, prising the flakes of dried blood from his skin. "You know your father. He has such grand reactions to the smallest things."

Loki leant into her hand, letting her push his hair behind his ear as she washed out the cut. He remembered what Amora had said, and asked before he could stop himself. "Is he afraid of me?"

Frigga smiled. "Such heavy questions."

"They shouldn't be." He sat up, and her hand fell away from his face. His shoulder was damp from the dripping cloth. "They wouldn't be if Thor asked you."

"But you are not your brother."

His temper flared, and he stood up so fast he knocked the stool over. "As if I'm not reminded of that every day." He started to cross to the door, then realised he didn't actually want to leave her, because where would he go? The last thing he wanted to be was alone. So he turned back to his mother, standing before her dressing table. "Why won't he let me study sorcery?"

"Loki—"

"He knows I can't compete with Thor on the battlefield, so why does he insist on placing me in races I will never win when I could best him easily in other fields? He wants me to fail." His voice was rising. "He wants me to look weak. He wants me to look unfit to be king so he can rest easy when he chooses Thor for the birthright instead of me because I've proved myself unfit. If I cause Ragnarok, it will be his fault. I don't want to hear your riddles and your vague excuses for him, I want the truth. Answer me!"

He was shouting. He hadn't meant to shout. Frigga placed the bowl on her dressing table, then waved a hand and the stool righted itself. Loki watched her, wanting to reach out, but his hands stayed fisted at his sides. Frigga sat down, her palms pressed against her thighs, then looked up at him. "Who told you that you will be the cause of Ragnarok?"

"I..." He fumbled. "It's what he saw, isn't it?"

"Did you see it as well?" she asked.

His ribs were still hurting. He wanted to sleep. He wanted to sleep for days. "No. I heard him say it to you. Thor and I were listening."

Frigga pursed her lips. The city light glowed on her skin, making it shimmer like she was fashioned from the dusk. "Your father," she said at last, "saw his son leading an army of soldiers risen from the dead. He believes it to be a vision from the end of the world."

"Was it me?" When Frigga didn't reply, he pressed on, "What if I chose now to never leave the palace, or Father put me in prison, or I fled to somewhere far away from here and never returned to Asgard?"

"You cannot live to fulfil or avoid what may come to pass," she replied.

"But that's what father does when he looks in the Mirror, isn't it?" Loki asked. "He looks for dangers he can avoid."

"You are not dangerous, Loki, but sorcery is. Magic is corrupting – only the strongest sorcerers are able to control it. Most are controlled by it. Your father has seen kingdoms fall to magic. He is wary. That's all."

"Then let me learn to control it! If he is so afraid it will overtake me, why doesn't he teach me to prevent that from happening?"

"Because learning control means learning magic. His hope is, in keeping you ignorant, he will keep you from accessing the full extent of what you can do. It is" – she paused, and he felt her selecting her next words as carefully as a fine silk scarf from a drawer – "not a decision on which your father and I agree. But he is the king." She looked up at Loki, her eyes sparkling. "I know what it's like. I know that hunger. I know it doesn't pass. It only grows stronger." She took his face between her hands, the same way she used to when he was small and would press her nose against his forehead. "But you are so young and so powerful. You have so much before you, so much to learn."

"So let me learn."

"I will."

He had not expected that. "You... what?"

"I should have taught you long ago about the power you have, and how to use it," she said. "Your father and I both should have." She picked up the damp cloth again and wrung it out, the blood turning the water a rusty brown. "If you wish to learn sorcery, I will teach you."

"Teach me what?" he said, his voice biting. "How to start fires and shift my form and other little tricks to impress the court, but not too much to scare them? You're too late to civilise me. You let me live feral for too long."

"I'll teach you how to control your magic. How to wield it." Frigga's voice came suddenly from behind him, and when he turned, she was standing in front of the window, her hands folded over her stomach. For a moment, he wasn't sure which was real, his mother framed by the light or the one sitting at her dressing table watching him. They both turned to him, her eyes on every side of him, and he felt pinned between them. "There is magic in everything upon our planet. It is energy, and it lives in the air, the earth, you and me. And some of us are born with an innate ability to control and manipulate that energy." The edges of her form at the window began to fade, then curl and smoulder like paper catching fire. He turned to her at the dressing table. Her eyes were fixed upon him. "I will tell your father I am teaching you. But what you are learning will stay between us."

Loki stared at her, unsure what to say. He had always thought of Frigga in perfect union with Odin, her soft touch balancing his battle-hard edges. She supported him. He conferred with her. They fell in line together, their opinions and policies stronger for the absolute support of the other.

But Frigga was not his father's. She was her own.

"The energy of Asgard is drawn to you," she continued. "You can't help that. How you use it is just practice, like strengthening your muscles and learning memory from repetition, but how you control it – that is the skill. To own your magic instead of letting it own you." She stood up and held out a hand to him. "I can teach you that. I should have long ago."

He didn't take it. "Is that what Karnilla was meant to teach Amora?"

Frigga's hand fell. "Amora is different from you. Your father and Karnilla both had concerns that she would be too powerful to control. Odin's decision to imprison her was not a sudden one. It has been a subject of discussion between them for some time. Her actions today only accelerated it."

Loki swallowed hard. The guilt creeping up his throat burnt. "What will happen to her?"

"That will depend upon your father and Karnilla."

"And what will happen to me?"

He had meant it as *What will my punishment be?* But

when it came out of his mouth, it weighed so much heavier than he had expected. *What will happen to me? What will happen to me and this power I have?* What would happen if he chose to fight it? And, more than that, what would happen if he didn't?

Frigga reached out and touched his cheek. "Patience, my son."

Chapter Six

Odin did not assemble the court for Amora's trial. It was only the king on his throne, with Frigga, Karnilla, Thor and Loki all standing at his side as she was brought before them, her wrists chained behind her. She was still wearing her feast day dress, smeared with dust and blood from the vault, and her hair was lanker and coarser than Loki had ever seen it.

Loki wasn't certain what his presence here would accomplish, but he kept catching himself leaning onto the balls of his feet, like his body was bracing for an attack. Perhaps he would be punished alongside her. Perhaps Odin wanted him to witness whatever he would do to her as a warning. The chains round her ankles clinked against the floor, a delicate sound that seemed more suited to putting on jewellery. No one had sponged the blood off her face. No one had healed her bruises.

Odin did not stand when the soldiers halted their progress at the bottom of the stairs that led to the throne. He just adjusted his grip on Gungnir. Across the platform from Loki, Thor and Frigga, Karnilla stared down at Amora, her lips pressed tightly together. With two dark braids falling around her face, she looked even paler than usual.

"Amora of Nornheim," Odin said, his voice the one he used for court meetings and assemblies, though there was no one else present. The resonance made the room feel even emptier. "You have been charged with treason, theft, destruction of a sacred relic and robbery. Do you have anything to say for yourself?"

With her head still bowed, she replied, "The charges are a bit redundant."

At his side, Loki felt Thor stiffen. Odin's brow creased. "Excuse me?"

"Are not theft and robbery the same, my king?" she asked. "I think you're trying to inflate the list of charges against me with synonyms."

"Silence!" Loki had expected the shout to come from his father, but it was Karnilla who raised her voice instead. Amora flinched. Karnilla stalked down the stairs, her cloak rasping with every step. "I gave you everything. A kingdom to inherit. Schooling to use your powers. A home."

"A cage," Amora retorted.

"And this," Karnilla said, her voice rising again, "is how you repay me. You disrespect your king. You disrespect me. You take the tools you have been given to control your power and you cast them aside. You let your strength corrupt and control you."

"I do not want to be controlled," Amora argued. "I am powerful, so let me be powerful!"

"And it is that power that is your undoing," Odin interrupted. "I asked Karnilla if she would speak on your behalf. I asked your delegation from Nornheim if any of them wished to vouch for you. Not a single one of them did. No one will speak for you, Amora."

Loki should have spoken. He wanted to speak. He felt the words on his tongue, ready: *It was me. I'm the one you should punish. I'm the one who is too strong, too dangerous.*

When he looked up, Amora was watching him. She had given herself for him, but neither of them had expected this. He bent his head and stayed silent.

"Your powers are too strong to remain unchecked, and you refuse to check them," Odin continued. "As such, you will be banished to Midgard, where you will remain for the rest of your existence."

Loki had to bite back a gasp. Death at the executioner's hand would have been more merciful, for this was death in its slowest form, its cruellest. On Midgard, there was no magic, no power to be channelled, power that her life force was tied to. Her magic would fade, and she would fade with it. The thought of it made Loki's skin crawl, the idea of losing his magic slowly, slowly, slowly, one drop at a time extracted from him by the world he was forced to live in. It was dishonour. It was pain. It was death. Were Odin any kind of merciful king, he would have let the axe fall fast and finished it here and now.

Amora's eyes widened, that rare flash of fear blazing incandescent, consuming her whole being. Whatever she had expected when she had spoken for Loki in the vault, it was not this. "Please, no."

"You will be taken now to the observatory, and the Bifrost opened for you," Odin continued, as Amora's voice rose in a scream. "It will not open to you again."

"No! Please!" Amora struggled. "Karnilla, please, don't let him do this to me! Please!"

At a nod from Odin, the guards began to drag her away, but she was thrashing like a tethered falcon. *Say something,* Loki told himself. *Save her.* But he couldn't speak.

"Karnilla, please! Your Majesty, have mercy! Mercy!" Her knees hit the ground, and Loki felt it like an earthquake tremor. "Put me in your dungeons. Let me rot there. Trap me on Nornheim, throw me through a wormhole, but please, not this!"

The guards abandoned their chains and hauled her up by her elbows, dragging her backwards down the hall.

"Karnilla!" She twisted, her supplications shifting. "Frigga! My queen, my lady, please, have mercy! Intervene."

"Mother," Loki said very quietly, but he felt Frigga's fingers against his back.

The guards were almost to the door now. Amora's voice was now a blistering scream. "My queen, please! Please— Frigga! Loki—wait! Loki please, tell him—"

The doors slammed, and Odin finally stood, turning to Loki. He felt Thor shrink away from his side, dodging the beam of their father's anger, even if it wasn't directed at him.

Frigga took a step forwards in between them. "Odin, let it be—"

But Odin held up a hand. "Let me speak to our son."

Frigga fell silent but didn't retreat as Odin approached them. His step seemed heavier than usual, and he leant heavily on his staff as he stood before Loki. "Consider this your warning, my son," he said, "of what will happen if you too become reckless with your power. Your title will not protect you again. I will not let you be the undoing of this realm."

And there it was. What Odin had seen in the Godseye Mirror, laid bare at his feet. Now he knew. Thor knew. They all knew which prince would turn against Asgard.

Loki felt his throat tighten, his hands closing into fists at his side.

He could have spoken up. He wanted to. He wanted to be like Thor and argue with his father and come away from it feeling righteous and right, knowing Odin would be secretly pleased with his hot-headedness and the way he stood his ground. But he was not his brother. Insolence would not be a sign of strength, but defiance. He and his brother may play the same game of his father's devising, but the rules would never be the same. Darkness moves in a different way than the light. It is always there before the light. It has to be faster, and smarter, and stealthier.

Loki was not his father. He was not his brother, or his mother. He was Amora, and she had been led away in chains and banished to Midgard. He had to be smarter and stealthier than she had been. He had to learn everything he could, and never let on how much he knew.

He did not feel like a prince. He may never be king. He wasn't made to be a soldier, and he wasn't certain if he wanted to be a villain. He wasn't certain if he had any say in that matter.

The only thing he knew for certain was that he was powerful.

Powerful enough to end the world.

Part Two

ᚠᚱᛁᛗ

Chapter Seven

*T*hor was the first one to complicate their diplomatic assignment to Alfheim.

He and Loki had been thoroughly briefed on the culture of the Ice Elves and protocol within the Ice Court. A culture that dictated that guests do not speak first in the presence of royalty. And yet the moment that Prince-General Asmund entered the antechamber where they had arrived, Thor said, "Asmund!" The greeting carried all the way to the high ceilings, making the icicles hanging from it tremble. Thor's voice, like everything else about him, seemed to have been created for a battlefield.

Perhaps it had been an unintentional mistake, or

perhaps Thor had remembered and simply ignored the rules, wanting to assert his dominance, as he had grown more and more fond of doing lately. Perhaps Thor had truly fallen asleep during their lecture instead of just 'resting his eyes' as he had claimed and he was truly oblivious to his error. Whatever the case, Loki made a mental note to remember that, whether or not this mission went badly, it was Thor who had mucked it up first.

It likely wouldn't matter – Loki was sure he would somehow still be blamed if this assignment didn't go as planned. Loki could have been three realms away and tied to a chair, and Odin would somehow still find a way to pin responsibility on him for any trouble.

But Loki usually wasn't three realms away from trouble. And certainly never tied to anything.

Loki did not travel often with Thor on assignments from their father across the Nine Realms. He had never excelled on the battlefield, and had been told that in negotiations, his gaze was disconcerting, so sharp that the nobility of the other realms may cut themselves upon it.

He and Thor were old enough to be considered men in the Asgardian tradition, but Loki was still the less muscled, the less blond of the princes. Every conversation with foreign leaders began with some comment about how little he looked like his father, or how much his brother did in contrast. Perhaps Odin didn't like to send him out simply to avoid wasting time on those observations. And while Thor was aggressive and loud in a way that could be misconstrued with leadership skills, Loki spoke softer and didn't put his fist through as many walls; somehow people read that as him being slippery.

There is something about you, Thor had told him once, *that people just don't trust.*

But he was trying. He had spent the last several years throwing himself into his studies, working hard, working smart, working to be a better soldier, a better sorcerer, a better prince, a different man than the version of him his father had seen turned traitor to Asgard in the Godseye Mirror.

Odin was growing weary. He stood slowly, complained of his joints, fell asleep after two goblets of mead, sometimes at the table before the feast was even over. And the princes were of age. But with every day that passed, no matter how hard Loki worked, it grew more difficult to pretend that Odin truly was weighing his options when considering an heir. The day was coming when Odin would hand over his crown, and it felt already decided whose brow it would rest upon.

That was the trap of seeing the future, Loki had begun to think – if Odin had never looked into it, never seen Loki leading an army, he might be considering him for kingship. And if he were king, why would he lead an army against his own people? Perhaps the future was only inevitable once you began to shape all your actions to fit it.

But Loki was trying, every day, to prove himself different from what the future had promised his father he would become. And now he was on Alfheim, with Thor, on an assignment from the king – brief the Ice Elves on the situation of the missing Norn Stones and assure them that Asgard had the situation entirely under control.

And at least it had been Thor who had made the first mistake.

Prince-General Asmund paused in the doorway, ranks of guards behind him, glancing at each other. One of the guards, his long white hair braided into elegant strands around his face, let his hand wander to the pommel of his sword, like he might be personally called upon to dispatch the son of Odin.

Asmund crossed his arms over his chest, the silver threads in his tunic catching the wintry light and gleaming. His hair was long and blond like Thor's, but while Thor's was the colour of sunlight, Asmund's was blond in a way that seemed to lack pigment. His skin was white too, so pale it had a blue sheen to it. The skin of all Ice Elves was like this, as if they were forged out of the heart of a glacier. They all seemed formed from the snow, built to blend into the frosted landscape that covered their homeland. Just the sight of the fair-haired Prince-General, the faint ridge of frost upon his brows, made Loki more acutely aware of how cold it was here, but how little he felt it. Thor had been shuffling and shivering wrapped in his fur-lined cloak, but Loki didn't mind the frigid temperatures. Curious.

When Asmund stopped, clearly taken aback by Thor's breach in protocol, Thor took it as an invitation to stride forwards, a hand extended for the Prince-General to clasp.

Loki winced delightedly. Mistake number two – the Ice Elves did not shake hands. The Ice Elves avoided physical contact whenever possible, believing even a tap upon the shoulder to be a gesture of unbearable intimacy.

Asmund looked at Thor's hand, then up to his wide smile and bright blue eyes. Loki waited, half hoping his brother would get slapped across the face for his boldness and half ready to jump to his defence if he did. Then, laboriously, one finger at a time, Asmund took Thor's hand. It was a stiff gesture, the performance of an act he'd heard described but never seen himself, but Thor immediately grasped him up to the elbow and slapped him on the back hard enough that a few ice crystals flew from his hair. "It's good to see you, General."

And Asmund smiled.

Loki could have set the world on fire. Here he was, in a deep knee bow that was making his muscles shake, having studied Ice Elf etiquette until his eyes had crossed in preparation for this assignment, and Thor had done the decorum equivalent of kicking down the door, yet the prince had not called for their immediate removal. How did Thor manage to win over every man he met with just a smile?

"Welcome, Thor, son of Odin," Asmund said, the words reaching Loki's ears in Asgardian as the Allspeak translated for him. Asmund's eyes flicked over Thor's shoulder, to where Loki was still bowing so low he was about to become one with the floor and said, "And to you, Prince Lonely."

Loki gritted his teeth. "It's Loki."

"Isn't that what I said?" the Prince-General replied.

Thor laughed. Loki grimaced. Wonderful, now there were two of them.

"My father sends his regards," Thor said, as Loki straightened, every bone in his spine making itself heard in the cold. "And his gratitude for welcoming us into your court."

"It is our honour," Asmund replied.

Amora would have been amused, Loki thought. She also would have started calling him Prince Lonely – she would have found that hysterical. In her absence, he sometimes found himself imagining her there with him, what she would say and how she would laugh. She would have said it was funny that no one cared about the Norn Stones until they disappeared. What a strange thing it was that became more frightening when it was no longer in sight.

Amora. He felt her absence every day like sand beneath his skin, an irritating grain that rubbed up against his every thought, every spell that built upon his fingers. Where was she now? After her banishment, she had fallen out of Heimdall's sight. No one knew where she was. Perhaps she was dead. Perhaps Midgard had drained her strength and magic so fast she had withered into nothing. Perhaps she was hiding in some corner of the cosmos where those who did not want to be found harboured each other. He clung to that hope, that some day, if he was crowned, he could find her and bring her back to Asgard to serve as his sorceress, as Karnilla was Odin's. It was a foolish fantasy for a whole list of reasons, the first being that Amora likely had no powers left. The second being that it was deeply unlikely he'd ever be king.

But who would he be if Amora had not been cast out? A stronger sorcerer? A better contender for the throne, with her imparting knowledge from Karnilla's classroom? His mother's lessons in sorcery had strengthened his control over his own power, but she would never push him to test himself like he knew Amora would have. Perhaps he wouldn't be in Alfheim, his knees cracking loudly as he rose from his bow, with Thor giving him a look like he was the embarrassing one.

Asmund said, raising a bony hand to gesture down the hallway behind them. "We have a feast prepared."

"We have not been sent to feast with you," Thor replied. "Only to brief you on the situation—"

"But we can speak over dinner. Come, follow me, you must be famished. I insist."

"We would be happy to join you," Loki interrupted, and when Asmund's eyes slid to his face, slow as a glacier, he bowed again, though not so low this time. He was afraid he'd never be able to get up if he went all the way to the floor. "By Your Grace's leave."

Both Thor and Asmund looked at him like he was something stuck under their shoe. Loki did a metaphorical throwing up of his hands and decided to abandon all the protocol he had studied. Apparently, the court of the Ice Elves cared only selectively for manners.

*T*he Ice Elves served them twelve courses, each one colder than the last, with talk solely permitted between them, so that the only sound during the meal itself was wet chewing, which entirely ruined Loki's appetite.

Thor fidgeted beside him the entire time, wolfing down his food and then doing a poor imitation of waiting to discuss the business they had come for. Across from them, Asmund ate slowly, licking his fingers and nibbling at the bones of the snowy hares that had been served to them skinned and whole, finding things to pick at upon his plate until the next course was prepared so no one was permitted to say a word. Even Loki was struggling to hide his frustration at this obvious delay. He stared up at the ceiling, the vaults angular and shimmering like fractals of a snowflake, each embedded with blue orbs that gave off light but no heat. The walls of the banquet hall looked as though they had once been dripping water that had been frozen midstream, with scenes from Alfheim's history carved round their bases. How furious the artists would be, Loki thought, if the climate suddenly changed and all their hard work melted. It almost made him want to start a fire.

As the last course was finally cleared, Asmund wiped the corners of his mouth with his napkin, then folded it into careful thirds. Its lace edges were stained faintly from the meal. "So. The business that has brought you here, Sons of Odin."

Thor leant forwards, elbows on the table. A vein in his forehead was throbbing from the effort it had taken to keep silent. "No doubt by now word has reached you that a set of Norn Stones has been stolen from the sorceress Karnilla."

Asmund raised a hand for his glass to be refilled, and Loki noticed the glistening rings that adorned his fingers, each spiked and sharpened so that his knuckles were lined with icicles. "Ah, yes. Karnilla's Norn Stones. The most powerful magical amplifiers in the Nine Realms."

Loki glanced at Thor, trying to read if his brother was getting the same creeping feeling of dread he was. "Indeed, Your Majesty."

"And she managed to misplace them."

"She's lost a set," Thor said. "Five of many."

"And she hasn't lost them," Loki clarified. "They were stolen from her."

"And she has not been able to sense them?" Asmund asked.

"Only if they're used," Loki replied. "And their intrepid thieves have not yet used them."

"But we are here at the behest of our father, to discuss with you Asgard's plans for their reclamation, and how you and your people might aid us in that."

"And what will happen to them, once the Norn Stones are reclaimed?" Asmund asked.

"They will be returned to Karnilla in Nornheim," Loki replied.

"From which they were already once stolen."

"No fortress is impenetrable," Loki countered. "But security has been increased since the theft."

One of the servants stepped between Loki and Thor, a silver decanter in hand to refill their goblets. The white liquid looked like icy slush. Loki had only had to sniff his own cup to know the drink was far too sweet for his tastes.

Asmund puckered his lips, his finger tracing the rim of his glass. "If Asgard requires our assistance to reclaim the relic they lost, then we would like to discuss spreading the Nine Realms' dangerous artefacts around more liberally."

"You want the Norn Stones?" Thor demanded.

Asmund quirked an eyebrow. "Just a set. Every realm

should possess one, so that we are able to amplify our own powers and protect ourselves, rather than allowing Asgard to do it for us."

"You are safe under our father's protections," Thor replied.

"But the Norn Stones aren't?"

"Asgardians are protectors of the Nine Realms. That's how it has been for centuries. We did not come here to discuss a major shift in political powers. You are being told what will happen after an incident that may affect your realm, in hopes you will be able to better protect yourself for it. It's a courtesy we did not need to afford you."

"What my brother means," Loki argued as Thor's hand flexed at his side, "is that the Norn Stones belong to Asgard."

Asmund took another sip of his sweet wine. "They belong to Nornheim."

"A province of Asgard," Thor snapped.

Loki gritted his teeth. "The Norn Stones are safeguarded by our royal sorceress as a way of amplifying her power so that people across the Nine Realms may benefit from it."

"It also means that Asgard possesses magic that can be projected to my kingdom," Asmund replied. "Into any kingdom."

"An Asgardian sorceress has never used her magic against another realm," Thor interrupted. This was likely the single piece of information he had woken from their history lectures long enough to retain.

"And yet she managed to lose a pouch to a common thief." Asmund stared at Thor, then smiled again, but it didn't reach his eyes. "Do you understand the power the Norn Stones possess? They are limited only by the imagination of their wielder. They can reshape matter, create portals between realms, cast illusions, magnify abilities, raise the dead. Why should Asgard's sorceress have all those powers for herself? Keeping the Norn Stones all in one place makes them too powerful for any one realm. Their power should be divided."

"And you think your realm is worthy of possessing them?" Thor asked.

Asmund's face remained placid, but Loki saw the line of his jaw sharpen as he clenched his teeth. "As worthy as Asgard. I have the support of the southern court of the Ice Elves as well, and our delegation on Vanaheim has assured me they will join our cause."

"So there is a union of the Nine Realms assembling against Asgard," Thor said. "Have you summoned us here only to entrap us?"

"If Odin wishes to discuss the subject further, he can come himself rather than send his two boys."

"We speak for our father," Thor replied.

"Your father would never be so forceful and clumsy as you have been, Sons of Odin."

Thor stood up, his legs ramming the table so hard that it jolted. That ice-white wine sloshed from the glasses onto the table, soaking through the lace table runner. Loki stood too, grabbing his brother by the arm – like that would do anything to stop Thor, but his presence alone had sometimes been enough. He said a small spell, one for slowing a heart rate, calming someone in distress. Thor took a deep breath, the skin along his arms shuddering.

Asmund had not flinched. His goblet was still in his hand, and he took a delicate sip. "You are welcome in our court for the night, Sons of Odin. Perhaps we might discuss the matter further tomorrow."

"Of course," Loki said over whatever protest Thor began to raise – beneath his hand, Loki felt his brother's muscles flex again. "Thank you for your hospitality. We'll be retiring."

He turned from the table and ran straight into the captain of the guard, who had been approaching in case

Thor actually did overturn the table. They both grabbed on to each other to keep from falling.

"Apologies," the guard murmured.

"My fault," Loki replied with a smile, then turned to his brother. "Thor? Coming?"

Thor stared at Asmund, his eyes narrowing, then stalked away, pushing past both Loki and the guard and storming from the room, the dining hall doors clattering against the wall with the force of his exit.

Chapter Eight

"**W**hat is this madness?" Thor demanded as they followed their escorts down the hall to their chambers. Loki was struggling to keep up – even with the spikes on the bottoms of his boots, Loki found it hard to find his grip on the ice floors. "Those Stones do not belong to Alfheim, or any other realm. They belong to Asgard!"

"Technically, Nornheim," Loki replied.

"A province of Asgard."

"Yes, I heard you the first time. Good to know you listened to the first five minutes of our geography class. Your tutor would be so proud." Loki's feet slipped on the ice floor and he skated a few steps, nearly toppling over. Thor grabbed him, hauling him upright, though the thoughtfulness of the gesture was undermined by the tightness of the grip and the glare that accompanied it.

"Don't test me, Loki. I am not in a sporting mood."

"You seemed to be feeling very sportsmanly as you rubbed yourself all over the elvish royalty."

"I was being friendly."

"You were being informal. Didn't you read the brief from the librarian?"

Thor made another growling sound and swatted the air like he was batting that sentence away. "I do not have the time for reading."

"I know, kissing with Lady Sif among the haystacks must take so much out of you."

For a moment, he thought Thor might slam him into the wall, and wondered if that would count as an inter-dimensional incident or a domestic one. Did a squabble between brothers mean more or less of a crisis if it took place off their own world? Thor had shoved him plenty of times without it inciting some sort of war.

"My lords," one of the guards interrupted, and Loki realised they had stopped in front of a door.

When the guards let them into their room, Thor stomped past them without a word and Loki followed, sparing the men a brief nod of thanks. The room had the same angled ceiling as the banquet hall, though the walls were smooth and lined with thick tapestries. Loki imagined this must be the room for guests who were not accustomed to the cold. The beds were layered with snowy grey pelts, with a window built into the wall across from them. Thor flung himself onto a bed, ignoring the thump of his head hitting the ice headboard. Loki didn't dare hope his brother had actually knocked himself out and he would get some peace to think. He crossed to the window and looked out over the courtyard and the guards patrolling the grounds below.

"Wasn't this meant to be simple?" Thor asked suddenly. "Father said this would all be simple."

Loki replied without looking, "There are no simple assignments from Father."

"Not when you're involved there aren't," Thor snapped.

Loki's eyes flitted to Thor. He knew his brother well enough to discern when Thor was being mean simply for the pleasure of getting a rise out of him, and knew the most infuriating response he could give in return was a calm, even tone. "You mean because those assignments don't involve punching your way out of trouble?"

"I have… other skills!"

"But using multi-syllabic words isn't among them."

"Then you can be the one to return to Father and tell him in as many syllables as you choose that we left with instructions to articulate a plan of reclamation and returned with an inter-dimensional war," Thor snapped.

"You're so dramatic."

"What will we tell Father?"

"We needn't tell him anything if the Elves agree to drop this ridiculous proposition on their own accord."

"And how do we convince them to do that?"

"We prove their Prism is nowhere near as safe as they claim."

"Their Prism?" Thor repeated.

"The centre of the palace – the most secure location in Alfheim. Its magic is used to power the entire court and creates heat-less light. Really, at least *skim* the briefs, won't you?"

"And how do you propose we make our way into the Prism chamber?"

"Let's start here." Loki reached into the pocket of his coat, withdrew a set of heavy keys and threw them onto the bed beside Thor.

Thor sat up, staring at the keys, then looked up at Loki. "Where did you get these?"

"They were a gift."

In truth, when Thor was putting on his show at dinner, Loki had waited until the guard had passed behind his chair before starting to make his exit so he could smash straight into her. She was high-ranking – she had a plume on her helmet that none of the others wore, and the hilt of her sword was more ornate. When they collided, she was distracted with apologies and keeping her balance and the Elves' natural distaste for physical contact. Loki had taken the keys he had seen bulging in her pocket and replaced them with his cutlery set from the feast table so their weight wouldn't be missed. He wasn't certain when their absence would be noted, but so far no alarm had been raised. She'd probably be too embarrassed to admit the oversight for at least another day. She'd make her fellows use their keys, search clandestinely. If Loki was feeling generous, maybe he would plant them somewhere to be found later and the guard would never have to admit she'd misplaced her keys.

The moment Asmund turned the talk against them, Loki had begun to plot what they could do next. Thor might not have seen the turn coming, but Loki had felt it brewing in the air. The Elves wouldn't hear their arguments and were clearly using the missing Norn Stones as a means of starting a fight they had long wanted to pick with Asgard, so the only way to stop them would be to prove their shortcomings. Force them to retreat quietly without his father ever knowing there had been rumblings of an insurrection.

He could not afford to fail this assignment. Perhaps Thor could, but Loki had far too much to prove, and far fewer chances to do so.

"We can continue our negotiations tomorrow," he said, "reach a tense impasse with the Prince-General, and return to Asgard to tell Father that we allowed the Prince-General of the Ice Elves – a man whose entire puny kingdom could barely fill a cupboard in the Asgardian palace – to push us around, and also there is apparently some sort of inter-realm coalition forming against Asgard's ability to keep its relics protected, calling into question our authority across the universe."

"Or?"

"Or we prove that, even at their best, the Ice Elves' security pales in comparison to what we have on Asgard. They could not protect the Stones – let alone any other relics – the way we can. Asmund is put in his place, and we return to Father with the compliance of the Alfheim Prince-General in assisting in finding the Norn Stones."

Thor didn't answer.

"But if you aren't willing to take control of the situation,"

Loki prompted, "that's fine. Perhaps your next assignment will be more negotiations with the Ice Elves. Though I imagine Odin will oversee them this time, as we failed alone. But Father will stand with us. For us, actually. We probably won't be permitted to talk, since we mucked this up."

Thor kneaded one fist into his open palm. Loki swore he could hear him thinking – it was a rusty, crunching noise. "Stop baiting me."

"I'm telling you the reality of the situation," Loki replied. "Those Stones are the property of Asgard. They are powerful and dangerous, and should not be in the care of a court whose captain of the guard doesn't notice her keys have been taken from her own pocket. So if not us, who will be the next thief to gain access to them? If the Ice Elves had a set of the Norn Stones, they'd be on the black market of Svartalfheim before the next feast day."

Thor snatched up the keys, threw them in the air once, and caught them. Then he smiled at Loki – certainly the first smile he'd given his brother since they'd arrived. Probably in longer than that. "This was supposed to be an easy assignment."

Loki pulled his fur cloak back over his shoulders. He could feel a spell sparking at his fingertips. "But wouldn't that be boring?"

Chapter Nine

The hallways of the Ice Court were all coated in a layer of fine snow, but it turned crunchy and frosty the closer Thor and Loki drew to the centre of the palace. They had waited to leave their chambers until darkness fell, but the orbs trapped inside the ice floes along the halls still emanated an eerie blue light. It was, Loki thought, the perfect light for sneaking around.

The temperature continued to drop the deeper they moved into the court. Even the few guards they came upon – each of them easily dispatched with a small spell encouraging them to look the other way or, if Loki wasn't quick enough, a hard thump on the back of the head from Thor – were wearing heavier cloaks than the guards who stood watch at the table for supper. The material looked slick and oily, like fish scales. "Why aren't you freezing?" Thor hissed at Loki. He had his arms folded hard against his chest, holding his cloak closed tightly over him. At his belt, his hammer, Mjolnir, created an unfortunate bulge in the fur.

There were three sets of doors that had to be breached to reach the Prism of the Ice Court, all roughly hewn from thick ice, built for strength rather than aesthetics. Each opened with a different key from the captain's belt. Alfheim did not have the magical undercurrents to power more advanced defence systems the same way Asgard did.

Behind the final set of doors, the room's ceiling was cathedral-high, and an enormous cylinder of pulsing blue light was encased in ice at its centre. Loki felt the hair rise on the back of his neck, the strength of so much concentrated magic in a single space vibrating through him. A spindly bridge ran from the door to the walkway surrounding the Prism. It looked so delicate that Loki was sure it would crack beneath his and Thor's weight. Beneath the bridge, water pooled, its surface glistening with chunks of ice. A thin trail of frigid water dropped from the ceiling and trickled down his back. He looked up. The ceiling above the bridge was lined with rows of icicles, translucent and trembling as though they were ready to fall. Their tips looked as sharp as swords.

Thor took a tentative first step onto the bridge. It crunched under his step, and they both winced, but the bridge held. Thor took another step, then another, until he was several feet from the doorway, and gave an experimental jump. The bridge trembled, but there was no crack. Nothing snapped beneath his feet. He turned back to Loki. "It's stronger than it looks. Come on." As he followed, Loki noticed Mjolnir in Thor's hand, though he wasn't sure what fight his brother was preparing for.

Loki felt a prickle across his skin, a different sensation than the one raised by the Prism's power. The creeping sense of a dread he couldn't place was snaking through him, and he almost glanced behind them to see if someone was coming. It felt like they were being watched.

"So." Thor reached the walkway surrounding the Prism and spread his arms as he turned back to Loki. "We have breached the centre of the Ice Court. Proven the Elves unfit to hold the Norn Stones. What do we do now?"

Loki stepped up beside Thor and glanced down. In the cerulean light, his skin looked blue, his hands unfamiliar.

"We could shut it down," Thor said. "Or destroy it.

That would likely be less technical. Though it might be a bit more hostile... what's the matter?"

"Something's wrong."

"What do you mean, something's wrong? This was your idea."

Loki tried to take a step after Thor, but it was a struggle to lift his foot from the ground. Ice cracked, and he felt the cold shards through his trousers. He looked down. A thin film of ice had begun to form round the bottom of his boots. He kicked his feet free, trampling the ice back to snow. "In suggesting this idea, I did not say it would be entirely devoid of complications."

"Then let us proceed before we encounter them. Shall we—" Thor had started down the walkway, but then pulled up suddenly. He looked down, and when Loki looked too, he realised Thor's leg was encased in a creeping skin of ice almost to the knee. Thor tried to thrash his way out, but the ice had him trapped. He growled with frustration and began to hack at it with Mjolnir, but the slow progress he made was undone as the ice kept creeping up his leg. His other foot was coated in it now too.

"Loki! What's happening?"

Loki felt something tightening round his legs and looked down. His feet were caught in the ice, thick trunks of frigid crystals pinning him in place. He tried to pull free, but the ice was unrelenting. He conjured a ball of hot energy between his hands and attempted to melt the ice, but it regrew too quickly.

Loki felt another drop of water on his head and he looked up. The ceiling seemed to be glowing orange, a colour that felt so foreign in the anaemic hues of the Ice Court he thought certainly it must be a trick of the light.

Then the first icicle fell, puncturing a hole in the ice bridge leading back to the door.

"This is a trap!" Loki slid his set of Asgardian blades from his sleeves, and jammed one hard into the side of the Prism, trying to pull himself up and out of the ice. He felt a wrench in his shoulders. Thor had managed to get one leg free with Mjolnir, but the ice was creeping up his torso on the other side. He grunted with effort, twisting round to get a better angle for a strike, but his hammer bounced off the ice. He thrust his hand in the air, urging Mjolnir to pull him free, but he was as rooted as a tree.

Another icicle fell and a section of the bridge was knocked into the ice below, sending jagged splinters flying in the air. Loki felt them sting his face. The next icicle knocked out the centre of the bridge altogether. Long streams of water were dribbling down from the ceiling, freezing again as they struck the pools below.

The ice was up to Loki's waist now. He took a breath, trying to summon all the magic he could to blast it from him, but it was too strong and climbing up him too fast. It was constricting his chest, making it hard for him to breathe. And even if he had managed to break free, their only exit had been destroyed. The water below was rising as the icicles dropped into it, its surface turning foamy and white. Thor shouted in pain as the ice closed round his hand, still clutching Mjolnir, straining the bones of his fingers into a tighter and tighter fist.

Then the doors to the Prism chamber flew open, and Loki heard shouting. He craned his neck and saw soldiers assembled, spears and bows all trained on him and Thor. In their centre stood the Prince-General, his own blade drawn but held casually before him. He did not look surprised to see the Asgardian princes in the centre of his fortress and up to their necks in ice.

Loki's heart sank. While he preferred capture over being swallowed by an icy river, this would mean Odin would certainly hear of what they had done. And this plan to show the strength of Asgard had turned into slightly more of an inter-dimensional incident than Loki had planned for.

Beside him, Thor must have sensed what he was feeling, for he said softly, "Worry not, brother. Father will understand."

Chapter Ten

Odin did not understand.

"After so many years" – he stared down at his sons, both kneeling before his throne with their heads bent; his gaze that could have melted the Ice Court to the ground – "of so many people devoting their lives to your tutelage, your study, your understanding of diplomacy, what insanity is it that compelled you to believe that the appropriate action in this situation was to stage an elaborate raid of the fortifications of an allied realm in an attempt to prove the unworthiness of their claim to a relic?"

"It's not their relic to claim," Thor mumbled. Loki glanced over at him. He was glaring at the floor, picking at a loose thread on his trousers and looking more indignant than he had a right to in the middle of one of their father's lectures.

"Silence!" Odin slammed Gungnir on the ground, the clang of the spear on stone reverberating through the empty throne room. Loki felt the shudder in his knees, all the way through him. It rattled his teeth. Odin had not yet shared their failure with Frigga, or his advisors, or any members of the royal court, which was a small blessing. Prince-General Asmund had personally returned them to Asgard, both princes soaking wet and burnt from the cold. He and his soldiers had marched them from the observatory down the Bifrost Bridge and into the throne room with a stride so purposeful that none of the posted sentries stopped them. The only small mercy was that, in the early dawn hours, few members of the court were there to witness their shame. Odin had to be woken from his bed, and was still in his robe as he stared down at them. Odin may have been the only being in the Nine Realms who was able to look intimidating in his pyjamas.

Loki shifted on the hard stone. His knees, still not recovered from being encased in the ice for so long, were beginning to ache.

"We were tricked," Thor said, standing without invitation. Odin did not snap at him. Had it been Loki who stood, the hall would have echoed with Odin's disapproval. "The

Prince-General lured us to his court in an attempt to withhold his assistance unless we promised to surrender control of the Norn Stones to them."

"And in return," Odin replied, "you attempted no negotiations, nor did you consult me. You committed an act of destruction and subversion."

"We were provoked," Thor argued.

"Of course you were provoked!" Odin replied. "My sons caught attempting to sabotage the power source of the Ice Court is a reasonable justification for saying that Asgard is unfit to retain its most powerful artefacts."

"Father—" Thor began, but Odin snapped, "Enough from you."

He adjusted his grip on Gungnir, then said, his voice lowered but still sharp edged, "You have disappointed me, my sons. Perhaps, in my age, and my hope that you would prove yourselves worthy of your birthright, I gave you too much responsibility too quickly."

"The idea was not mine," Thor burst out. His cheeks were bright red, and a vein throbbed in his forehead. "Loki was the one who proposed it as a show of our strength. He orchestrated it."

Loki wondered, momentarily, what their father would do if he turned Thor into a ferret in the middle of the throne room.

Odin's eyes slid from Thor to Loki, his gaze as slippery and flammable as an oil spill. "Is this true, Loki?"

Loki, still on his knees, glanced up, first to his brother, who would not look at him, then to his father, who was staring far too intently. Even if it had been his fault, Thor didn't have to say it quite so bluntly. They could have at least shared the responsibility.

"I had no choice but to go along with him," Thor said.

No, Loki decided, ferret was far too good for Thor. He'd rather turn him into a spider. Something small and irritating that could easily be squashed underfoot.

"Loki," Odin said.

Loki swallowed, eyes still downcast. The sunlight through the throne room windows felt too bright and buttery against the golden tiles. He wanted to close his eyes. "It's true, Father."

"Very well." Odin stared them both down for a moment, drumming his fingers against the handle of his spear. Then he said, "Thor, a king does not attempt to pass the blame for his actions to others. He accepts the consequences. A king is strong enough to take ownership of his mistakes, and admit when he has made a poor decision. He does not claim he had no choice, for he knows there is always a choice. You would do well to remember that."

"Yes, Father," Thor mumbled.

"And Loki…" Odin turned to him, and Loki swore he saw the circles under his father's eyes darken. Odin heaved a sigh, then said, "Leave us please, Thor. I would like a private word with your brother."

Thor did not need to be told twice. He darted from the throne room, determinedly looking everywhere but at Loki. The door thudded behind him. Odin pushed himself up with the aid of Gungnir, then began to descend the stairs from his throne. His tread was heavy. "Rise, my son." Loki obeyed. He was slimmer than his father, but close enough to the same height that he could look him in the eye when they stood on even ground. But Odin stopped two steps before the bottom so he was still looking down upon him. How was it that Odin had the sort of piercing gaze with only one eye that most men could not have achieved were they made of eyeballs?

"We are given our instincts for a reason," Odin said, and Loki braced himself for one of his father's morality lectures that sounded profound until you actually tried to puzzle out what it meant. Most of his court would think the king's words were simply too philosophical for them to understand, but Loki had endured them often enough to know they were usually nonsense.

Odin went on. "Our instincts protect us. They keep us safe. Our first instincts come from our truest heart, the purest ore of our desires. And I worry, my son, that your instincts are corrupt." Loki raised his head to argue, but Odin held up a hand. "I hoped very much that you were ready for this assignment. After years of studying with your mother, I wanted you to be ready. I wanted you to be worthy of such a task, and able to put your own foolish heart behind you to see it completed. I wanted this to be an opportunity for you to demonstrate that you are ready for further undertakings and the responsibilities that belong to members of the royal court. I fear I was wrong."

Loki clenched his jaw. Of course Odin's parting words to Thor had been about the role of a king, but when he spoke to Loki, he barely treated him as a courtier.

"The Ice Elves were plotting against us," Loki said before he could stop himself.

"So you felt it fair to plot in return?" Odin replied, the question somehow both rhetorical and sincere.

Loki sucked in his cheeks. "I owed them nothing."

"You were guests in their court," Odin said. "Diplomatic ambassadors. You owed them your respect. All your actions, your base instincts for the situation, were the opposite of how you should have behaved. There are some things that cannot be taught, and one is how to change our hearts. Our true selves always show themselves in the end."

A thousand retorts crossed Loki's mind, ranging from *It was your meat-headed golden boy who was ready to knock out the Prince-General over dinner* to *Maybe if you had been a more benevolent ruler of the Nine Realms, we wouldn't have these diplomatic squabbles at all* to *If you would stop thinking of me as nothing more than the enemy you saw in the Godseye Mirror, perhaps you would have as much patience and forgiveness in your heart for me as you do for Thor.*

But all he said was, "Yes, Father."

Odin turned, heaving himself back up the stairs again, and called, with his back to Loki, "Thor and I will return to Alfheim to make a formal apology to the Ice Elves before we continue the hunt for the stolen Norn Stones."

The muscles in Loki's thighs were burning. He wanted to run. "What about me?"

Odin paused, face turned away. "You will remain here in Asgard."

Loki's head shot up. "Father—"

"You may continue your studies," Odin said, like he hadn't spoken. "And attend court meetings while we are away."

"Am I meant to be grateful for that?" Loki said, his voice laced with bitterness.

Loki knew he shouldn't say anything more. He was

treading dangerous waters already. "I don't want to stay here while you give Thor another opportunity to prove himself worthy to be king," he said. Odin stopped, one hand now resting on the arm of his throne. Loki pressed on. "Give me another chance. Another chance to prove I am capable. My instincts are not corrupt, I simply made a mistake. I admit that. Is that not what you said a king should do?"

Odin sank into his throne, running a hand over his beard as he studied Loki. "You think I have not given you adequate chances to prove yourself worthy of the crown?" he asked.

Loki could feel the snare closing around him, but he answered anyway. "No, Father."

"And you ask me for another chance."

"Yes."

"Then you can take on one of the duties that your foolishness has robbed me of time to oversee. There is a question of magic on Earth—"

"Midgard?" Loki snorted. "Never mind, I'll stay on Asgard."

"You asked me for another chance," Odin said.

Loki resisted the urge to slam a fist into the throne room floor. Leave it to his father to turn his words backwards upon him. "What assignment do you have for me on Midgard?" he asked through clenched teeth.

"There is an organisation there that monitors movement from other realms into theirs. The people of Midgard remain largely ignorant to the existence of realms beyond their own, and we wish to keep it that way. They call themselves the SHARP Society."

"That's a ridiculous name," Loki muttered, but Odin either did not hear or ignored him.

"They suspect a series of mysterious deaths in the city of London are a result of magical forces from another realm, and they were hoping for our support in an investigation." He raised an eyebrow at Loki. "Does that not sound exciting enough for you? Death and magic?"

Loki shrugged. "They're just humans."

"Are their lives so much less important than yours?"

Well, yes, they're humans, Loki thought, but he didn't say it.

"You will travel to Midgard on my behalf," Odin continued. "Meet with the SHARP Society and investigate their claims. You will offer them any advice and assistance they may require."

Advice and assistance. Thor was searching for the thief responsible for stealing one of Asgard's most powerful magical artefacts, while Loki was being sent to smile and nod as humans acted hysterical in his general direction about how they were being murdered by Asgardians. Like Asgardians didn't have better things to do.

"You will return when I have deemed you worthy of a return," Odin said.

It was banishment in miniature. *Sit in the corner until you've learnt your lesson.*

Loki was plotting a way out of this, when Odin let out a long sigh, two fingers to his temple. Even the slope of his shoulders looked weary. He always looked weary these days, but this time he seemed to be specifically weary of Loki. "Do not test this kindness," he said. "The effects of your foolish mistake will be great enough to justify a larger punishment. You should thank me for my mercy."

Loki stared at his father, his muscles clenching. He could have set the throne room on fire, but that seemed a little obvious.

Instead, he did what he had long ago learnt was best when it came to his father: he bowed his head and swallowed his pride. He had years of practice pretending to be at peace with Odin's choices. He was accomplished at sitting quietly and letting anger simmer unseen inside him.

"Yes, Father," he said, and when he left the throne room, Odin did not call him back.

Chapter Eleven

*L*oki returned to his chambers, feeling more a prisoner in his own bedroom now than he had when his father had exiled him there as a child as punishment for minor offences. Though just like in the days of his youth, Loki allowed himself a very dramatic flop of despair onto the bed. He stared up at the hangings, rage funnelling through him despite his best attempts to quell it. How many times had Thor behaved far more recklessly than he had while on missions for Odin? He'd never been benched like this, forbidden from participating in the assignments that were so clearly meant to test the princes for how well suited they were to kingship. Was it the baiting that had been his downfall? The premeditation? Or was Odin simply looking for a reason to keep him as unfit for the throne as possible?

Thor didn't knock, but Loki recognised the sound of his entrance. No one else's tread was quite so galumphing. "Leave me alone," Loki said, his cheek still smashed into the fur blanket on his bed.

"I'm sorry," Thor said.

"No, you're not." Loki sat up, resisting the urge to comb his fingers through his hair. He knew he'd messed it up on the bed covers, but vanity had a way of getting undercut by one's anger in moments like these. "If you were sorry, you would have taken the responsibility that was yours. Weren't you listening to Father?"

"None of it was mine."

"Oh, that's strange, I remember a blond giant with me when we broke into the Ice Elves' Prism chamber. He was trying to smash his way out, but that must have been a hallucination of my small mind."

"My presence does not mean I am responsible," Thor countered.

"But you supported me," Loki said. "You could have told him that at least."

"I'm sorry, Loki, but I cannot risk our father's anger

right now." Thor's voice was so devoid of anything besides righteousness that it made Loki want to scream.

"And you think I can?" Loki demanded.

"I'm trying to help you. So is Father."

Loki fell backwards onto the bed again. "Go away, I'm sulking."

"Please don't be angry with me."

"Oh, I think we're a bit late for that. You're lucky I haven't set my horde of tiny dragons upon you. Their teeth are very sharp and their appetites insatiable."

"Loki, if I have caused you some offence—"

"*If?*"

Thor let out a heavy sigh. "I don't know what it is that I have done," he said, his voice softer than usual.

Loki snorted. "Oh, please."

"I'm trying to apologise."

"And yet you can't even work out what for, so I don't think it counts."

Thor stared at him, his hands working in and out of fists at his side. Loki braced himself, ready for Thor to strike something, possibly him, but instead he said, his tone soft with hurt, "You are so determined to despise me, aren't you?"

It would have been better to be struck. Loki flinched as though he had been. "I don't—"

But Thor held up a hand. "Spare me, brother. Whatever you hold against me, whatever I have done to wound you, I hope you know that I am not your enemy. I want to fight by your side, not against you."

They stared at each other. Loki wished he knew how to explain the way he could not separate his brother from all the unseen forces that had shaped them both. It was everything that had dug the trench between them. He did not know how to exist in this world that had been built around them, the world they had kept building for themselves because they knew no other way. A world that had decided that what waited for him was the fate of a traitor.

At last, Thor said, "Father and I are returning to Alfheim."

Loki rolled onto his back, pulling his knees up to his chest. "Send me a raven when you get there so I know you're safe," he replied dryly.

Silence. Then, "I wish you were coming."

"Not me," Loki replied, staring at the wall. "So glad to be going to Midgard with all the humans and their adorable little human faces and greasy food and magic-less blood."

"Be careful," Thor said.

Loki flicked his fingers in Thor's direction. "Begone."

Loki stared at the ceiling, counting the dimples in the coffered tiles and waiting for the sound of his brother's boots to retreat, followed by the soft snap of the door. He finally pushed a hand through his hair – it had grown long, nearly to his shoulders. He wound it round his palm and curled his fingers into it, the way Amora used to when she was thinking, but rather than unfurling like hers always had, it tangled into a knot. Loki let his hand fall away.

Be the witch, he told himself. Be cleverer and sharper and quicker than everyone else. Come up with *something*.

But his brain felt thick and stalled with jealousy and fury. For the first time, he wished that he too had a hammer. He wanted to break something.

But perhaps there was some destruction he could do on Midgard. Not much. And not obvious. Just enough to get him noticed. Just enough to be the hero when he cleaned up a mess of his own making.

Chapter Twelve

*W*hen the shimmering haze of the portal that had sent him from Asgard to Earth cleared, Loki discovered that he had been dropped in the middle of nowhere. Midgard was already fairly middle-of-nowhere as far as the Nine Realms went, and in this particular spot, there was also no discernible speck of civilisation. And it was raining. He hadn't even taken his first real step on Midgard and he was already up to his ankles in mud.

The countryside around him was not altogether unpleasant, but it was just that – countryside. Rolling hills in riotous green where small white dots of sheep grazed, soggy and bleating in annoyance. Loki wished he could join them in their protestations. He took a step, prising his foot from the sucking mud. He nearly left a boot behind, and was shocked when his foot landed not in another puddle of squelching mud but on something hard. He looked down. He had been deposited on some sort of track, two parallel iron bars driven into the ground connected by perpendicular wooden boards.

An ear-splitting whistle startled him so badly he nearly tipped over. He looked up. Something was barrelling at him along the track, spitting black smoke into the sky. The rain spat and fizzed off its metal siding. It let out another shriek, clearly having no intention of slowing down, and Loki leapt out of the way, conjuring his knife on instinct.

It was a train – he only realised it as it chugged past him, pistons pushing the wheels along the track. From his perch in the engine, the driver shouted something that Loki was certain was an obscenity. He struggled to his feet, tucking his knife back into his sleeve. He had forgotten just how primitive Midgardians were, how fantastically behind their technology was compared to the Asgardians'. Steam trains were archaic. What backward hole had his father dropped him into?

Loki watched the train pass, the first few carriages lined with windows behind which Loki could make out the dim, crouched shapes of humans. The back half of the train was black window-less carriages. On the sides an emblem had been painted – a snake eating its own tail surrounding a skull with crossed bones beneath it. There were words as well, but the train was moving faster than the Allspeak could translate them.

He looked down at himself, mud now splattered up to his knees and his clothes sticking to him from the hot rain. He sighed, then conjured a small spell to shield himself from the rain. Frigga had warned him that Midgard would drain his strength faster than Asgard, and without magic thick and native like it was on his home realm, his power would be slower to replenish. Small spells would take more energy, and in excess, would eventually bleed him dry. Magic didn't live in the air here like it did in Asgard – he would have to rely on the built-up reserves of strength his mother had taught him to carry like canteens of water on a desert expedition.

But surely his own comfort constituted some kind of emergency.

His father had given him the name of the meeting site where the SHARP Society would be waiting for him – the Norse Wing of the British Museum in London. Like that meant anything. Whatever it was, he was certain it wasn't in the middle of this emerald landscape and driving rain. He followed the train tracks up the hill, and when he crested it, he could see where the sky darkened ahead, black smoke from stacks turning the sky smudged and thick. Even the rain seemed to flinch away from it.

London, he thought, and began to follow the tracks towards it.

*A*fter a lifetime on Asgard, he had known Midgard would disappoint him. But did it truly have to be so dramatic about it? The shift – from the crystalline skies over his father's golden palace, streets so clean they sparkled and white water dripping from the fountains in every square, to the streets of London, where the skies were grey in a way that made it hard to tell if it was twilight or hazy and towers spat hideous smoke into the sky – was disorienting. The air felt chewy, the streets swampy and all the people seemed as grey as the sky. Figures passed along the street, hunched inside ratty clothes, shouting and screaming at each other over the clanking of great machinery out of sight. On the corners, tiny boys in ragged clothes thrust newspapers into the air, shouting headlines in chorus with the screams from brothels and taverns, though it couldn't have been more than midday. People pushed greasy hair away from their faces, their skin as rugged and brown as old boot leather, while they led half-starved-looking horses, their flanks vibrating with flies, the contents of their stomachs emptied onto the street, then left to lie where it landed.

He hoped it was just mud on his boots.

But London was not entirely unpleasant, if one subtracted the filth. It felt like a battlefield, somewhere raucous and dizzying, where it took an over-abundance of wits just to stay on your feet. Asgard was as quiet as a funeral procession in comparison. Perhaps this was how Thor felt when he stared down an enemy across a battlefield and primed for a fight. This chaotic energy, this heat emanating off the city, this was Loki's kind of fight.

If Asgard failed him, perhaps this could be his kingdom. The city seemed in desperate need of some leadership. They may even build a statue of him.

It took a few moments of observation before he changed his clothes from the green-and-black tunic he always wore on Asgard to mimic what he saw the Midgardian men wearing: a dark suit and a high-winged collar cinched with a tie. He held out a hand, conjured a tall, dark hat, and put it upon his head. A glamoured outfit wasn't a sustainable spell, but it would do until he could find the SHARP Society and some actual clothes. Though he wasn't planning on staying long enough to truly need to replace them.

He walked along for a street or so, decided the hat was far too tall, and pushed it down into a soft wool cap.

It only took questioning a newsboy to get the location of the British Museum – a newsboy who demanded a coin for his trouble. Loki gave him a rock he enchanted to appear as a shilling, and the boy was pleased enough by this that he offered to take him there.

The British Museum was puny compared to the libraries and galleries Loki had grown up visiting in the capital, but with the black city surrounding it, he guessed it was meant to be impressive. The stone front was lined with curl-topped columns and had a peaked roof, the stone still sparkling beneath the layer of grime from the factory smoke. Inside, more stone arches were stacked atop each other to form the entry hall, and voices echoed off the high ceiling, shouts of laughter and greeting occasionally breaking free from the tumult. Loki followed the map he had taken from the entrance, past two taxidermic animals with long necks at the top of the stairs, through the hallway with low glass cases where gold tombs were laid out in a row as neat as piano keys.

Loki didn't know whom he was looking for, or how

he was meant to find the SHARP Society, but he knew as soon as he reached the Norse Wing. It was strange, to be surrounded by so many things that looked like items from his home, but not quite. Perhaps if Asgard had rolled around in the mud, cracked off a few edges and then decayed for several thousand years it would look something like these relics. The shapes were familiar. The engraved bronze, lines interweaving and twining like the roots of Yggdrasil, the round domes of dragon heads carved on axe pommels, ornate shields and goblets that, had they been shined up and decorated with a few jewels, he could imagine the lesser nobles of his father's court drinking from over a feast table. The cases were crowded, and a second tier of galleries closed off to the public held ancient-looking books bound in heavy, creased leather. Tables topped with glass ran down the centre of the hall, with pendants, cutlery and small fragments of stone lined up on cushions inside each.

It was absolutely mad, Loki thought as he examined what looked like two shapeless lumps of rock that a small plaque identified as a pair of dice, the things the humans saved as vestiges of their ancestors and deemed worthy of putting on display. Who wanted to be remembered by their fork or their comb? That told you nothing about the way people were.

"It's fascinating, isn't it?"

Loki turned. A young man was standing behind him, his ruddy-brown hair curling out in unruly tendrils from under a flat cap, and his pale skin covered in so many freckles it looked like he had been splattered with mud. Perhaps he had been – Loki didn't trust this filthy city. Loki was no expert in judging the age of Midgardians, but the man must have been young, though he was leaning on a cane, his weight carefully balanced on one leg.

Loki tucked his hands into his pockets, then turned back to the case, adopting what he thought was an unmistakable *leave me alone* posture. "It's fine."

"Fine?" The young man was either relentless or oblivious to social cues, for he limped up to the case beside Loki and prodded the glass, leaving behind a smudged fingerprint. "Do you even know what it is that you're looking at?"

"Cutlery," Loki replied.

The man frowned at the fingerprint, then pulled his sleeve up over his hand and tried to wipe it away, only succeeding in lengthening the smudge. "Cutlery from a civilisation of people who lived thousands of years ago."

"Are you some sort of docent?" Loki asked. "Because I'm not looking for a tour."

"No, I'm just deeply offended when I see people not appreciating the artefacts. Look at those." He turned to the case behind them. Inside the case, two skeletons were laid out and arranged like they were still lying in the earth. The bones looked brittle and shaggy, but someone had folded the fingers of each over the pommel of their swords, the blades gone black with age. One of the skulls was caved-in on one side, the other wearing a helmet with a protective stave carved upon the front.

The boy was watching Loki's face, like he was waiting for a reaction. Loki purposely kept his features as blank as possible, just to annoy him. "They're warriors," the boy finally prompted.

"No, those are definitely skeletons."

"In life they were warriors."

"Does that matter?" Loki asked. "Death makes every man the same."

"Well, they weren't both men, for a start," the man interrupted. "That one's a woman. The swords were exchanged as marriage rites. Better than rings, I think. More practical."

"If you're a warrior."

"Or if you don't care for jewellery." The man offered a hand. His nails had dirty crescents beneath them, and his skin was dry and chapped. "I'm Theo, by the way. Theo Bell."

Loki gave his hand a disdainful pat, then turned away. "I'm not interested."

"Aren't you impressed by all this?" Theo asked.

"Am I supposed to be?" Loki replied.

"Well yes, since this is one of the most interesting wings in one of the most interesting places in London."

Loki laughed. "They're not very impressive for the finest treasures of your realm."

"Realm?" Theo repeated.

"Your... world."

"It's your world too."

"Doesn't mean I have to be impressed by what someone dug up in their back garden and stuck a plaque to." He nodded to the case, where a pair of objects sat that a sign said were called 'pans', though they looked more like lumps of fused metal, roughly hewn and chewed round the edges by rust.

"Do you know the stories?" Theo asked as Loki turned away. "The gods and the myths. And the ships and swords and things. Odin and Thor and Loki."

Loki stopped and glanced backwards over his shoulder. Theo must be trying to give him some sort of sign, and

Loki was desperately trying to ignore it. If this was the representative for the SHARP Society, he was turning round and heading straight back to Asgard. He'd rather scrub the palace floors with his fingernails while his father and Thor searched for the Stones than deal with humans.

Theo smiled at him. His ears were too big for his face, and they stuck out like leaves. "You're not from round here, are you?"

Loki sighed, resigning himself to the fact that this was indeed his contact. "Well, aren't you *sharp?*"

Theo's grin broadened. "Can I show you something else?"

"You might as well."

"Try not to sound too resigned to the fact."

Loki followed Theo across the gallery, towards a closed door that Theo unlatched using a key from his pocket with a quick glance around the room before ushering Loki through. He thought it would lead to the next exhibition, but instead it seemed to be a dark storage area with no windows and nothing but long wooden crates that looked eerily like coffins, their insides spilling over with soft white straw to protect whatever had been carried inside. They looked big enough to transport the married skeletons and their swords.

The door snapped shut behind him, and Loki turned to face Theo, arms crossed. "What am I supposed to see in this closet? More skeletons? Don't you humans have a saying about that?" Theo didn't reply. He had leant his cane against the door and was fiddling with a small silver case. "What's that?"

"Do you take snuff?" Theo asked, flipping the latch.

"No."

"Probably good." He shrugged. "I haven't got any."

Loki frowned. "What?"

Before Loki could react, Theo flipped the case open and blew a coarse black powder, like charcoal from a dying fire crushed underfoot, into Loki's face. Loki inhaled before he could stop himself, and felt the burn as the powder coated his throat. He coughed, then coughed again harder, the dark haze hanging in the air from the powder somehow turning thicker. His vision flickered. "What was that?" he managed to choke out between coughs.

Theo had already tucked the silver case back into his pocket and was reaching for a hook beside the door, stripping off his own jacket to replace it with another that looked like part of a uniform. This couldn't be the group that was meant to welcome him as an ambassador of a foreign land – this was a trap.

Loki fumbled for his knives, but his magic was becoming harder to reach. A blade slid into his hand with painful slowness. At the sound, Theo looked up from his buttons and frowned. "For God's sake." He put the tip of his cane to Loki's chest and, before Loki could swipe it away with his blade, pushed. It was not a hard push. Certainly not hard enough to fell an Asgardian. But Loki's legs gave out with very little persuading, and he tipped backwards, landing hard in the open crate behind him. A cloud of straw fluttered up around him, settling on the fabric of his suit. The knife slipped from his hand and skittered across the floor.

Theo snatched it up and tucked it into his boot, the motion too smooth for it to have been his first time handling a weapon. He shoved his cane beneath the handle of the door, then limped to the box. Loki fought to sit up, though his limbs all felt gelatinous and like they were taking too long to understand what his brain was asking of them.

Theo watched him struggle for a moment, like he was debating what to do next, then fumbled in his pocket for the case again. He threw the remaining contents into Loki's face.

Loki's muscles went slack, and he fell back into the box. He blinked slowly, and when he opened his eyes again, there was a slam overhead and everything went dark. Was he unconscious at last, whatever that powder had been finally consuming him? But then he heard a hammering, and the darkness was interrupted by a small line of light, a crack between panels as the lid was nailed into place above him.

He couldn't get a spell gathered, nor could he make his knife appear again in his hand, though he would have loved dearly to stab it upwards through the lid of this box and try to guess where it had landed by the sound Theo made. He was still not entirely conscious when he heard voices, and then the box was tipped – tipped in the wrong direction, so that his head was pointing downwards and he slid the length of it, landing hard. The strength of the blow was almost enough to knock him back to sense.

Outside the box, he heard Theo yelp. "Oh, no, that's the wrong way up!"

"He'll be fine." The box thumped again and Loki felt his teeth rattle together. *Wake up,* he tried to command himself. *Move! Think! Fight!*

But all he could do was lie there, a knot at the bottom of what may be his own coffin, as he was carried forwards to who knew where.

Chapter Thirteen

The effects of the powder got worse before they got better, or perhaps it was just the disorienting feeling of being upside down in a dark, confined box that had him so properly dead to the world. He didn't know how much time passed between Theo knocking him out and when the box was at last deposited with a heavy thud. Or how long after that it was that he heard the crack of a crowbar against the lid, breaking open what Theo had nailed into place. The powder must have mucked with his senses more than he had realised in the dark, for he couldn't see anything. Only a few snatches of conversation flashed through his consciousness.

"—used all of it?!"

"I had to!" He recognised Theo's voice, but not that of the woman he was conversing with.

"Do you know how hard that is to come by?" the woman said. "That was enough to knock out a Frost Giant."

"How do you know what it would take to flatten a Frost Giant?" Theo asked.

A third voice – another man's, this one deep and gruff. "They'd be knocked out by the smell of your pits."

"Shut up," Theo snapped.

Then Loki heard the clatter of the crowbar thrown aside, and the heave of the lid. It hit the floor with a wooden crack. He could feel the faint press of light against his eyelids, but he kept them shut. Someone grabbed his wrist, and he wondered if they were checking for a pulse to make certain he was still alive. He could feel the straw against the back of his neck, feel someone's touch on his skin.

Then he heard Theo's voice right over the top of him. "So that's him, is it? Loki, Prince of Asgard, Lord of Darkness and Mischief and Chaos and Everything Evil?"

Had he had his wits slightly more about him, he would have protested soundly against that last honorific, and particularly the certainty with which it was delivered. He was a prince of Asgard, but Lord of Darkness, etc., had never been inked on his birth record.

A few short, ringing steps, heels on stone. Then the woman's voice. "I don't believe that's his preferred title. But yes, that's him."

"Bit smaller than I was expecting," said the third voice from what seemed a few feet away. "Sort of like you, Bell."

"Can it, Gem," the woman said. "Get him up."

Loki still wasn't certain how much of a hold the powder had on him, but he wasn't prepared to go anywhere limp and helpless and without a fight. He opened his eyes, springing up at the same moment. Theo, who had been leaning over him, reeled backwards with a cry of surprise. Loki's limbs still felt liquid and wobbly, but he had enough control and enough focus to grab Theo with one arm round his neck and press him to his chest, making sure Theo was between him and whomever it was he had been delivered to.

He summoned his dagger to his hand, raised it to Theo's throat, and found... nothing. His hand was empty.

He looked up. He was standing in a dingy coffin-shaped room, narrow and low-ceilinged and lined with more crates and cases like the one he had been so unceremoniously thrown into. The only illumination came from a few lanterns, their light swirling as moths collected around their frames, and one small window at the crook of the ceiling. Through its small, grimy panes, he could see boots passing by on the street. On the other side of the box he had been carried in, staring back at him in surprise, were two people, one of them a big-shouldered man with hair so close-cropped it looked painted on. The breadth of his shoulders would have intimidated even Thor. He had snatched up the crowbar that must have been used to pry the lid off the crate and raised it for a fight. Beside him, with a cautionary hand thrown out to ward off that fight, was a woman, her greying hair pulled back into a tidy bun. She cut an immaculate figure in wide-legged black trousers that Loki thought for a moment were a skirt until she took a step forwards. She was so thin she looked like a skeleton with flesh rolled thinly out over her like pastry draped over the top of a pie. She was regarding Loki with a careful gaze, but no fear.

He reached for his dagger again, shaking out his arm that wasn't clamped round Theo's throat. Nothing. Theo clawed at Loki's grip, trying to pull himself free, and Loki almost let him go. His grand plan of taking a hostage and using his life as a bargaining chip against whoever his captors were had backfired entirely, as he had no weapon.

Or any spells. Something had happened between the Norse Wing of the museum and here that had knocked the glamour off his clothes – he was in his Asgardian tunic again. He fumbled for something else, to conjure another weapon, or at least summon something on the ground to his hand that could do enough damage if swung around with great enthusiasm. But he couldn't find a drop of magic in this bone-dry air. It felt like thirst in the desert – worse for how incurable it was. He almost gasped for it.

"Well, that was" – the woman folded her arms – "dramatic." Her voice had a clipped, formal accent to it, in sharp contrast to the big man's haphazard vowels and slurred consonants.

"Who are you?" Loki demanded. "And where am I?"

"First, let Mr Bell go and then we can have a proper conversation."

"Not until I know what you want with me." He flexed his hand, desperate for a knife, and he actually growled with frustration when it failed to manifest. It felt just out of his reach, like his fingers brushing the edge of a cliff as he fell.

"If you are attempting some sort of conjuring, you can desist," the woman said. "Unless you wish to exhaust yourself."

"Why can't I use my magic?" Loki demanded.

"We have placed restraints upon you," the woman replied.

"Restraints?" Loki held up his free hand and noticed a metal band round his wrist. They must have clamped it on him while he was mostly incapacitated. There was one round his other wrist as well, and he recognised the metal at once – it was Asgardian, the same chains they used in the palace dungeons to keep prisoners from using magic. And if they were the same as the ones in Asgard, the wearer couldn't remove them. He cursed under his breath.

"Mrs S," Theo said, his voice hoarse, and Loki realised he had been tightening his arm round Theo's neck without meaning to. He relaxed his hold and Theo gasped, though his fingers were still digging sharply into Loki's arm.

"We were planning to have you bound more securely when you woke," the woman – Mrs S – said. "To prevent exactly this sort of confusion and in hopes we might have a reasonable discussion first."

"I don't think there's much room for reason when one party is bound," Loki replied.

A small smile tugged at her lips for the first time. "Clearly you've been wearing the wrong bindings, my dear. Now, why don't you let Mr Bell go and we can all introduce ourselves. No one will be tied to anything."

"You'll take these off me?" Loki asked, holding up one of his hands to refer to the restraints.

"Not just yet," Mrs S replied. "But I think we can all agree that so long as they stay in place, you holding Mr Bell is rather pointless."

"I can fight you without magic."

"I'm sure you can, my dear. But this will all go much smoother if you don't prove it."

"Do you have more of the blackout powder?" the big man – Gem – said, his fist flexing on the crowbar, like he was ready to use it if the answer turned up negative.

"I should," Mrs S mumbled with a dark look at Theo. Even Loki thought that criticising a man currently being held hostage was a bit of a low blow.

"It wasn't my fault!" Theo choked. "He's stronger than you thought!"

"For God's sake," Mrs S muttered. "He's turning blue. Your Majesty, please release my associate. This is an unseemly show of force for a man of your standing."

"How do you know who I am?" Loki demanded.

Mrs S quirked an eyebrow, and reluctantly, Loki let his arm fall from round Theo's throat. Theo staggered away, catching himself on the edge of the box when his bad leg gave out. Gem picked up Theo's cane from where he had dropped it and threw it to him.

Though none of them were particularly threatening,

apart from Gem – though he was threatening in the same way as Thor, so it felt familiar – Loki was suddenly very aware that he was outnumbered, in an unknown place, unarmed and unable to access any source of power. He'd never been cut off from his magic before, and that alone made his skin itch. His eyes darted around the room, searching for something he could use as a weapon if they came at him, but the best instruments had already been claimed, namely Gem's crowbar and Theo's cane. The room was bare but for the straw-lined crates strewn around, and rooting through them in hopes of finding something pointy didn't seem like the most effective use of his time. He flexed his hands absently. He knew how to fight unaided by spells, but not having them there if he needed them was creating a logjam in his brain. He couldn't seem to think up any plan that wouldn't require magic.

"Your Majesty," Mrs S said, "Would you like to sit down?"

"On what?" Loki asked.

Mrs S shrugged. "I'm simply being polite. Though I'm happy to have Gem squat into a bench formation if you need it."

"Who are you?" he demanded.

"We are representatives of a vast secret organisation

called the Society for Hospitable Activities from Remote Planets."

"You're the SHARP Society," Loki said.

Mrs S gave him a small bow. A ring on her left hand flashed. "We are."

"My father said you knew I was coming."

"We did."

"So why did you knock me out and take away my magic?"

"We manage inter-dimensional threats, and you are an inter-dimensional visitor of unknown power," she replied. "One cannot be too careful when dealing with someone like... you."

"What do you mean, someone like me?" Loki demanded. "I'm here on behalf of my father." Surely Odin hadn't told them what a delinquent he was, but it seemed the only explanation for how far and incorrectly his reputation had preceded him. He was certain they wouldn't have knocked out his father and dumped him in a box if he had showed up himself.

"You're a foreign being on our planet. Forgive us for taking precautions."

"You are absolutely not forgiven."

"I would remind you," Mrs S said, "you are a guest in our realm."

"I'm here on behalf of my father, the king of Asgard," he snapped. "I have a *right* to be in your realm."

Mrs S's mouth twitched. "How very colonialist of you. You are a guest of the SHARP Society—"

"That's a daft name, so you're aware," Loki said. "SHARP Society. It doesn't mean anything and the S is redundant."

"It stands for the Society for Hospitable Activities—" Mrs S began, but Loki interrupted.

"Yes, I heard you the first time."

"We picked an acronym and worked backwards," Theo murmured.

"Perhaps you could find something more accurate. You could call yourselves the Society where Hospitality is Ignored Totally. Or, for short—"

"Regardless of those trivialities," Mrs S interrupted, "we at the SHARP Society are dedicated to observing and intervening as necessary when beings from other realms travel to our planet. And though you are our guest, it is still our responsibility to keep you in check while you're here."

Loki wanted to protest that he had thus far done nothing to prove he needed any kind of 'keeping in check' and also that he was here to help them, not make more trouble, but it was a circle he was tired of running in.

"Has your father informed you why you've been summoned here?" Mrs S asked.

"*Summoned* seems like a rather grand word," Loki replied. He wanted so badly to sit down on the edge of the crate – his legs were still wobbling beneath him – but he was determined not to show any weakness. "I'm here as a favour."

"Quibbling over trivialities is so much less amusing than you seem to think," Mrs S replied. Her voice was fraying. He was testing her patience. Good. "We have requested help from Asgard because of a string of inexplicable deaths here in London."

Loki threw up his hands. "Easy, I've already cracked it."

A moment of silence, then Theo asked timidly, "Have you?"

"Yes." Loki folded his hands before him, as if he were about to deliver devastating news, and said very seriously, "You humans are being murdered by... other humans." When none of them laughed, Loki did it for them. "You think an inter-dimensional being dropped in on your pathetic realm just to murder a few humans? No offence to your fragile little lives, but I could wipe out whole continents if I chose to. Most hospitable *aliens* have better things to do with their time."

"Our people are dying, and a magician is to blame," Mrs S said. "You cannot look past that."

"You have no proof of that."

"But once you see these corpses, you'll understand that their deaths were not caused by humans. There's magic involved."

"Looking at corpses. Tempting." He rubbed his hands together. "But I think we're done here."

He headed towards the door, but Mrs S, Gem and Theo all stepped in together, barring him. "We need aid from Asgard," Mrs S said, and for the first time, he heard a slight fray of desperation in her voice. "We cannot fight a sorcerer without Asgard's help."

"I don't think you're going to have to," Loki replied. "This city seems like the kind of place where plenty of people die completely unaided by magic. So if you could show me the way out, I'll be getting home." Gem glanced at Mrs S, then started to reach for the box again, but Loki interrupted, "Absolutely not, I am not going anywhere in a coffin."

"I'll take him back to the fairy ring," Theo said.

"Are you sure?" Mrs S's eyes flicked to his cane, but if Theo noticed, he didn't acknowledge it.

"Gem has to be on patrol soon. I'll go."

"Just directions to the surface will suffice," Loki replied. He wasn't keen on spending more time with these humans than was necessary. "And take these off, please." He thrust his wrists to Theo, nodding at the cuffs.

Theo glanced at Mrs S for direction. She still had her arms folded, and he was beginning to wonder if her eyes were permanently narrowed. "Not just yet."

"If I can't glamour my clothes, I'll look like a damn fool walking around your city streets."

"We'll risk it, for the safety of Mr Bell," Mrs S said.

"Don't worry," Theo added. "You'll be far from the most foolish-looking man in London. Come on, follow me. This place can be hard to get out of."

Loki snorted. "You're a hobby detective squad, not the secret police."

"We're a secret society," Mrs S replied. "Not much point if you don't actually try to keep your secrets. Go with him, Theo. And we'll see you soon, Your Majesty." She gave him a small bow.

Loki offered a curled lip in return. "I certainly hope not."

Chapter Fourteen

*A*s reluctant as Loki was to admit Theo was right, the tunnels beneath the British Museum were difficult to navigate. Each one looked the same – dark, narrow stone, poorly lit and lined with more crates, some larger than the one Loki had been trapped in, some pocket size. A few were cracked open to reveal their contents – statue heads carved from grey stone, a golden brooch, a breastplate inlaid with intricate filigree. By the time he and Theo emerged into the sallow sunlight of the London streets, he had lost all sense of where he was or in what direction they had gone.

Theo tapped his cane against the bottom of his boot, scraping off something sticky that had adhered itself there.

"You need to get back to the fairy ring."

"What's that?"

"Where you arrived – the spot of connection between Asgard and Earth," Theo replied. "There are hundreds of them on Earth, but that one's the closest."

"Why do you call it a fairy ring?"

"Oh, humans have all sorts of names for them. Stonehenges, fairy rings, portals. Places where the worlds overlap."

"You could have met me there then instead of at that museum."

Theo shrugged. "Well, we drew straws and no one wanted to stand in the rain and wait for you. And Mrs S works for the museum, so it's convenient, and they have enough odd items lying around that no one asks questions about ours. And it's easier to meet an enemy on familiar turf."

"Am I your enemy?" Loki asked. "I thought I was your much-needed aid from Asgard."

Theo either didn't hear him or ignored the question. He looped his scarf round his neck, and blew a short breath onto his bare hands. "Come on, then, if you're so keen to be home."

But Loki didn't move. "I'm not going to hurt you."

Theo smiled. "I sort of believe you."

Neither of them spoke as they walked. Theo paid a lamplighter for a candle and shade as the night began to fall. It cast a dull shine along the road ahead of them as the city gave way to countryside, the tenuous pavement of London's roads turning to muddy paths rutted with wheel tracks and the deep impressions of livestock hooves.

Theo was the first to break their silence. He tipped his head back, ruddy curls cascading from his face. In the twilight, his skin looked slick, like he had just surfaced from underwater. A small smile settled over his lips, and he lifted a hand, pointing upwards. "Look."

Loki raised his head to follow Theo's finger, not sure what he was meant to be seeing.

"The sky is so clear tonight," Theo said. "You can never see the stars in the city."

And Loki realised Theo was only looking to the stars. He looked up too, the thick sugar of a galaxy trailing through the darkness, flecked on all sides by sprinkles of planets and constellations. At their backs, the city glowed golden with lantern light, its own small galaxy beneath the sky. London was brass and silver, draped in steamy clouds with empty hollows and pockets that swallowed the light.

"Can we see Asgard from here?" Theo asked, his head still thrown back, like he was drinking in the view.

Loki knew the answer – the stars were closer to him than home – but he still found himself searching the sky. "No."

"Do you have stars in Asgard?" Theo asked.

"Do we *have* them?"

"Can you see them?" Theo clarified. "Or is your sky empty at night?"

"We can see the stars in Asgard," Loki said. "More than you can see from Earth. A dozen times this amount."

"What about beer?" Theo asked.

"Can we see beer from Asgard?"

Theo tore his eyes from the sky long enough to give Loki a disparaging look. "Do you have beer in Asgard?"

"All kinds," Loki replied, not certain where these questions were leading, but amused in spite of himself that Theo's thoughts had slid so deftly from the sky to the drink. "And honey-sweet wines and fizzing cordials and apple mead that will keep you young and vinegar spirits that will knock a grown man out cold."

"Music?"

"At every feast."

"And dancing?"

"What else does one do when music plays?"

"And dogs?"

Loki frowned, stumped for the first time. "I don't know what that is, so I don't think so."

"Well, that's going to count against Asgard."

Now it was Loki's turn for the disparaging glance. "As if Midgard could hope to compete with Asgard."

Theo threw back his head and laughed. "Midgard? Is that what you call us?"

"Is it funny?"

"No, no, I like it. *Midgard*. Does that make me a *Midgardian*?" He puffed out his chest when he said it. "It sounds powerful."

"Perhaps it's not translating quite right, then."

"Give me a moment, will you?" Theo stopped and leant up against a tree, stretching out his bad leg with a wince. "Sorry I don't move so fast."

"Here." Loki held out a hand, and Theo surrendered the lantern to him. "Is it broken?"

"My leg?" Theo chuckled through his heavy breath. "A long time ago. It never healed right."

"We could have taken the train," Loki said. "There's a track that goes straight through the… whatever you called it. Fairy ring."

Theo snorted. "You don't want to be on that train. It's the Necropolis Rail. The train that carries the dead from London to the cemeteries to be buried."

"Do you not bury your dead in your own city?"

Theo shook his head. "No room left. They started stacking bodies in the streets after the cholera outbreak." He let out another heavy breath, and Loki suddenly felt strange, watching him wince and catch his breath in silence. He glanced around the countryside, the treetops making dark clouds against the sky. A pack of bats flew overhead, blotting out the moon.

When he turned back, Theo was looking at him with a strange smile on his face.

"Why are you looking at me like that?" Loki demanded.

Theo's face didn't change. "Like what?"

"Like you find me amusing."

"I wouldn't say amusing." He took up his cane from where he'd leant it against the tree and pushed himself back to his feet with another wince. "I've worked with Mrs S for a while now, but I've never actually met someone from another realm. And it's *you*." Theo held out a hand for the lantern, but Loki didn't surrender it.

"What do you mean it's me?"

"You're..." Theo gestured vaguely through the air. "You're Loki."

"I'm aware." They stared at each other through the darkness, the air between them golden and dancing as the lantern flickered. Theo knew something about him – Loki was sure of it. Sure the whole Society knew it. But he couldn't fathom what it was that made them treat him so strangely. What had his father told them? *I'll be sending my son who I have foreseen bringing about the end of the world by leading an army against me. Have a wonderful time, feel free to take his magic and make assumptions!*

He wouldn't put it past his father.

Theo straightened his cap, then started down the path again. "We're nearly there."

When they reached the ring – a bare circle in the grass, bisected by the railway tracks – Theo threw aside his cane and sank down on a nearby stone, pulling off his cap and wiping his arm over his forehead. Loki waited for him to say something – some sort of farewell or thanks for coming or, based on the way Theo had looked at him earlier, perhaps a request to sign something in memory of their time together. But Theo just gave him that stupid grin.

Loki held out his wrists. "Remove these."

"Not even a *please*?" Theo asked.

"You've taken away my magic, so forgive me if I'm not in a mood for politeness."

Theo took Loki's hand in his and turned it, palm to the sky, as he began to fiddle with the mechanism at the hinge. Loki almost asked him how he'd come to possess a modified set of Asgardian restraints, but it wouldn't matter soon. He'd be home.

If his father would let him come home.

The cuffs came free and Theo patted Loki on the pulse point before tucking them into his jacket pocket. "There you are, Your Highness. You're free."

Loki flexed his fingers, feeling magic begin to swell below his skin again. Slower than it did in Asgard, but still a relief. He shook out his sleeves, then faced Theo. "Well. I'd say it was good to meet you, but I do hate lying."

"All right, then."

Loki didn't move, not sure why he was so annoyed by Theo's refusal to even give him a wave. Theo stretched out his legs, hands behind his head, a theatrical gesture of unconcern. "Pay attention – you're about to see inter-dimensional travel. If you enjoyed my general presence, you may faint from the excitement of this."

"We'll see," Theo replied.

"What do you mean *we'll see*?"

"I mean we'll see if Asgard wants you back."

"Why don't you think Asgard wants me back?" Loki said, the belligerence rising in his tone to cover the panic. His father had said he'd be forced to stay here until his work had been deemed satisfactory, but surely Odin would let him limp back to Asgard and beg forgiveness.

"Because you were sent here to help us, and you haven't done that," Theo replied. "Mrs S says your father won't let you return home until this is finished."

"Fine. Well, watch this." He stalked to the centre of the fairy ring and then, just to make a properly dramatic show of it so that Theo would feel the true fool, threw his head back to the sky and opened his arms. "Heimdall!" he called. "Bring me back!"

He waited for the sky to open. The air to shimmer and crack. The clouds to part and the Bifrost to open to him.

Nothing.

The night was silent.

"Heimdall!" Loki shouted again. "Heimdall, bring me back!"

Still nothing.

Loki went on staring at the sky, sure that the ferocity of his stare could penetrate the Bifrost. "Heimdall, this isn't funny. Bring me back. Tell Father to bring me back. Heimdall, you son of a—" Behind him, he heard a soft crunch, and he whirled on Theo. "Are you *eating?!*"

Theo froze, one hand dipped into a greasy paper bag. "I missed dinner because I was tending to you."

"I'm trying to access an inter-dimensional portal and you're snacking?"

He held the bag out to Loki. "Would you like some? They're peanuts. Do you have peanuts on Asgard?"

Loki threw his head to the sky again. "Heimdall, get me out of this realm. Heimdall, come on!" He turned back to Theo. "I suspect he's occupied elsewhere."

"Of course."

"Or he wasn't expecting me."

Theo threw a nut in the air, missed it with his mouth and it bounced off his forehead. "All right."

"So Heimdall is probably… napping. Or something."

"Of course," Theo said with a solemn nod, though Loki could see that cheeky smile just beyond his lips. "Napping. Would you like to wait around and try him in a bit? When he isn't… napping?"

Loki wanted to stamp his feet in frustration. Waking Heimdall from his probably improbable nap wasn't an option. His mother had mentioned that while one day he might learn to project himself between realms, that one day was still in the future. Even on Asgard, his projections still struggled to move between rooms in the palace. "Do you have a way to contact Asgard?" he demanded of Theo. "I need to speak to my father."

Theo wiped his mouth with the back of his hand. "Back at our headquarters."

Loki almost rolled his eyes. Of course this amateur squad had a *headquarters*. "Fine. Take me to your headquarters."

"First you have to come with me to Southwark."

"Where?"

"A neighbourhood in the southern city. That's where the bodies are being kept." Theo shoved the bag of peanuts back into his pocket and smiled. "As long as you're waiting for Heimdall to wake up, you might as well have a look at what we brought you here for."

Loki sighed through his nose, an action he knew made his nostrils flare out in an unattractive away – at least that's what Amora had told him – but he indulged the drama. What he truly would have liked to do was collapse onto the ground, cross his arms and refuse to be budged until Heimdall sucked him up out of this godforsaken realm through the Bifrost. He would rather have lain down in this soggy grass and let it swallow him whole than go back to London. He should be on Alfheim. He should be with his father and his brother. He should be doing work fit for a king, which was certainly not done in so much mud. Or if it was, there should have been a sword involved.

"I will not abide restraints again," Loki said.

Theo shrugged. "Fine, but I won't abide any magical mischief you might make."

As if you could do anything about it. He was tempted to turn Theo into a frog, just to remind him who was truly in charge here. But a spell that large would be too hard to justify on this magic-less planet. No matter how satisfying it would be.

Loki let out a feathery sigh. "Fine. Take me to the Southern Erk."

"Actually it's Erk of the South," Theo corrected.

"What did I say?" A small smile tugged at Theo's lips. Loki glared at him. "You're mocking me."

"They did warn me you were quick."

"Who's they?"

"All the books."

"Books?" Loki repeated, but Theo had already taken up his cane and started walking down the pathway again, back the way they had come.

"Come on, Mrs S is waiting at the morgue."

ᚠᚱᛏᛗ

Chapter Fifteen

$\int$outhwark clung to the banks of a rancid river, the smell of which made Loki pull the collar of his shirt up over his nose, though Theo told him that was both rude and conspicuous. Even in the frail light of the gas lamps, the brick houses were dark with soot, and plaster crumbled off the siding, dropping into the streets like rockslides in miniature. Children with charcoal-smeared faces sat along the edges of the collapsing roofs, spitting seeds or possibly teeth at each other. The cobbles bulged at random, like great tree roots were pushing them up from beneath, and the gutters spilt onto the streets, their contents thick and sluggish.

"This is your home, is it?" Loki asked, his lip curling as

he stepped deliberately over a spill of rotting produce that had been mashed into the stones. "You must be so proud."

"Come, now, I'm sure there are more decrepit corners of Yggdrasil," Theo replied cheerfully. "Not many, but at least one."

"If there are, I have yet to see them."

He followed Theo down a short lane, then round the back of a red-shuttered tavern with crooked window-panes and an upper storey that seemed to jut out at a dangerous angle over the first. To Loki's surprise, the alley was flooded with people waiting to get into the building ahead of them, and the noise of excited chatter echoed off the narrow corridor. Sellers stalked through the crowd, hawking orange slices and biscuits for sale.

Perhaps something had been lost in the translation, but this was not what Loki had expected when Theo had said he was taking him to see bodies. He had thought of a graveyard, or at least a quiet basement. The underground corridor of the museum seemed a more appropriate place for a viewing than this, with the crowds and the noise and an atmosphere of merry excitement. This felt like a fairground.

Theo seemed unconcerned by any of it. He navigated them through the mob of people to where Mrs S was waiting for them, sitting on a coal bin and knitting. She hardly glanced up as they approached. "Good to see you weren't robbed on your way here," she called as they approached.

"I'm sure His Majesty would have protected me from any roving thugs," Theo replied. "Or at least protected himself and accidentally saved me as well."

"Still have your wallet?" she asked.

"Yes," Theo replied confidently, but Loki saw his hand dart to his trouser pocket. "What are you knitting?"

"A hat for the prince," she replied, holding up the shapeless bundle of yarn. "Something with horns."

"What is this place?" Loki interjected.

Mrs S flicked her eyes to him. "Didn't Theo tell you?"

"He said it was a morgue," Loki replied. "So what are all these people doing here?"

"They're tourists," Mrs S replied, tucking her knitting into her carpet bag and dusting off her trousers as she stood. "They started putting the dead on display in Paris, and now it's all the rage in London too. Charge sixpence a head for a prime view of the many ways you may leave this world. The grizzlier the better. This spate of recent mysterious deaths has given them quite a boost." She nodded at the onlookers. "Perhaps they should pay your people some sort of commission."

"They all are here to see the dead?" Loki asked. "That's morbid."

Mrs S shrugged. "That's human. Come along, boys."

As they made their way to the entrance, shuffled forwards by the flow of the tourists, Loki noticed another group gathered round the doors, this one holding signs in the air or wearing them on strapped boards looped over their shoulders. Some of them were chanting the same message as was painted on many of their signs: LET THEM LIVE. Mrs S brushed past them without sparing a glance.

As Loki went to follow her, a woman wearing one of the signs over her shoulders leapt in front of him and shoved a leaflet into his hand. "Those you see presented as dead in these halls are not yet gone to their great reward!" she shouted, sort of to him and sort of so the whole crowd could hear. He felt her spit speckle his face. She must have been near Mrs S's age, with dark hair flecked grey and a small, neat hat secured to it with a pin. Her dark skirt was starting to ride up where her sign had caught the hem. "The police and the papers would have you believe them dead, but they merely sleep!" she shouted, thrusting a leaflet at Theo, who stuck his free hand into his pocket and looked purposefully in the other direction. "To bury these dead would be to bury the living!"

"Come on." Theo removed his hand from his pocket and grabbed Loki's arm, dragging him through the door and away from the woman. Loki glanced down at the leaflet. The text was blotchy from her sweaty palms, but the illustration at the top depicted a skeleton reclining in a scrolled frame, one bony hand wrapped round a curled scythe. The bold, striped letters beneath it read DO NOT LET THE LIVING SUFFOCATE IN A GRAVE. THERE IS STILL HOPE FOR THOSE THOUGHT DEAD.

There followed several long paragraphs in a font too small to make out without proper study, but it looked like the woman with the sign had a lot to say on the subject. Loki shoved the leaflet into his pocket, then followed Theo and Mrs S into the morgue.

*T*he morgue hallways were so stuffed full of people that Loki had to crane his neck to see into the dimly lit cases, and even then he hardly got a proper view. On each side of the aisle, floor-to-ceiling glass windows separated the spectators from corpses laid out on slabs, tilted so their bodies could be viewed. Cloth had been artfully draped across the bodies in strategic places, with the corpses' clothes hung on pegs behind them. Dark water dripped from a pipe along the ceiling, presumably cold to keep the bodies preserved. A few policemen roamed on both sides of the glass, though they seemed unperturbed by the spectacle.

Disgust curdled inside him. Though it wasn't at all the death; death did not bother him. All lives ended – he and Thor had been taught that from a young age. Warriors gave their lives for Asgard every day. Even those who died old and at peace would have been worn down in the service of the realm. Instead it was the indignity of this, the twisted display, the gawkers, the small children with their noses pressed against the glass, smearing their faces as they gaped at open wounds. They were only humans, but in that moment, he wished he could place each of them in a ship and see them off to Hel.

"This is barbaric," he murmured.

Beside him, Theo was staring at the floor. "At least we have dogs."

Mrs S stopped at the back of the largest group and waited, one foot tapping out an impatient rhythm. As they moved towards the glass, Loki heard someone behind him whisper to her friend, "I've been waiting all week to see the living dead."

He whipped round. "What did you say?"

The girl, short and spotty and still young, started at his attention, but then jutted out her chin defiantly. "That's what they call them in the papers," she said. "The ones that's dead for no reason." She poked a finger towards the glass. "She should be living."

The words rang inside him, the memory of what his father had seen years ago the last time he looked in the Godseye Mirror. *Leading an army of the living dead.*

He felt Mrs S's fingers coil round his arm, pulling him away from the girls. "Take a look, we won't have long."

Theo hung back in the crowd, but Loki followed her to the front of the group until they were nearly pressed up against the glass, staring at the woman's body laid out before them. She was naked, her long hair uncoiled and hanging in limp threads to cover her breasts. In the icy light through the glass, she didn't look dead at all: she looked asleep. Her skin hadn't taken on the clammy, pale quality that other corpses did, and there was no discolouration, no sign of sickness or injury. In spite of how reluctant he was to appear interested in this assignment, Loki found himself stepping so close that his nose brushed the glass.

It was only then that he looked down the row of corpses and realised they were all this way – still asleep and entirely not-dead-looking. There was no blood, no injury, no visible signs of what had felled them. They had nothing in common but death.

He suddenly understood how Mrs S had been so certain

that it was magic that had killed these people. There was nothing natural here. Nothing human, nothing native to Midgard.

"How many are there?" he asked, his breath fogging the glass.

"Two more hallways full," Mrs S replied. He could see the hard set of her mouth reflected in the glass. "Scotland Yard won't allow any of them to be buried. They're keeping them all here for observation."

"Observation?" Loki repeated. "What are they expecting to observe, exactly?"

"They're not sure," she replied. "But because none of the bodies are decaying, some believe that they're not actually dead. There's no heartbeat or breath, but they're not corpses. The police could prove death or life definitively with an autopsy – an examination of a body to determine how they died—"

"I know what an autopsy is," Loki interrupted, though he hadn't.

"—but none of the families of the dead have granted permission."

"Why does it matter if there's an autopsy?" Loki asked, trying to say the word with confidence, but it felt strange in his mouth.

If his pronunciation had been questionable, Mrs S didn't comment. "Because of their unusual state, it's the only way these people can be declared officially dead and then be buried. And since there's still some debate as to whether or not they're actually dead, the coroner can't legally perform an autopsy without the family's consent. But no family wants to be the one to volunteer their darling brother or sister or mother or father to be cut open and taken apart if it turns out there's a way to revive them. So no autopsy, no burial. The bodies just pile up here on display. Groups like that lot outside" – she jerked her thumb over her shoulder the way they'd come – "have got to all the families and convinced them not to authorise an autopsy, because they think they're not actually dead."

"You mean the protesters?" Loki asked.

Mrs S nodded. "I don't know how things are done on Asgard, but here it's preferable not to put a living person in the ground – if they weren't dead already, they would be then."

"Yes, I believe that is universally true across the realms, except for a few subterranean dwellers who bury their dead in the sky."

Mrs S laughed softly. Loki could still see her faint reflection in the glass separating them from the body. "Each time I think I have learnt the strangest things about this universe, something stranger unveils itself. Sky funerals." She rubbed a hand over her chin, and he could tell she was picturing it, her mind unspooling.

"How did you find out about all this?" Loki asked.

"We have a man on the inside of the police force," Mrs S replied. "He tips us off. And it's our responsibility to know these things."

"Your responsibility by whose authority?"

"Your father's."

"And what does he give you in return?" He turned back to the glass. "You're wasting your time working for aliens, Mrs S."

"Well, will you be wasting it with us a bit longer, Your Majesty? I noticed you're not back in Asgard."

"My travels have been delayed." As much as he didn't want to admit it, to this woman or his father if he was ever allowed back in his realm, he was intrigued. Whatever magic it was that had a hold of these people, he hadn't seen it before.

"Have they, now?" Mrs S asked, and he ignored the amusement in her voice.

"So I suppose I'll stay and investigate this with you."

Her reflection smiled. "How very generous, Your Majesty."

Chapter Sixteen

*T*he SHARP Society office was located at Number 3½ Finch Street, like it had been forgotten until the last minute and then squashed into what was meant to be an alley. Hardly large enough to house a vast secret society. It had fewer windows and a narrower front door than the shops on either side. At its back, a factory belched black smoke at intermittent intervals. In the pale light of the early dawn, Loki could see a small hanging sign that read B. A. SHARP, ANTIQUITIES.

Though a bell over the door rang when Theo led Loki in, the shop looked deserted. Glass cases and shelves were bare, their corners collecting dust and cobwebs. The counter had begun to mould where a drop of water from a leaky pipe overhead kept up a steady stream. "Is the shop itself meant to be the antiquity?" Loki asked.

"What?" Theo looked up from fumbling to light a lamp. "Oh, no, it was Mr Sharp's. We only use the back room now – our office is through here. Come on."

Theo led him round the counter, through a musty velvet curtain that smelt like the water had once been dripping on it before taking over the counter.

This was barely an office. Loki was beginning to suspect they were barely a society.

The back room, in contrast to the shop, was packed. Books were stacked to the ceiling. A heavy round table crowded into the centre was sagging beneath the weight of papers and crates and one very rusty sword. A workstation had been shoved into one corner, wires and gears littering its top.

As Theo took off his coat, Loki picked up a ring with an obviously fake jewel. The stone was prised away from the setting and propped up to reveal a set of miniature gears.

"Don't touch that," Theo said quickly.

"What does it do?" Loki asked.

"It shoots darts tipped in a sedative. Or, it will, once it works. It's temperamental."

"Where did all this come from?" Loki asked.

"Me, mostly."

"You made it?"

"Some of it. I was an engineering student once. I was going to be an engineer as well, but that plan was rather... ruined." He shrugged. "It's probably all silly compared to what you have on Asgard."

"Yes."

Theo cast Loki a glare from where he was piling kindling into the stove. "You're not supposed to agree with me."

Loki shrugged. "You said it."

"Yes, but mostly in the hopes that you'd raise some kind of protest. *No, it's so impressive, worthy of Asgard, and you're wonderful and brilliant and handsome, Theo.*" He struck a match from a pack on the table and dropped it into the stove. It smoked, struggling to catch the kindling. "Asking too much, I suppose."

Loki picked up a set of tarnished gold gauntlets that looked more like something from his homeland than from Earth. "What do these do?"

Theo glanced up from a second match. "Nothing. They're antiques Mr Sharp found on an expedition."

"Mr Sharp. The mysterious purveyor of the empty shop."

"Not so mysterious," Theo replied. "Mrs S's husband. He was an archaeologist – collected Norse artefacts for the British Museum. They both were. Him and Mrs S. He was the one who first made contact with your father and Asgard, entirely by accident, after he found the fairy ring near Brookwood."

"Mr Sharp," Loki repeated. "Your daft society name makes so much more sense now." Theo snorted. "You should petition to change it, so you have something less embarrassing to put on your calling card."

"Not handing out many calling cards these days." Theo blew on the stove, then added, "And it's not much of a secret society if you go handing it about."

"Have you considered putting it to a vote?" Loki asked, running a finger along the grimy window sill. "The many, *many* other members of your clearly enormous secret organisation may be more likely to show up to your offices if you had a more fetching name."

He glanced at Theo, who was chewing on his lip, staring intently down at his matchbox.

"It's a tribute, the name," Theo said.

"A tribute?"

"To Mr Sharp."

"I assumed. What happened to him?"

"He died a few years back," Theo replied. "Before I met him. You can't conjure fire, can you? Now that I've taken the cuffs off." He threw the third blackened strike match into the stove. "It's bloody cold in here, and I can't get this to catch."

Loki considered him. Considered saying no. Theo did a dramatic shiver and chattered his teeth. "Fine." Loki crossed to the stove, rubbing his hands together partly for showmanship and, partly because it was indeed frigid in the tiny back room, gathered a flame between his fingers and dropped it into the belly of the stove. The kindling roared to life, bathing him and Theo in a rosy, warm glow. Loki pressed his hands to the top of the stove, then glanced at Theo. "What?"

"That's..." Theo ran a hand over his chin, and Loki suddenly felt strange, the way he always had on Asgard whenever his powers would manifest. But then Theo finished, "That's brilliant."

"It's a simple spell."

"Yes, well, some of us can't do spells at all." Theo hung his cane on the back of a chair at the table and sunk down into it, shifting the rusted sword off the stack of papers in front of him.

"Did you make those cuffs as well?" Loki asked, baiting

him, taking the seat across from Theo's and kicking his heels up against the stove. "The magic-suppressing ones."

"No, those came from Asgard," Theo replied. "Your father sent them to Mr Sharp so that any magical beings he detained could stay detained. Apparently, there were a few incidents."

It seemed to Loki that if you were enlisting humans to fight powerful magical beings on your behalf, the least you could do was arm them with the proper weaponry from the start, but before he could voice the thought, Theo pulled a stack of papers from the bottom of a tottering pile and began to fan them out over the table between them. "So, here are the police reports—"

"Hold on." Loki clamped a hand over the top of the first report just as Theo reached for it, and for a moment their hands were smashed together. It was inelegant and unintentional – the brief feeling of skin on skin startled them both, though only Theo shied away, rubbing his hand like it had been burnt.

"You promised to help me contact Asgard if I came with you to the morgue," Loki said.

"Did I?" Theo rubbed the back of his neck.

"I remember it like it was yesterday." A pause. "It was, in fact, a few hours ago."

"Yes, I recall, thank you." Theo heaved himself to his feet and retrieved a ceramic jug and bowl from a shelf by the workbench, then placed it on top of the police reports. He uncorked the jug, then emptied the clear liquid from it into the bowl. "This one is also from Odin."

"Aw, he gave you a jug of water?" Loki pressed a hand to his chest. "He's thoughtful like that, my father."

"No, he gave us a *bowl*," Theo corrected. "It works as a two-way means of communication between here and Asgard." Theo stepped back. The surface of the liquid shimmered, and from his angle, Loki could tell an image had formed, but he couldn't tell what it was. "Would you like some privacy?" Theo asked.

"Why? Can you hear both sides of the conversation?"

"Why?" Theo mimicked. "Are you going to be talking about me?"

"Possibly. Only disparaging things, I assure you."

Theo snagged his cane off the back of the chair, cast a longing gaze at the stove then called over his shoulder as he pushed through the velvet curtain, "Tell your father I said hello."

Loki bent over the bowl, its surface trembling slightly as though the ground below it was wavering. He had expected to see his father's council room reflected back, or Heimdall's observatory. Perhaps even the throne room. At the very least, the map-maker's offices or the library, the sort of places other dignitaries were shown when they visited or communicated with the Asgardian court.

But instead, he found himself staring at blank stones that it took him a moment to realise made up a ceiling. It was so wholly unremarkable and unadorned that there wasn't a chance it could be anywhere significant in the palace. Whatever place Odin had decided to accept communications from the SHARP Society, it was no place of honour. Loki felt a stab of anger at his father again for condemning him to this place, this embarrassment. Working with these humans Odin couldn't even spare a corner of his council room for communications with. He'd never make contact with someone in Asgard in this dark, hidden corner of the palace. He'd be lucky if a boy emptying chamber pots passed.

He straightened up, looking around for Theo. He considered going to fetch him, to ask how it was they ever made contact with Asgard if this was all they had, or if there was some schedule for when a guard on patrol would pass by. Then something flashed on the surface of the water, and Loki dipped back to it, his nose nearly skimming the surface.

"Thor!"

A long pause, then the shuffle of footsteps, and a shadow

fell over his line of vision, blotting out the ceiling. It was Thor, his hair knotted and stringy with sweat and his chest bare.

He let out a shout of surprise. "Loki!"

"Please tell me you're wearing pants," Loki replied.

"What are you doing in a washbasin?"

Is that where he was? Worse than expected. Odin had banished all communication with the SHARP Society to the changing rooms off the training arena where soldiers sparred. It was somewhere the king himself never went. "What are you doing answering the call of a talking washbasin?" Loki returned. "Are you at the training fields?"

"The changing rooms under them. You can't just…" Thor shifted, grabbing a towel from somewhere outside Loki's line of vision and throwing it over his shoulder like he was trying to cover himself. "What if I had been undressed?"

"Then I would have been forever scarred," Loki replied dryly. "Believe me, this isn't my first choice of location either."

Thor rubbed the towel over his head, then threw it onto the floor. Had he been present, it would have taken a good deal of effort for Loki not to retrieve it. "That won't dry if you leave it bunched up like that," he said.

"What?"

"The towel."

"Did you appear here just to discuss my… grooming habits?"

"Could you have picked a more upsetting way to phrase that?"

Thor let out a huffy sigh, cast his eyes down at the towel then seemed to make a conscious decision to be contrary and not pick it up. "Where are you?" he asked.

"On Midgard," Loki replied. "Where I was banished."

"You weren't banished," Thor replied indignantly. "You're on an assignment."

Loki gave him a saccharine smile. "Aw, that's precious you believe that. Why aren't you on Alfheim?"

"Father's gone alone," Thor replied. "He's sending me and a brigade to search for the Stones at a smuggling port near Vanaheim. One of our spies there thinks they might have passed into the black market."

Loki almost fell forwards into the basin in anger – and also a bit in the hope he'd fall straight into Asgard. "Another heroic quest to add to your generous supply."

"He thought it would be a better use of my skills—"

"Of course he did," Loki interrupted. "And my talents are better used playing detective with humans."

"It's important work for a king—" Thor began, but Loki cut him off.

"No, it's a waste of time meant to punish me. You have to get me out of here."

Thor frowned. "Call for Heimdall."

"I did. I think Father has told him not to bring me back. The Bifrost is closed to me."

"Then I shouldn't bring you back either."

Loki realised he was gripping the side of the basin without meaning to. "Brother, please."

"But your assignment—"

"There is no assignment. Father made up some sham reason to get me off Asgard and to placate these pathetic humans who think what happens to them matters to us. Let me come with you to find the Stones. I'd be so much more valuable to him there. He's out of the realm, he doesn't even have to know until I return with you."

Thor chewed the inside of his cheek, that familiar vein of consternation popping out in his forehead. "I'm sorry, brother."

"Thor, please—"

"I wish you luck with your assignment, and I'll see you when you return to Asgard."

"Thor!" Loki shouted, but his brother was already gone. Then he came back just long enough to snatch up the towel he had discarded, fold it clumsily and stalk away again.

Loki fell backwards into the chair, pressing his fists against his forehead and allowing himself a groan of frustration. He had, perhaps, exaggerated in saying that there was no reason for him to stay on Earth. Something magical truly was happening to these humans of London, but he didn't want to be the one to work it out. He wanted to be scouting the realms for the Norn Stones with Thor, not in a room so narrow he could barely spread his arms, surrounded by human approximations of Asgard and air so dry it made him itch. He wanted to be home. He wanted to be given a chance.

Loki stood abruptly and pushed through the curtain, almost smashing into Theo, who was leaning against the counter directly across from it.

"What happened to privacy?" Loki demanded.

"There was a curtain," Theo replied, the apples of his cheeks pink. Then, he asked, almost like he couldn't help himself, "So we're pathetic humans that don't matter to your father, are we?"

Loki blew a long sigh through his nose. "I'm sure the work you do is very important to your realm and its safety and balance and order and all those diplomatic vocabulary words. But you don't understand the grand scale of the universe. The biggest thing that happens on Midgard is a blip. A moment. The inter-dimensional equivalent of a sneeze. My brother is about to leave on an expedition across multiple realms to track down one of the galaxy's most dangerous magical amplifiers, so forgive me for not dedicating all my energy to the death of a handful of humans in this goitre of a city."

Theo's jaw clenched, and Loki sensed he wanted to say more than he did. "Those people have families."

"Everyone has a family."

"That doesn't mean their lives don't matter."

"Oh, please." Loki snorted. "Life is the opposite of precious and rare. It's everywhere. If you wept for every life lost who *mattered*, you'd weep until the world ended."

"They deserve justice," Theo pressed on. "And the people here deserve to be safe from whatever it is that's killing them, as much as your people deserve to be safe from whatever artefacts your brother is searching for."

"Are you attempting to move me?" Loki spread his hands. "Do you expect tears? I'm not the crying sort."

"No, I suppose that's too much to ask of *you*." They were interrupted by the bell over the door, and Theo spun round. "We're not open—" he started. "Oh, it's you."

It took Loki a moment to recognise Gem away from the dark hallway beneath the British Museum and dressed in a smart blue uniform with a tall domed hat. Even if he hadn't seen the officers in the morgue the day before, it wouldn't have taken much understanding of Midgardian fashion to realise Gem was a policeman. Soldiers looked the same everywhere.

Gem was red-faced and out of breath, his enormous shoulders heaving like a mountain upset by an earthquake. "They found another one."

Theo's elbow slipped off the edge of the counter. "What?"

"Scotland Yard," Gem replied between gasps. "One of the constables over in Clapham, behind the Plough. Another body."

Theo cursed under his breath. "Does Mrs S—" he began, but Gem interrupted him.

"I called on her at the museum. She'll be on her way by now. You know where it is? The blokes can't see me with you."

"I can find it. I'll grab the kit. And my coat." Theo turned towards the back room and almost smashed into Loki. "Oh, and you. You're coming too."

"To a murder?" Loki asked.

"To a crime scene," Theo replied.

Chapter Seventeen

*T*he crowd surrounding the Plough Inn was nearly as large as the one that had been waiting outside the morgue. Loki wasn't sure whether he should be impressed or disgusted by humanity's stalwart dedication to morbidity.

At the back of the crowd, Mrs S was waiting for them, a dark cloak thrown over her high-necked bodice. She was wearing trousers with wide legs that flared over her short boots, and her bony arms were crossed over her stomach. It may have been meant to look like she was waiting impatiently, but Loki had a sense she was simply warding off the cold. She had a pair of dark spectacles perched on her nose, their frames so small that they were hardly bigger than her eyes. "There you are," she said as they approached her. "I've been able to get precious little information from those infuriating policemen, but Gem should have more for us later. It's Ashford and Baines," she said to Theo, names that clearly meant something, for his mouth puckered. "Now." She turned to Loki. "Just to prepare you a bit for what is about to happen—"

"I'm about to see a dead body?" he offered.

"Oh." She paused. "Yes, but that wasn't what I was going to prepare you for. The police force here is rather hostile."

"To everyone?"

"Yes, but specifically us."

"Now, Mrs Sharp." Loki mirrored her stance, arms crossed over his stomach. "Why would anyone be hostile to you?"

"My point being," she said, "that what precious little time we have to access the crime scene and the body should be used to its fullest extent. You have the kit?" she asked Theo, and he patted the leather bag slung over his shoulder. "Excellent. The prince is your responsibility."

"I'm capable of being my own responsibility," Loki interjected.

Mrs S raised an eyebrow, but didn't comment. "Follow me, now."

This crowd was less animated than the one outside the morgue had been. No more than whispers passed between people, like mourners at a funeral trading gossip about the deceased. Loki noticed several people lean into their friends when they saw Mrs S, their gazes lingering on her peculiar spectacles and wide trousers. None of the other women on Midgard wore trousers, Loki realised.

Two policemen were standing at the front of the crowd, their arms locked to keep people back. One of them was Gem, doing a good imitation of not noticing them. The other officer was just as broad as Gem, his hair cut in the same uneven crop. He cast them a derisive sneer as they approached. "What a very expected surprise."

"Good afternoon, Paul," Mrs S replied. "You're looking well."

"You've got to call me Officer now, Mrs Sharp," Paul replied.

Mrs S clicked her tongue. "Now, I don't think your mother would appreciate you taking that tone with me."

Paul blushed. "She doesn't want nothing to do with you any more, and neither do we."

"So she's told me," Mrs S replied. "May I speak with your commanding officer?"

"Mum says you went loony after your husband kicked it," Paul went on.

Mrs S's smile went tense. "It's so kind of your dear mother to speak of me so. And for you to bring it up now." She turned to Gem. "Sir, will you please let us pass so I may speak with your commanding officer? Since your brother will not?"

Loki saw it then, the resemblance between Paul and Gem. It was subtle – he had thought they looked alike in the way all men with large hands and mountain ranges for shoulders looked alike. But they also had the same flat nose and small eyes, foreheads so wide you could have papered them with broadsides.

Gem cast a glance at his brother. "They don't do no harm, Paul."

"Detective Baines doesn't like—" Paul started, but Gem dropped his arm and said, "You can go on, Mrs Sharp."

"Thank you, Gem," she replied, and she, Theo and Loki passed between the two men. "Tell your mother I am still in possession of my mental faculties in totality, and I hope she's well."

Gem nodded. "Ma'am."

The body of the murdered man looked like the others in the morgue, slack features and lifeless limbs, but in the way of sleep and not death. He was dressed in knee-high socks and a rough coat. His hands were black around the knuckles, and a set of long-handled brushes fastened to his back had tumbled into the mud, their strap pulled tight round his neck.

A few men in the same uniform as Gem were meandering around the alley, turning over crates and kicking at the dirt, looking for anything left behind. A man with a spindly legged tripod was setting up a camera to take photos. Two men were conversing over the body, one with a thick moustache, the other a lanky redhead with a wispy beard, and they looked up as the group approached. The man with the moustache smiled, his face absent of any emotion to accompany it. "Look lads, the ghost gang has arrived."

Mrs S's smile was equally steely. "Good evening, Detective Ashford." She turned to the red-headed officer and nodded curtly. "Detective Baines."

"Mrs Sharp." Ashford held up a hand to halt their progress. "You're trespassing on an official Scotland Yard crime scene. Again."

"Would you like to go through the usual theatrics where you make protestations requesting I leave and I object?" Mrs S asked.

"I'd rather just arrest you," Ashford replied.

"That doesn't sound like you, Detective." Mrs S held

up her hands, palms flat, and wiggled her fingers. "You generally prefer not to get your hands dirty."

Ashford hitched up his trousers with a mirthless chuckle. "So what is it that killed him this time? Spooks? A phantom? Was he strangled by a poltergeist? Or did he cross the same witch as every other bleeding corpse in London?"

"You got a new beau there, Bell?" Baines called to Theo, before Mrs S could answer. "He's a greasy cat, isn't he? I thought you liked the intellectuals."

It seemed inadvisable to perform any spells in front of these policemen, or even voice the threat to do so, so Loki simply gave the man a look that said as clearly as he could, *I will turn you into a toadstool.*

"Ignore them," Theo murmured to Loki, though his voice was tight.

"What do you think of my trousers?" Mrs S intervened, and Theo nudged Loki's leg with his cane.

"Come on, we need to take a better look while she has them distracted," he said.

"They let me wear these at the museum now," Loki heard Mrs S say as he followed Theo around the fringes of the crime scene.

"Got to be your own husband now that yours is dead?"

Baines asked with a nasty smile. "Why do you try so hard to look like a man, Mrs Sharp?"

"Because," Mrs S replied without wasting a withering look upon him, "you lads need a good role model."

Theo gritted his teeth, then crouched down beside the body, a tight breath of pain escaping his lips as he shifted his weight off his bad leg. Loki bent down beside him.

"Here." Theo fished in his bag, pulling out a pair of spectacles like the ones Mrs S wore.

"What are these for?" Loki asked as he took them.

"You can see the residue of the spell."

"I didn't know spells left a residue," Loki replied.

"Only here on Earth, because the air is so absent of magic. I suspect in Asgard, you're so thick with it you'd never find a mark."

Loki held the glasses up to his eyes. The colours around him turned acidic, the light taking on a sickly quality except for a small sliver of white air that hovered above the dead man, like a fine dusting of snow over his whole body. When he peered over the top of the lenses, the glow was gone. He pushed the glasses up his nose, then looked down at his own hand, bringing a spell to his fingertips without executing it, and to his surprise, his own fingers took on the same ghostly glow.

"Did you make these?" he asked Theo.

"The glasses?" Theo unfolded his own glasses onto his nose with a shrug. "I put them together, but it's not my idea. They operate with the same basic principles as the double exposure of spirit photography."

"I don't know what any of that means."

"It's not that impressive," Theo said. "Do you know what sort of spell this is?"

"I don't think spells look different. Here." He held up his hand for Theo to examine, summoning the energy again.

Theo frowned, peering over his glasses and then through them again.

"And I don't know any spells that can do this to a human. Or any being." Loki leant backwards, misplaced his hand and nearly toppled over. He reached out to catch himself; his hand grasped wildly for purchase and landed upon the bare forearm of the dead man.

He felt the spell, though he couldn't say quite what it was. Beneath him, the man's body, still warm even in death, spasmed. His fingers reached out, grabbing Loki round the wrist. His eyes flew open and they stared at each other.

Then the man fell slack, dead again.

Loki scrambled away, ripping off his tinted spectacles

and staring at the man. He was dead. He was. He had been. And then, for just a moment…

He realised suddenly that he wasn't the only one who had noticed. The policemen had stopped talking and were now shouting in confusion about what had just happened. Several people from the crowd, who must have been able to see over Gem's and Paul's massive arms, screamed. Someone grabbed Loki by the collar of his coat and dragged him out of the way, then bent to take the man's pulse. "Nothing," he called to no one in particular.

Detective Ashford was white-faced, his eyes wide. "I saw it. I saw him—"

Baines looked up. "I saw it too. We all saw it."

"Bloody hell."

"What did you do?" Theo murmured to Loki under his breath.

"I haven't a clue," he replied.

Detective Baines whirled suddenly and shoved Theo, knocking him backwards into a puddle. His tinted spectacles flew from his face and skittered across the stones. "You trying to bloody trick us, are you?"

"I didn't do anything!" Theo protested.

"Like hell you didn't," the detective growled, taking a deliberate step onto Theo's spectacles. They crunched under his foot like a breaking bone. "You crackpots show up at the same time something strange and inexplicable happens? What a bloody coincidence."

"Leave him alone," Mrs S called.

The detective kicked some of the rancid puddle onto Theo, who flinched. "Don't think I won't arrest you again."

He raised his foot once more, higher this time, like he was still deciding where the blow would land, but Loki leapt to his feet, stepping in between the detective and Theo. He was itching to slide one of his knives into his hand, but didn't think that would make a good case for not arresting them. The detective halted, foot still raised. He and Loki stared each other down, then the man slammed his foot to the ground one more time, splashing them both, before they turned away.

"Mrs Sharp," Loki heard Ashford say. "I think it's best if you and your men leave immediately."

Loki turned and offered Theo a hand. Theo took it, and Loki could feel a faint tremble as he pulled him to his feet. Mrs S retrieved Theo's cane from where it had fallen, then nodded towards the way they had come.

As they pushed back through the crowd, several people started jeering at them, repeating many of the same insults the red-headed detective had used. A few jumped in front of them, begging to know what had happened; they hadn't been able to see. One man said he was with a newspaper and asked for a comment. Mrs S ignored them all.

"You need a plague," Loki said as they finally broke into Clapham Common, the streets stuffed with carriages and wagons but the pavements less congested and far less hostile. "Something to decrease your surplus population a bit."

"We had one," Mrs S replied. "Several, actually, but somehow the bastards just keep hanging on." She stopped, turning back to Theo. "Do you want to sit? Are you hurt?"

Theo shook his head, though he looked distressed. "Let's go home."

"Right. Of course. I'll find us a cab. Stay with him, won't you?" she asked Loki, then stepped into the street, trying to wave down one of the passing carriages.

Theo slumped backwards against the wall of a butcher's shop. Loki leant beside him, staring down at the bricks beneath their feet, stained dark from the rubbish littering the butcher's alleyway.

"Thank you," Theo said after a time.

Loki shrugged. Gallantry made him uncomfortable, but it seemed needlessly cruel to tell Theo he hadn't meant to intervene. Hadn't even realised he was standing until he was halfway to his feet.

"Is it always like that?" Loki asked. "With the guards."

"You mean the policemen?" The ghost of a smile flitted across Theo's face. "Usually. Sometimes they spit on us. More name-calling. It was rather tame this time."

"Do you have to work with them often?"

"It's generous to say we work with them. But we cross paths. Often. Usually when there's something magically disruptive, the police are called to investigate its disruptiveness. Thinking it's non-magical, of course. And we're usually there, and they usually would rather we weren't, so words are exchanged." He took off his cap and ran a hand through his knotted curls. "But we've got Gem on the inside. And… others." He pinned on the final word with no resolve.

"Your vast network of secret society members," Loki remarked.

Theo glanced sideways at him. "Right. Vast."

Mrs S returned then. "I've got us a cab back to the office." She reached out and looped an arm through Loki's. "Come along, Your Majesty. It would be my honour to show you how we humans deal with our frustrations."

"How's that?" Loki asked.

"We get well and truly drunk."

Chapter Eighteen

They drank back in the SHARP Society office, sitting round the table that was too large for the small back room. Mrs S had a bottle of a clear liquid in a cupboard and poured three glasses, draining hers twice before the others had picked theirs up. Loki sniffed his – it smelt excessively acidic and a bit floral. He managed only a few sips before his eyes began to water, and he put his glass down, certain the alcohol had done some sort of corrosive and permanent damage to his insides. Theo picked up his glass, took a long drink and seemed to regret it immediately. He pressed a fist to his chest, lips held tight together and cheeks puffed like he was trying not to splutter it everywhere.

"So," Loki said after a silence. "You're not really a vast secret society, are you?"

Theo looked to Mrs S, who was pouring herself yet another drink. "We are not a government-recognised organisation, if that's what you're asking. No uniforms or salaries or protection by law or any of that."

"How many of you are there?"

"Three."

"Only three additional men?"

"No. We three are the entire society." Loki had suspected it, and expected to take some pleasure in hearing her say it, but instead pity swelled inside him. Mrs S swiped her thumb over the corner of her mouth and reached for the bottle again. "Small in ranks, but we make up for it in personality. Didn't Lord Byron write that?"

"No," Theo said without looking up.

Mrs S waved a hand. "What's the bit about the band of brothers, then?"

"'We few, we happy few, we band of brothers,'" Theo recited. "'For he today that sheds his blood with me / Shall be my brother.' Though that was most definitely not written by Lord Byron."

Mrs S nodded at Theo proudly, then said to Loki, "One of us has a university education."

"Half," Theo corrected. "Half a university education. They threw me out, remember?"

"We have attempted," Mrs S said, holding up her glass to the light of the fire, like she was examining it for flaws, "to explain our situation to the police before and request their assistance. And to warn them about threats that may be beyond their understanding. But we have been met largely with ridicule and disbelief."

"Exclusively," Theo corrected. "We've been met *exclusively* with ridicule and disbelief."

"How do you know about my father?" Loki asked. "And Asgard and the Nine Realms and all of it?"

Mrs S pulled her drink into her and said, very seriously and in a low, confidential tone, "My mother was a Valkyrie."

Theo looked up, his mouth hanging open. "Hold on, really?"

Mrs S didn't say anything. Her eyes were locked on Loki's, one eyebrow making a slow, precise ascent towards her hairline. He scanned her face for a moment, then leant back in his chair and shook his head. "I don't believe you."

Mrs S laughed loudly. Theo rolled his eyes, then heaved himself to his feet. "I'm going to the loo."

As Theo disappeared behind the curtain, Mrs S leant back in her chair, pulling one leg under her and staring up at the ceiling. She was silent for so long Loki thought she must have forgotten the question, but then she said, "My husband and I were archaeologists. We travelled the world and collected antiquities, primarily for the British Museum, though we did some private trade. Hence" – she waved a hand vaguely at the shop – "we purchased what we thought were Viking relics at an auction in Paris, but when we brought them back to the museum, they refused to authenticate them. Said they were fakes. My husband was quite determined to prove them wrong, and in the process discovered that they weren't fake, they were Asgardian, and the seller was a smuggler from Vanaheim stealing from your father. Odin's men showed up to reclaim the stolen items, and in thanks, he sent my husband and me a ship full of gold—"

"A whole ship?" Loki interrupted.

"Just a wee one." Mrs S held up her hands in demonstration. "But it's been enough to keep me comfortable. After that, my husband and I volunteered to keep an eye out for any other inter-realm crises on Earth, and your father accepted, which is when our partnership began."

"What sort of crises?" Loki had never heard Sharp's name from his father's lips before he was sent here.

"All kinds of things. Some time-travelling thieves using the doors of Prague as portals between dimensions. A demon summoned from Hel possessing monks in Italy." She took a sip of her drink, then said, her tone grave, "My husband died in your father's service, hunting down animated gargoyles that were terrorising Paris. It was a foolish task to try to take on alone, but by the time your father was able to send assistance, it was too late. For my husband," she added quickly. "Not for Paris. It's still kicking."

"How long ago was this?" Loki asked.

She shrugged. "Not so long. A few years."

Loki frowned. He had sat in on every court meeting in the last two years and was almost certain he'd never heard about gargoyles on Earth. He also knew he'd never heard of the SHARP Society from his father. Whatever cries for help had been sent from Midgard, they'd never found their way to the Asgardian court.

Mrs S ran her thumb along the top of her glass. "We keep watch over the fairy ring outside the city as well. Not sure what you'd call it on Asgard. They're spots where, when things break through the Bifrost and fall into other realms, it's where they land. Portals. Ley lines. Thresholds. The places where things fall from the sky." She finished her drink, then pushed the glass away from her. "Don't let me have another. I'm going to attempt to pour myself one but you must tell me no."

"So you took up the work alone?" Loki asked.

Mrs S nodded. "It's difficult to be a lady in any professional field, but particularly one no one believes exists. It's amazing the ways men find to box you out of even imaginary places."

"Where did you meet Theo and Gem?"

"I've known Gem since he was a tiny thing. His mother and I were friends. But she and her husband decided not to associate with me and mine once our professional interests shifted. Thought we were batty. Gem had just returned from military service in South Africa and came to tell my husband and me about a woman with green skin he'd met there, who said she came from outer space. I think they had a bit of a romance. I never asked." She started to reach for the bottle, then paused. "Whatever had happened between them, it affected him enough to seek us out. And now he's a police officer, but helps us as well. It's nice to have a man on the inside. And a bit of muscle."

Loki snorted. "What about Theo?"

"Ah. Theo is a bit more complicated." She glanced at the doorway, making sure Theo wasn't returning, then said in a low voice, "He was at Wandsworth." When Loki stared back at her, uncomprehending, she clarified, "A prison."

"He's a criminal?"

"I know, he looks so harmless, doesn't he? The leg really fools people. Though I suppose whacking someone over the head with a cane is as good a way as any to commit a murder. He's not a murderer," she qualified quickly. Her fingers flexed round her glass, knuckles splotching. "Just after my husband died, I was investigating what I thought may be the use of other-worldly technologies in the munitions factories belonging to this man called Stark—" She cut herself off with a hand wave. "The details are not important. But it led me to Wandsworth to interview some of the men who had been arrested in relation to the factories, and one of them was a lad called Theo Bell who looked like he hadn't eaten a square meal in a year and had a broken leg because someone had found out he was a… what he was… and stepped on his femur and no one had done a bloody thing for him."

"And he was involved in this factory scandal?" Loki asked. He was surprised by how sincerely engaged he was in all this. He had thought humans so small and uninteresting, and had been so determined to particularly despise these ones who were responsible for calling him here. And yet here they were.

"Only in as much as he was present in the factory when a mass arrest was made. He was a student working on a project updating factory machinery."

"He shouldn't have been arrested if he was just there," Loki said. "That's not fair."

"So little is. I suppose it's the same in your realm as well. I think that's one of the universe's rare consistencies." She leant back in her chair, tipping her head to the ceiling. Outside, evening was creeping in, and in the faint gloom, the lines of her face looked as precise as a straight edge. "They let everyone else go, but they held him on an indecency charge."

"Indecency?" Loki repeated.

Mrs S lolled her head forwards and squinted at him, then let out a hissing laugh through her nose. "My, it really must be an idyllic paradise of equality where you come from – do women have the vote there as well?"

"Can women not vote on Midgard?" Loki asked.

Mrs S stared at him, like she was trying to decide if he was in earnest, then said, "Theo's a boy who likes boys. Not boys exclusively, I don't think. We've never discussed it at great length. But that's a criminal offence in our realm. To have intimate physical relationships between two men."

"Oh." Loki didn't know what to say. He knew what it was to be cast out and unwanted and taunted for the fabric you were stitched from. To want to find strength and pride in the things that made you *you* in spite of the world telling you that you should hide them. It was a particular kind of dissonance that was hard to understand until your ears rang with it.

"Don't mention I told you – he's not keen on chatting about it," Mrs S said, leaning in confidentially, though there was no one to overhear them. "I'm a little drunk. I didn't promise you good spirits, but I did promise strong ones." She knocked her empty glass against his, which was still full. "You aren't having any."

"It's vile."

Mrs S pressed a hand to her chest. "How dare you speak ill of my national drink. How would you like it if I came to your planet and insulted your mead?"

"You wouldn't – it's very good." Loki took another sniff of the liquid, thinking he might try to muscle down one mouthful to make her feel better, but instead nearly vomited. "Particularly in comparison."

Mrs S laughed just as the curtain behind them parted with a dusty *flump* and Theo appeared again, this time with Gem stomping behind him. "Look who I found."

Mrs S tottered to her feet, opening her hands to them. "Geo!"

Gem raised an eyebrow at her. "Are you drunk?"

"A bit. Not as much as that slip-up would lead you to believe." She hooked a foot round a chair and pushed it towards Theo before seating herself again. Gem huddled over the stove, warming his hands. "What do you have for us, Gem?"

"The man's called Rory Garber. Twenty-one years old, chimney sweep. Had three girls show up at the morgue to identify his body."

"Daughters?" Theo asked, but Gem shook his head.

"Wives."

"He's a Mormon?" Theo asked, his mouth falling open.

Before Loki could ask what that meant, Gem shook his head. "Just not very nice. All three of them thought they were the one and only."

Mrs S let out a loud laugh. "Oh, that's a devastating realisation over a deathbed. Pour me some coffee off the burner, won't you Gem?" As Gem handed her a teacup, she said, "Anything more about the cause of death? Or the time?"

Gem shook his head. "There's nothing, same as the others. No cause of death as far as anyone can tell.

According to all three of his wives he was in perfect health. Not a clue of when or how."

"No witnesses, I suspect," Mrs S said.

"None. But he did have six shillings, a penknife, a calling card and a set of dice in his pocket."

"Whose card?" Theo asked.

Gem squinted, trying to remember. "The Inferno Club. One of those grizzly death saloons over in Covent Garden. A lady's name was on it as well – some medium. Likely had his cards read or some such."

Theo glanced at Mrs S. "Worth investigating the club?"

Mrs S pressed a hand to her forehead. "I swear to God, every body that's been found has a different card in its pocket, and none of them have been even suspicious yet. This city is obsessed with fancy stationery. Oh, there is one more thing we should probably discuss." Mrs S leant forwards on her elbows towards Loki, her long fingers curled round her cup. "You, my dear, did something to that dead man."

"I don't know what."

"You brought him back to life," Theo said.

Loki glanced at him. "I don't think so."

"No, you definitely did," Theo replied. "We all saw it. The whole flamin' street saw it."

"I can't bring the dead back to life," Loki protested, his defences rising, though he wasn't certain why. "My magic doesn't work like that."

"You certainly animated him in some sense," Mrs S said.

"I didn't do anything!" Loki protested. "I was showing Theo what my magic looked like in contrast to whatever spell it was that killed the man, and then I touched him and…"

"And gave him a momentary breath of life," Mrs S said.

The living dead. Loki felt a shadow pass over his heart. He heard the words in his father's voice.

"Are all them protesters right?" Gem asked. He had poured himself a cup of coffee and the teacup looked doll sized in his massive hands. "Maybe they can be brought back."

He looked to Mrs S, but she didn't reply. Her lips were pursed, and she was drumming one finger on the tabletop. Theo stretched out his bad leg, massaging the knee with the heels of his hands. "It doesn't make any sense."

"Be more specific," Mrs S said.

"There is no pattern to these deaths. They've nothing in common – even the Ripper had a type. He killed prostitutes in Whitechapel. Whoever's doing this is all over the flippin' map."

"What are you suggesting?" Mrs S asked with a frown.

"It's definitely magic, but maybe it's not a killer," Theo said. "Perhaps it's something else."

Gem snapped his fingers suddenly. "The Enchantress!"

Loki's head snapped up. "What did you say?"

"The Enchantress," Gem said. "She's the medium in Covent Garden. She's the one who was on the card."

Loki felt his face get hot, all the blood rushing to his head with a speed that made him dizzy.

The Enchantress. Years and realms between them, and had he found her *here?*

It couldn't be her.

It had to be.

"Friend of yours?" Theo asked.

"No," Loki replied quickly, though he knew his face had already betrayed him. His heart was beating so fast he sounded winded. "I just like the name. Perhaps I'll use it for myself one day. *Loki the Enchantress.*"

Theo snorted. "You do know what it means, don't you? It's the feminine version of *enchanter.*"

"Does that matter?"

"It would to most men," Mrs S replied. "Wouldn't want to be feminine; that's weakness." She let her head fall backwards, staring at the ceiling. "We should look into the club. We've got no other leads."

"I'll do that," Loki said, trying not to infuse his voice with excessive enthusiasm and failing entirely.

Theo arched an eyebrow. "Will you?"

"I mean, it makes the most sense, doesn't it, if there's some sort of magical something going on, for me to be the one to investigate it, since I am the only one here who can actually do magic? Not that there is magic. Or that she can do magic. She's not a, you know, real enchantress. I don't think so, anyway, but I wouldn't know, because I don't know her!" *What is the matter with you?* he chided himself. *Be normal!* He swallowed hard, then said, more casual this time, "Besides, Theo's leg is sore and Gem was just on patrol and you're drunk. So. I'll go."

Theo was still frowning at him, and Loki was certain he was about to protest, but Mrs S, who was either growing drunker or simply didn't care, spoke before he could. "Good to see you finally investing in our cause, your lordship." She raised her empty glass. "To the prince of Asgard. May he conspire with the humans for many happy years to come."

Chapter Nineteen

*B*y the time he arrived at the Inferno Club, the sun was a sluggish splash of amber over the tops of the buildings. He passed a flock of black sheep grazing on a dying lawn, only to realise they weren't black sheep at all, rather white sheep that had spent too long in the city and been turned a dingy grey. The streets were crowded with people everywhere he went, and the city felt like it was overflowing. Canvas awnings hung over the pavement, shop fronts discoloured with mud and whatever noxious chemicals were living inside it. The streets were congested with carriages and people darting between them, and in the narrow alleys where the carriages didn't fit, feral cats roamed, dodging backed-up drains and piles of stinking rags.

Chapter Nineteen

Humanity was truly disgusting.

The entrance to the Inferno Club sat in the middle of the building, amid the sooty, stained shops and the flats with laundry strung between them. In a block of ordinary facades, it was a gold tooth in a rotted mouth – the door was guarded by two stone demons wrapping themselves round the frame, wings extended and tails curled over the lintel. They looked down at the queue of people waiting to get in, their mouths open in a wild, toothy cackle that flanked the words painted in gold: *The Inferno*. Below that, in vertical letters along the sides of the frame, ALL HOPE ABANDON, YE WHO ENTER HERE.

Which was a tad dramatic.

Loki joined the back of the queue waiting to get into the club. The patrons were all dressed extravagantly compared to what he'd seen most people wearing on the streets – veils and tall hats with stuffed birds perched upon them and long swirls of crepe dragging along the ground. Everything black. He considered letting his nails go back to the black he usually painted them, but no one else in his sights had coloured nails. Best not to press his luck. From within the club, the strains of a screeching string instrument floated, haunted and ghostly sounding. The crowd was buzzing, high on their elevated heart rates and a small thrill of fear that was already lurking.

Humans were both disgusting and easily amused.

Beyond the door, there were stairs leading downwards, and the walls and ceiling around them had been shaped to form a sort of tunnel. The tunnel was lit with unshaded gas lamps, burning open and hot along the walls, just enough light to illuminate the fact that the tunnel was lined with more of the demons from the door. They curled upon each other, scrabbling over their fellows and pushing each other into the ground. Their heads were bald and round, small horns poking out and each face pointed and wicked. Below them, reliefs were carved of naked humans screaming in agony, like the torch flames were the fires of hell sucking them under as the demons pressed them down. Behind him, Loki heard a woman give a small shriek that then broke off into a delighted laugh, her group of friends joining in with her.

The steps down through the tunnel ended in a black curtain, which, when Loki pushed it back, revealed the club itself. The lighting was lower here, with lanterns hanging in cages made from bones at random intervals. The walls were draped in heavy black curtains, pulled back into elegant folds. But the whole thing was rather sensationalised. The tables were shaped like coffins, the walls between the curtains decorated with skeletons and bones and devilish faces. Scenes of battles and beheadings were painted above the bar, along with a sign proclaiming NOXIOUS POISONS. Below it, a list: *cancer of the liver, consumptive germ, cholera from a corpse.* The man behind the bar was dressed as a monk, a heavy crucifix made of bone hanging off his neck. As Loki passed him, the man sucked his teeth, then spat a wad of grey saliva into an ashtray.

The room was already crowded, the tables stuffed with people dressed like mourners, some of them looking giddy with the horror of the place, others sweating and sickly. "I've had too much," a man at the bar cried, swaying on his stool. "Too. Much. Plague. It isn't good for you."

In the corner farthest from the tunnel entrance, the black curtains were closed, and a man dressed in a funerary suit seemed to be standing guard before them, his arms as wide around as Loki's waist. The sign above his head read THE SEVENTH CIRCLE, and below that, THE ENCHANTRESS. Loki's chest constricted around his thudding heart. *Breathe.*

The man at the doorway watched Loki approach from across the room, his eyes half obscured by his thick brows. The hood of his heavy cloak was slipping backwards down his bald head.

"Good evening," Loki said. "I'd like to see the Enchantress."

"Ten bob," the man grunted.

"Excuse me?"

The man raised one of his shrubbery eyebrows. "Ten bob," he said slowly. "Half sovereign. For a seat."

"A seat?" Loki repeated.

"Are you daft?" The man wiped his nose with the back of his hand, then smeared it on his trousers. "You buy a seat for the show, you see the Enchantress."

"Do I look like the sort of person who wants to sit through a show?" Loki asked.

The man gave him an appraising up and down. "You look like a witch."

Loki looked down at himself. He'd foregone the glamoured clothes he'd been wearing and purchased an actual suit on the way here to save energy – all black, complete with a tiny dark pin through the tie and the highest-heeled boots that Paxton's had for men – disappointingly quite low. "Thank you."

"Witches are girls."

"Does that make it less of a compliment?"

The man snorted – though not in a shared-joke sort of way. "Next show's still ten bob," he said, eyeing Loki head to toe. "Even if you put a hex on me, witch boy."

Loki was tempted, but he resisted. "Could you send

a message to her?" he asked. The man didn't say no, so Loki pressed on, "Will you tell her that her Trickster is here to see her?"

"*Her* trickster?" the man repeated, his emphasis much heavier than Loki's had been.

"Well no, not hers. Not..." Even if he couldn't feel his face getting hot, he would have seen it in the man's smirk. "The Trickster," he clarified, then added quickly, "Not that I'm *the* Trickster. I'm... Can you just tell her? Please?"

"For ten bob I will."

Loki turned away from the man guarding the doorway to the stage and stalked over to the bar. The man was still spinning on his stool, chanting about plague. He was obviously drunk, but his shoes were well shined and his hair evenly cut. Perhaps not a rich man, but one with enough means to get very drunk off the plague. Loki resisted rolling his eyes, then pulled his tie slightly askew and reluctantly ruffled his hair, before stumbling over to the man and grabbing on to him.

The man almost tipped off his stool. "Whoa, mate."

"Can you buy me a drink?" Loki slurred.

"Ah get lost." The man leant into his own glass, but Loki clung to him, leaning in close and lacing his voice with the honeyed magical compulsion. "I need ten bob for a drink, mate, I've just lost my job, and my wife's died, and all my seven children have measles, and we've got so little for food I'm afraid we may have to eat one of the children—"

"All right, all right!" The man looked more than a bit alarmed as he jerked away from Loki, then fished in his pocket until he came out with a handful of coins. "There." He shoved them at Loki. "Get your drink and let me alone."

"Cheers." Loki turned, readjusted his tie then returned to the man guarding the doorway and dumped the coins into his hands.

If the man had witnessed the means by which Loki obtained the coins, he was too busy counting them out to say anything. Once he had pocketed them with a grunt, he looked up. "You're lucky."

"Am I?" Loki asked.

The man nodded at the drunk at the bar. "He's a boxer. I've seen him knock out men twice your size."

"Is that so?"

"Must have been a pretty good hex, witch boy."

"Must have been," Loki replied.

Behind the curtain, the dark room was a tiered semi-circular theatre. The stage below was mostly taken up by a circular table, painted black and with a board in the centre displaying the Midgardian alphabet written in gold. The attendees filed into the chairs round the perimeter, most of them in black so that they blended into the dark fabric swooping from the ceiling and walls. The air in the room was already thick and smoky. Trays of incense hung on either side of the doorway, and as he ushered people in, the doorman dropped another match on each, sending even more heavily perfumed smoke billowing into the air. Loki swallowed a cough. Perhaps the Midgardians found these smells pleasant and calming, but they felt like an assault upon his senses.

He took a seat near the back, very aware that his heart was beating too fast. With each person who passed through the dark curtain, a small cloud of dust rose from the velvet. Loki looked around, trying to make out shapes through the darkness, but the room seemed to be designed to make its occupants feel stifled, stuffed into a space too small for them. Perhaps it was meant to make you feel like you were in a coffin.

"Good evening," said a voice from the stage. A woman on Loki's right shrieked and grabbed his arm. She had to be shaken loose like an insect before she seemed to remember that her husband was on her other side and she'd rather cling to him than a stranger.

"Welcome to the Inferno," the voice said, as smooth as honey and absent of London's guttural vowels and hard edges. The way she spoke felt balanced, every syllable in its purest form. Loki felt a shiver go through him. "I am the Enchantress. I will be guiding you tonight as we connect to the world beyond ours."

A woman stepped into the circle of pale light from the coloured glass lamp hanging over the table. Her face was veiled, the dark shroud obscuring her features too heavily to know if it was her. Loki leant forwards in his seat, like he could somehow draw close enough to see beyond that opaque veil. The voice was as slick as silk, deep and resounding, but it was too put-on to recognise if it was her or not.

It had to be her.

It couldn't be her.

The Enchantress sat upon a chair before the table, the many rings upon her fingers clanking together. They flashed, though there didn't seem to be enough light to truly catch them. "The truth of this cosmos is known to me, in a way few on Earth know it. The veils that hang between realms are as thin as paper. My connection to the other-worldly is real, and powerful, and beyond the understanding of most humans," she continued. "And if you approach tonight's session with an open mind and a willingness to accept that the truth often extends beyond our understanding and imagination, you will tonight, in this very room, hear and see things that may seem inexplicable but are simply beyond your small minds. And yet this does not mean they are not as real as you and I."

In the first row, a woman was already crying. The man beside her pushed her head into his coat, trying to look as though he was comforting her but likely trying to stifle her sobs. He gave the Enchantress an apologetic smile. "She's very emotional."

"You say that like it is a weakness," the Enchantress replied. "It is not weakness to be soft. It means you are open. You are sensitive to the movements of the universe in a way that others are not. What is your name, darling?"

"Žydrė Matulis," the woman replied, her heavy accent furthered muddled by her sobs.

"Join me on the stage, won't you? Both of you." She held out a hand. Žydrė and her husband climbed the short stairway holding hands, then stood awkwardly at the fringes of the gaslights casting a dim sheen over the stage until the Enchantress gestured them to two chairs at the table. "Whom is it you seek?" she asked Žydre, fanning her skirts round her knees for maximum aesthetic effect.

"Our daughter," Žydre said. "Our daughter Molly Rose. She's one of the dead in the Southwark Morgue."

"The living dead," the Enchantress murmured, and a collective shiver of fear seemed to pass through the room. "Tell me when she died."

"Two weeks past," Žydre replied. "We want to bury her, but they say... A man at the coroner's office told us she might not be dead. It might be that none of them are. We were hoping if you could find her spirit, she could tell us."

"Of course, of course." The Enchantress turned to the assembled crowd. "Might I call upon several more volunteers who might lend their energies to myself and these two grieving parents?" Her head swivelled slowly over the assembled crowd. Several people raised their hands, and she pointed at random with a long finger encased in black lace. Loki didn't dare move. He didn't want to raise his hand, didn't want to do anything to feed this wild hope inside him. Any movement felt like a bet he wasn't certain he'd win.

But then she froze with her face towards him. Though he couldn't see her eyes, Loki felt them on him. He felt pinned, examined, his skin on fire in a way it had only ever felt in a single gaze.

Then she extended a hand to him. "Join us, won't you, sir?"

It couldn't be her.

She reached up and pushed her veil off her face – just for a moment – and he saw a flash of her deep green eyes.

It was Amora.

He stood – his legs were trembling, why was he trembling? – and walked to the stage.

The Enchantress called up several more audience members until every chair round the table was full. Loki took the spot across from her, suddenly too aware of his skin, his breath, the way his hair fell round his face. He swore he could feel the warmth off *her* skin, or perhaps that was just his own burning from its proximity to hers. Its first proximity in years.

Žydre was still crying, and she reached out, grabbing one of Amora's webbed sleeves. "I have a lock of her hair—" she began, but Amora held up a hand, turning away from her.

She did not say a word as she assembled four candles in the centre of the table and lit them, one at each corner of the painted letters, then placed a planchette with a cut-out centre on top of the letter board. "The spirits do not speak to our earthly whims," she said to Žydre without looking at her. "Your daughter will not be reached right now. Instead they urge me towards... this man." She turned to Loki, her veil parting to reveal a single dark eye, and she opened her hands to him. "They wish to speak to you."

He swallowed. "I have much I'd like to ask them, too."

"Then take my hands."

Loki stretched his and took hers across the table. Beneath their linked fingers, the planchette over the lettered board began to spin. Žydre gasped, clutching her husband's arm and crying harder.

The planchette flew from one corner of the board to the other, pausing over the top of the word *HELLO* painted in one corner before darting in a frantic scrabble over the alphabet, spelling out words.

"Spirits!" another man at the table cried, his voice wobbly. "They're here!"

"What do they say?" Žydre's husband asked.

HELLOPRINCE.

"Prince?" Amora repeated with surprise, like it wasn't her making the planchette move. Loki wasn't certain how, but he knew she was doing it. It couldn't be magic – she'd been gone from Asgard so long that she surely wouldn't have strength to waste on tricks like these. "Your surname?" she asked, and the corner of her mouth turned up in a cheeky smile. "Or do we have royalty with us tonight?" A few nervous titters from the audience. "What is your first question, my dear prince?"

He stared at her, the glimmering green of her eyes beneath her veil. What could he say? Even without an audience of humans witnessing their reunion, what could he possibly say to the person who meant the most to him? The person he thought he'd lost long ago?

"How?" he asked, his voice hoarse.

The planchette began to move on the board, tracing out its answer: $MAGIC$.

When he looked at her, she was smiling, the tilted smirk like a crescent moon.

"I've missed you," he said, the words leaving him in a breath.

She tapped a finger against the back of his hand. "That's not a question."

"Have you missed me?"

She tipped her chin towards the board, as the planchette spun.

$EVERYDAY$.

"Why are you here?" he asked.

The planchette whizzed. *HIDING*.

"A last question?" she asked.

"Did you think I'd find you?" he asked.

"Oh, my darling," he heard her whisper, the words nearly lost under the scratch of the planchette across the letters.

INEVERDOUBTED.

Chapter Twenty

*W*hen the show ended, as everyone round the table stood and the rest of the guests returned to the audience, Loki felt Amora slide her hand into his once more, pulling him towards the wings of the stage.

"I haven't long," she whispered, and he felt her breath against his ear. "Come with me."

He followed, feeling the soft rustle of the curtains as they passed backstage. She led him down a narrow brick hallway lined with ropes and pulleys, then through a side door into what must have been her dressing room. It was dark, the fire in the grate reduced to pale cinders, and the walls were lined with mirrors, their edges foggy and cracked. The counters in front of them were covered in cosmetics, thick paints and brushes in disarray. A pot of powder had tipped over, spraying its sparkling contents into a shape like a bullet hitting snow.

Amora shut the door, then turned to Loki, ripping off her veil so that her hair tumbled out of its fastenings and down her back. "Loki," she said, and he didn't know what to say in return. Even her name would have felt like too much. He couldn't make his limbs move, so she came to him, pressed her hands to either side of his face as she stared into it. "I can't believe it."

"Amora." And finally he found himself again. He opened his arms and when she fell into them, he could remember no words, no sound, nothing in the Nine Realms but her name. The smell of her hair. The feeling of her pressed up against him. He had not realised the depths of his missing her until she was here with him again.

"What are you doing *here?*" she asked, her face against his shoulder.

"I'm on an assignment from my father."

"An assignment? That sounds very official. Kingly, even." She wrapped her arms round his neck, leaning back to peer into his face. "Did I call you by the wrong title? Should it have been King Loki – still believable."

He didn't want to tell her. He didn't want to talk about Asgard yet. He knew everything about what had happened between him and his father since Amora was banished – he wanted to know everything about her.

"Sit down," she said, gesturing him to one of the low stools by the fire. "Do you want some tea? I only have a quarter of an hour before the next show, but the fire's likely still warm enough."

"How did you ever end up here?" he asked as he took a seat. "Telling fortunes and summoning the dead?"

She unhooked the kettle from over the fire and began to refill it with a jug of water from one of the dressing tables. "Believe me, it wasn't my first choice. I've been all over this pathetic little realm, trying to find someone who could help me off or restore my powers. London is as good a place as any to exploit humans who think this spiritualism is real magic. If you speak gravely and seriously while wearing black, they'll believe anything you say." She grinned. "And I've always enjoyed the theatre."

"Is that what you call it?" he asked. "'Spiritualism'?"

"That's one name for it. Humans believe that certain people among them can communicate with the spirit world – that's what some of them call it, where the dead dwell."

"Can they?" he asked.

"Oh God, no." She laughed. "There's hardly a drop of magic on this planet – let alone enough to call up ghosts. But everyone's dying of cholera and typhoid fever and dysentery or being brutalised by men in Whitechapel – and that's not even including this recent scourge. So many bodies they can't bury them fast enough, and they often grow sick and die without any warning, so there's no time to say goodbye. That's all people want – to say goodbye or send their love or their apologies or impart final messages they never got to say to people. It's all tragically pathetic."

Amora replaced the lid of the kettle, then hung it over the fire. Loki leant forwards, ready to relight the flames with a spell to save time, but Amora extended a hand to the grate before he could. Beneath her fingers, the flames leapt to life.

Loki gasped. She turned to him, her delight equal to his surprise, and gave a small bow. "Surprise."

"You can still do magic," he said, unable to keep the shock from his voice. "How?"

"It hasn't come easy." She pulled a chair up beside him, their arms brushing. "Midgard almost drained me. Every bit of magic I used was gone forever. Can you imagine? Living without your magic? It's like losing a limb. No – more than that. It's like having your heart cut from your chest and being expected to simply learn to live without it. And when it leaves you slowly..." She shuddered, rubbing her hands up and down her arms like a chill had passed over her. "I was dying. Though *decaying* is perhaps the better word. It was that slow and horrific."

"But you found a way to restore it?"

She leant backwards beside the fireplace, stroking her fingers through the air as the flames curled in response. "Through this spiritualism nonsense, actually. I had all but resigned myself to a fate worse than death when I began working here and discovered that the humans who come to these shows are so raw and willing and open to my influence. And so willing to offer pieces of themselves up. Human energy doesn't provide much sustenance, but I can siphon off enough to get by. Enough to perform small spells. And there is no shortage of humans willing to give themselves to me. Though they don't always know that's what they're doing."

Something about her words, the roundabout, implicit nature of them, rattled inside Loki. He watched her as she took the kettle off the fire, poured the tea into two cups and handed him one by the saucer. The way she raised her own teacup to her lips, her nails long and sculpted as they tapped against the porcelain with a soft *chink*. Her skin still taut and pale. She hardly looked as though she'd aged since they parted, and wore none of the grime of this city like everyone else did.

He could feel her circling something, some truth she did not want to tell him but still wanted him to know. Something he had to guess.

She smiled at him, the corners of her lips turning up around the rim of her teacup.

"You're the murderer," he said suddenly.

She froze, cup still pressed against her mouth. "Excuse me?"

"You're the one leaving the living-dead corpses all over London," he said, certainty blooming inside him. "You're the one the SHARP Society is looking for."

"Dear gods." She placed her cup back in its saucer with a rattle that mimicked her laugh. "Has Odin got you playing detective with that band of misfits?"

"Do you know them?"

"Only by reputation. They take it upon themselves to tag every non-human being in range of their gadgetry. It's adorable how they seem to think they could do something to stop any of us if they tried."

"They work for my father."

Amora pressed her hand to her heart and gave him a sickly look, the sort one might give a child who, with no understanding of how gravity works, has offered up an explanation involving invisible glue for why their feet stick to the ground. "Sweetheart, they work for your father in the same way the men who clean the sewage from your palace stables do. That idiot Sharp caught on to the existence of Asgardians through a slip up on your father's part, and so your father gives him little jobs to keep him occupied so he doesn't go blabbing about the existence of the Nine Realms. No one wants humans involved in inter-dimensional affairs. They'd slow everything down."

"He's dead," Loki said. "Mr Sharp. It's his wife that runs the organisation now."

"Does she? Poor hen," Amora replied, lips pursed. "Earth is so determined to make everything that's hard for a man doubly hard for a woman."

"But you steal energy from humans?" he asked.

She shrugged, pulling her feet up onto the chair beneath her. "It was just small amounts at first – enough to keep me alive, but so little that they wouldn't notice. And then it wasn't enough." She took a sip of her tea, then glanced at his cup, still untouched in his hand. "I have sugar, if you want it. Though if I remember correctly, you prefer your brews... bitter."

"You drain humans of their essence to preserve your own, then leave their bodies in the streets? How does that restore your magic? Humans don't have any."

"But for sorcerers like us, our life essence is so tightly entwined with our magic that they're one and the same. To refresh one is to refresh the other." Her eyes combed him, that same intense, searching gaze he remembered. It made his skin itch. It made him want to look away. It made him want to touch his hair to make sure it wasn't out of place. At last, she leant back in her chair and said with a small pout, "You don't sound as impressed as I thought you would be."

"I didn't know you could do that."

"Neither did I, and there's a reason for that. It's best not to let your students know what exactly they can do with their powers for fear they might overtake you." The note of bitterness in her voice was unmistakable.

Amora took up her tea again, her lips skimming the rim of the cup in a way that sparked a queer strain of jealousy in Loki. He had missed her so much. With an intensity he hadn't realised until she was here again and he remembered what it was like to have someone to talk to. Someone to rely on.

She was murdering humans. He had seen them in the morgue, the chimney sweep limp in the street. She had taken human souls to sustain herself.

And yet, somehow, he still couldn't stop thinking about how much he'd missed her. How she was here. She was *here*, and he was here. He almost reached out to take her hand, just to prove to himself she was really beside him.

Amora placed her teacup on the dresser and pressed her

fingers together as she surveyed him. "Loki, look at you! You used to be so skinny and gawky, and now you're less skinny and less gawky."

He laughed. "You wouldn't believe how much bigger I am than Thor."

"How is your dear brother?" Amora asked. "Has he got himself killed in battle yet?"

Loki took a sip of his tea and nearly spat it out. Far too sweet, even without sugar. "No, he's still blond and as royal as ever."

"Has Odin named his heir?"

"Not yet." He took another sip of the vile tea, waiting for her to speak, but she didn't. She stared at him, watching. Waiting. "I will not be king," he blurted. The words landed like a blow – not to her, but to him. Had he ever said them aloud before? Ever truly looked them in the eye?

Her forehead crinkled. "Still he doubts you?"

"I'll never be more to him than the son that led an army against him in his vision of the future." He reached out and took her hand before he could stop himself. She let him hold it for a moment, then pressed both her hands round his. "I've missed you so much."

"I have to go," she said, standing suddenly and twisting her hair back into a knot. She reached for her discarded veil. "But I must see you again. How long until you return home?"

"I don't know. My father is off looking for the Norn Stones and has told everyone else not to welcome me back until he gives permission."

"The Norn Stones?" Amora repeated.

"A pouch was stolen from Karnilla's court."

"And she hasn't found them yet?"

"She can't sense them unless their power is accessed," Loki replied. "And it hasn't been yet."

"Well, that's interesting." She tapped a finger against her teeth. "Think what we could do with a bundle of stolen Norn Stones."

"The SHARP Society is looking for you," Loki said, standing up and following her as she checked her make-up in one of the mirrors, swiping her fingers through the spilt powder and dabbing it on her cheekbones. "They found your card on the last man you killed."

"The handsome chimney sweep? He brought his wife here for a reading and then dragged her out in the middle of it when I suggested turbulent times ahead in their love life. It's amazing how people draw their own conclusions when you're vague." She pinched her cheeks to colour them. "I don't fear the SHARP Society."

"I know you don't," he said. "But if they drop even a hint of your name to my father, he may take a more personal interest."

She stopped, staring first at her own reflection in the mirror, then him. "You think he'd come after me?"

"I don't know. But if he did, it would be more than banishment this time."

She laughed with her lips pursed. "Your father has already done his worst to me."

"Don't test him, Amora," Loki replied.

She reached for a silver-handled brush on the counter, and without thinking, he grabbed her by the elbow, pulling her back to face him. Her face was suddenly much closer to his than he had anticipated. "Please. There must be another way for you to restore your powers."

"Do you think I haven't spent every moment of my banishment trying to find one?" she demanded, her tone biting.

"Let me help you. We'll get you away from here. Somewhere my father won't find you, somewhere you won't have to steal souls to survive."

"How?"

"I'll find a way."

She stared at him for a moment, then looked down at the spot where his hand was still on her elbow. He let go, as quick as if he had been burnt, but she didn't move. She kept her arm raised between them, like an invitation to hold her again. He wanted to.

But then she turned, retrieving her veil from the counter and extending it to him. There was a tortoise comb attached to the top. "Tuck this into my chignon for me, won't you?"

He lifted the veil, twining the teeth of the comb into the soft blonde wisps of her carefully wound hair. His eyes grazed the bare back of her neck above her collar, the pale white curve of it. She must have sensed his gaze, or seen it in one of the mirrors, for she tipped her head luxuriously, running one finger along her throat as though in presentation.

Loki blinked, then dropped his hands. "There."

"Thank you." She turned and kissed him quickly on the cheek. "Come back and see me. There's so much more I have to say to you."

His heart hiccuped. "As soon as I'm able."

"And you can keep the SHARP Society away from me?"

"I'll try."

She stared at him for a moment, tongue darting out between her teeth to wet her lips. Her gaze felt hot and hungry. Then she leant forwards and kissed him again, this time just as he turned his head, so instead of landing upon his cheek, their lips brushed.

Amora pulled down her veil before he could see the look on her face.

ᚠᚱᛁᛗ

Chapter Twenty-One

*L*oki cut through the theatre and then across the club, the lightness of his heart reverberating into his step. He felt like he was dreaming. Like he was floating.

Then he spotted someone at the bar and came crashing back to Earth.

Theo was sitting on one of the tall stools, a pint glass in front of him with a book wedged open against it. And he was looking directly at Loki. He raised a hand and wiggled his fingers in a little wave, then patted the stool beside him.

Loki sighed, then crossed the room and slung himself onto the seat beside Theo. "I know I'm not from around here," Loki said, staring forwards at the chalked drinks menu like he might make a selection, "but I don't think many people bring books to taverns."

Theo let the pages fall closed with a dusty flump. "And no one has called it a tavern since the days of Shakespeare."

"Who?" Loki asked.

"You don't know who Shakespeare was?" When Loki stared blankly at him, Theo clapped his hands with a squeak of delight. "You don't know who Shakespeare was. Oh my God, this is incredible. I've never met anyone who didn't know who Shakespeare was. So he was a poet, sort of, but he also wrote the most frequently performed plays in the history of performed plays, and there have to be a certain number of syllables in every line, and at the ends of all of them – the plays, not the lines – the lovers either marry or they end up dead."

"Isn't that how all love stories end?" Loki asked.

"Well, I think history does have less extreme examples." Loki glanced at the spine to see if it was one of these Shakespearean epics. Small embossed letters spelt out *Tales from the North*, but before he had a chance to read the subtitle, Theo slipped the book onto his lap, out of sight. "But Shakespeare only leans into one or the other. He's probably the best-known writer on – what did you call us? Midgard? Everyone knows him."

"Oh, so he's sort of like your Rajmagarfen?" Loki asked.

Now it was Theo's turn to stare blankly. "Who's Rajmagarfen?"

"You don't know who Rajmagarfen is?" Loki did the same hand clap of delight – though without the squeal, as it was less dignified than he liked to be. "Oh my God, this is amazing. He's this brilliant writer from Asgard, and in all his stories, the dead end up lovers and the married end up dead."

Theo's eyes narrowed. "You're having me on."

"I would never jest about Rajmagarfen," Loki replied with grave sincerity.

Theo rolled his eyes and reached for his glass, mumbling around the rim. "Your father didn't mention what a pain you would be."

"You followed me here," Loki said.

"No, I just came here for a nice pint of…" Theo glanced into his glass. "For a pint."

"Of course. What a coincidence you chose to have it at the club you knew I was visiting."

"Such a coincidence." Theo used his finger to fish some floating chunk out of his drink, then wiped his fingers on his trousers. "Do you know her?" he asked lightly.

Loki turned to the bar. Across the room, a quartet

of musicians dressed as red imps were tuning their instruments. "Who?"

"The Enchantress." Loki continued to stare at the musicians, but he felt Theo's eyes on him. One of the men swore loudly when he poked himself in the chin with the pitchfork prongs at the end of his violin bow. "You were hardly subtle about it, you know," Theo said after a moment. "You've been dragging your feet since you arrived about getting involved in any of this, but then the moment you hear her name, suddenly you're an enthusiastic supporter of the cause. We all caught on."

Loki sighed through his nose, relishing the long, deep breath while he weighed what to say next. "We were friends once," he said at last. "As children."

"So then the answer is yes."

"Yes, I know her," he said. "But it was a long time ago."

"Is she an actual enchantress?"

"She was."

"Guess you can't use the name, then. She's already claimed it. Did you see her?" When Loki nodded, Theo prompted. "And what do two aliens talk about when they're reunited?"

"Oh, the usual. Discussed Ragnarok and court politics

and how much muscly-er I am than my brother. We *aliens* are just like you, you know." Loki squinted up at the chalk menu above the bar. "If I'm going to get a drink, do you think I'm less likely to be actually poisoned by the consumption germ or typhoid fever? Follow up question: Do you think the typhoid is a hot drink?"

"If you don't tell me," Theo said, "I can just assume the worst."

"What would the worst be?"

"That you two are plotting to conquer the Earth together."

Loki let out a shocked bark of laughter. "That's quite a jump from a chat with an old friend."

Theo shrugged. "I wouldn't put it past you. Perhaps I'll report that to Mrs S."

"She doesn't scare me," Loki replied.

"She should."

"I've stared down dragons."

"So have I," Theo replied, then drained the rest of his pint.

Loki sighed again, this time letting his spine relax so that he slumped over the bar, an overwrought gesture of surrender to cover his lie. "I asked her if she could get me back to Asgard, but she's in exile and has no magic after so long on Earth." He said this last part carefully to make sure Theo understood what it meant.

But Theo didn't comment. Instead he said, "You're truly so desperate to be away from us?" Loki might have been imagining it, but he sounded a little wounded.

"It's nothing personal," Loki replied. "But this simply isn't the best use of my time."

"Well." Theo swivelled forwards on his stool. "I'm sorry we're not as interesting as the stolen artefacts your brother is hunting down."

"You're not half as interesting," Loki replied. "The corpses aren't *not* interesting, I will admit, but they just can't compare."

"Did you ask her about them?" Theo asked. "The corpses?"

Loki felt his heart begin to pound, but he kept his face resolutely the same. "She doesn't have any magic left. She was banished here by my father years ago, and all her power has deteriorated."

"What does that have to do with it?" Theo asked.

"Because they died by magic, according to your spectacles," Loki replied. He was starting to feel hot and itchy, and suddenly wanted a drink, even if it was foul. "So she couldn't have killed them."

"What about magical artefacts?" Theo asked. "Maybe she's got some secret murder weapon?"

"As opposed to what other kind of weapon?" Loki muttered, but Theo ignored him.

"Maybe she's got your Norn Stones and is using them to kill people."

"She doesn't have the Norn Stones," Loki replied. "They were stolen long after she was banished. And they don't work like that – they're not powerful on their own. They amplify the power their wielder already has, and Odin's sorceress would've detected that amplification. Even if she didn't care about getting caught, using them to wipe out Midgardians would be ridiculous. Why waste strength on something that can be done just as easily with a knife in the dark?"

Theo's eyes darted sideways to him. He truly had an unbelievable number of freckles. Loki had never seen anything like it. It might have looked garish on another man, but somehow it just made Theo's face more interesting. A starry sky that could be studied for years and still there would be constellations left unnamed. "I was going to invite you to come stay at my place tonight, but if you're thinking of knives in the dark, I may reconsider."

Loki blinked. "You... you want me to stay with you?"

"As a house guest," Theo said quickly, the skin beneath those freckles reddening. "I thought you might need somewhere to stay, since we were out all last night. Mrs S said you could fend for yourself until you started being a bit less belligerent, but... I've got room. Not much. It's a pretty rubbish flat, but there's a roof. And a bit of floor you can kip up on."

"I can't have the bed?" Loki asked with mock affront. "I am a prince of Asgard, you know."

Theo looked momentarily concerned, like he had actually started some kind of inter-dimensional scandal by not offering him a bed, but then Loki raised one eyebrow, and Theo shook his head with a weary laugh. "It'll do you good to sleep on the cold hard ground for one night, Your Highness."

Chapter Twenty-Two

Theo's building was, as advertised, rubbish. The night was chilly, but somehow it was even colder inside. The wallpaper in the hallway had begun to decay, revealing soft plaster moulding and support beams beneath that looked like they were doing little to provide support. The flat was on the third floor, and Theo had to stop outside of his door, breathing heavily and stretching out his bad leg.

"You raised my expectations far too high," Loki said, lifting his foot as a large insect skittered down the hallway and into a large crack in the wall.

"Well, prepare to be impressed." Theo fiddled in his pocket for the key, then jammed it in the lock. It took him throwing what seemed like the entirety of his fairly insubstantial weight into it before it creaked open. "See?" he said as he strode in, Loki on his heels. "Fit for a king."

It seemed hardly fit for any kind of living thing. Loki wouldn't even keep the Southwark corpses here. The floor was uncarpeted wood, splintered and creaking underfoot. There was a pile of blankets bundled onto a limp mattress on the floor, and a small grate for a fire with a single set of cutlery and a tin plate and mug stacked beside it. There was a chipped washbasin below a glass-less window, its frame lined with oiled paper that was starting to tear around the nails. The room was made even smaller by the fact that two walls were stacked to the bottom of the window frame with mismatched books.

"You know," Loki said, toeing a volume that had tumbled from the pile. "You'd have more room if you kept fewer books."

Theo hung his cane on the edge of the grate beside the small fireplace and began to stoke the ashes. "I'd rather have books than space."

"Well, when the floor caves in, don't say I didn't warn you." He watched Theo struggling with the fire for a moment, then offered, "Do you want me to do that?"

"No, no," Theo said quickly. "Let me do something

hostly. Though this is not the place to host anyone." Silence fell over the flat as Loki watched Theo blow gently on the cinders until they blushed back to life. He suddenly felt very aware of both of them in this small room, barely able to be more than a few feet apart from each other even standing in opposite corners. He glanced around, looking for something to stare at that wasn't Theo, but there was so little else. It was too dark to see the titles of the books, and the rotting floorboards were hardly encouraging to look at. And he kept finding his eyes wandering to Theo, the curl of his shoulders, the concavity of his cheeks as he stoked the fire, the way he swiped his hair out of his eyes with the back of his wrist.

Why are you looking at him? said a small voice inside him; it sounded like Amora's.

Loki turned away.

Theo pushed himself up with a hand on the grate, then brushed his hands off on his trousers. They looked at each other, and Loki was suddenly sure Theo knew how intently he had been watching him. Then Theo smiled sheepishly and stuck his hands in his pockets. "Do you want some tea?" he said. "Or food. Or a change of clothes? I don't think we're the same..." He held up one hand, like he was comparing their heights, then let it drop. "Though I suppose you can do something about that, can't you? With your spells and things. If you really want—"

"I don't need anything," Loki interrupted. Theo nodded, tucking his chin to his chest. Then, after a few moments of silence, Loki added, "Thank you."

Theo nodded, teeth pressed into his bottom lip. "Suit yourself." He looked around, and Loki thought about offering to leave just to relieve them both of the awkwardness, but then Theo said, "I think I'll make some tea. For me. If you don't mind. I mean, you can have some as well, but... Tea."

He limped back to the stove, taking a kettle off the hook beside it. The firelight glanced off a pair of the green-lensed spectacles on the mantelpiece, abandoned after their time at the crime scene.

"Why do you do this?" Loki asked.

Theo glanced up from the kettle. "Do what?"

"Work for Mrs S and her Society. Or work for my father, I suppose. Why not do real work? Something that pays, so you..."

"Mrs S pays me," Theo protested. When Loki raised an eyebrow, he conceded, "A bit. She pays for the flat, anyway."

"Yes, but with a real profession, you could get a flat that wasn't condemned."

"I haven't got many options for employment."

"Because you're a criminal," Loki said.

The kettle lid slipped from Theo's fingers, clattering to the floor. He looked up. "So you know it all then."

Loki wondered suddenly if he'd made a mistake in saying it. He briefly considered leaving again. Instead he turned away and picked up the first book on top of one of the piles, flipping through it. "Mrs S mentioned something. After the police—"

"Flamin' Scotland Yard." Theo hung the kettle over the fire and pushed it into place. It bounced against the back of the fireplace with a clang of metal on brick. "Those idiots never miss a chance. Do you want to know all the sordid details, then? I can assure you it's a very thrilling story of unrequited pining and misreading signs and me making a complete fool of myself and then getting arrested for it. Ripped from the pages of a penny dreadful."

"I don't understand."

Theo mashed a hand over the back of his neck. "I kissed someone I thought was interested in me. He wasn't. I got rounded up as part of a factory raid, and this bloke was angry so he went to the police, and when they let everyone else go, they kept me for indecency."

"I understand the mechanics of it," Loki said. "What I meant is that I don't understand why you Midgardians are so small-minded."

Theo looked up. "What do you mean?"

"On Asgard, we don't have such a limited view of sex. Or love, for that matter. There are no rules about who can be with whom. Certainly no one is arrested for it."

Theo stared at him. In the pale glow of the fire, he looked as though he had caught a glimpse of something rare and precious, a wild flower opening its petals between a parted jungle curtain. "Do you mean that?"

There was nothing Loki could say in the face of such backwards justice. Why waste a cell – why waste your time – trying to punish someone for something that wasn't a crime?

Theo looked away first, turning back to the tea kettle. The firelight pocked and hollowed his face. "Do you have a preference? Between men and women?"

"I feel equally comfortable as either."

"No, I don't mean... not all of us can change our gender at will."

"I don't change my gender. I exist as both."

"You're not... That doesn't make sense."

"It does to me."

"Well, all hail Asgard, then."

Theo leant backwards, fingers pressed to his mouth and his eyes on the fire again. "You wouldn't take me back, would you?" he asked after a moment. "To Asgard?"

"In what capacity?" Loki asked.

"Dunno." Theo shrugged. "Kept man?" He laughed at his own joke, then said, "Never mind. God, this is all so strange."

"What is?" Loki asked.

"That I'm talking about Asgard with Loki, the brother of Thor—"

"Please," Loki interrupted. "Call me anything but the brother of Thor."

"—God of Mischief, and he's telling me that there's a place in this universe where no one gives a fig about whom you fall in love with, and *that* is the thing I find most unbelievable of all of it." He wiped his eyes with the back of his hand, then hooked the arm holding the kettle over the fire with the poker, pulling it out of the flames. "Are you certain you don't want any tea? I promise it's not as rancid as the gin Mrs S gave you."

"All right." Loki watched as Theo added leaves to two small strainers balanced over chipped mugs and poured the hot water over them, the steam wafting from the surface in lazy tendrils. He handed a cup to Loki and they lingered for a time in silence, Theo perched on a stack of books, Loki leaning against the wall, both with their lips pressed to the rims of their cups, waiting for the tea to cool enough to drink.

"Is this what humans do?" Loki asked. "Go to museums

and clubs and drink tea and sleep on mouldy mattresses in freezing flats."

"Sometimes," Theo replied. "When we're not fighting and working and dying in factories. What do Asgardians do?"

"The same," Loki replied. "Though we don't have factories. We die on battlefields, more often."

"We do that too. Sometimes." Theo took a tentative sip of his tea, his eyes flicking to Loki over the rim. "Do you die, in Asgard? I mean, not you personally. But... do people die? Are you *people*? What should I call you? Asgardians?"

"We die," Loki said. "Asgardians die. Not so easily as you humans do, though. Our lives are much longer."

"How much longer?"

"Several thousand years, give or take a millennium."

Theo spat a mouthful of tea back into his cup. "You do not. You're having me on."

"I'm not. Really!" He laughed when Theo still looked sceptical. "An Asgardian can live longer than humans can understand. Though perhaps it helps that we don't daily breathe air that is actively poisoning us."

"How dare you speak ill of London," Theo said in mock outrage. "She has her charms."

"I have yet to see them. Though I hear the dogs are good."

Theo paused, his teacup to his lips. "So are you at the prime of your life, then? For an Asgardian."

"I'm only just beginning." Loki took a sip of the tea. It was still hot, and he tasted the heat more than the tea itself, but the steam smelt spicy and bitter, and left a damp film across his cheeks. "You wouldn't be happy in Asgard."

Theo shrugged. "Got to be better than here."

"You'd be lonely if you were the only human."

"You'd have to keep me company then."

"I'm very busy."

"I don't mind." Theo took a sip of his tea, then said suddenly, "It's just really nice."

"What is?"

"It's nice..." Theo repeated, his thumb skimming the rim of his teacup. "To know that there's somewhere out there in the cosmos where people like me don't have to be afraid."

Chapter Twenty-Three

*L*oki woke to the sound of gentle rain on the window sill.

He had fallen asleep on the floor beside Theo's filthy mattress, but sometime in the night he must have shifted, for now they were both lying on it, burrowed like rabbits under their respective blankets. Theo was still asleep, his hands pulled up to his face and his mouth slightly open. Loki rose as quietly as he could, pausing only to help himself to the black umbrella leaning against the door. No point wasting the energy for a spell. Or raising the questions that might come with being the only one unaffected by rain on a busy city street. Theo would likely know where he'd gone, or at least guess. Perhaps he'd tell

Mrs S, or simply follow Loki himself. What did it matter? Though the SHARP Society did not have his father's most attentive ear, Loki was certain that if Mrs S delivered a report of his fraternising with Amora, he would be sucked back up the Bifrost and locked inside the palace before he could so much as breathe the same air as her again.

The walk to the Inferno Club wasn't long, but the air was bitter with the frigid rain, and Loki found his nerves mounting as he drew nearer. Why was he nervous? It was Amora. His friend. They knew each other. Perhaps that was exactly the problem. He looked down at himself, still in his all-black ensemble from the night before, and considered changing the colour of his tie to emerald to match the green veins in her eyes. But if she noticed, he'd likely die of embarrassment, and if she didn't notice, he'd die of disappointment. Either way, dead. Not ideal.

He wasn't sure Amora would even be at the club, or that he'd be able to get in, but he sent a note to her dressing room with one of the men sweeping up the tunnel, and a few minutes later he returned to tell Loki the Enchantress wanted to see him onstage. In the overcast dawn light, the club interior looked silly and garish. The tabletops were smeared with the sticky remains of last night's spilt drinks, the floor littered with oyster and peanut shells crushed underfoot. The plaster demons had cracks, and chunks were missing from their bodies. Loki recognised the man sitting on the bar reading a newspaper as the ticket taker from the night before, looking strange and out of place with his shirtsleeves rolled up and a kerchief round his neck. The headline on the front page read in block letters LIVING-DEAD KILLER STALKS SOUTHWARK; ANOTHER RIPPER?

He didn't glance up as Loki crossed the empty bar area and passed through the curtains leading to the stage. The theatre was as dark as it had been the night before, but the gaslights were glowing, casting slender beams that traced Amora's silhouette against the backdrop. She had pushed the chairs back from the table with the talking board and was on her knees, one arm craned to adjust something underneath.

When she saw him, she stopped and stood, her shadow falling long and dark behind her. "Loki. You came back."

He stepped onto the stage, into the same column of light illuminating her. It felt like a small universe the two of them shared. This close, and in the harsh lights of the stage rather than the dreamy firelight of her dressing room, her face looked softer than he remembered it. Amora was never the sort to let her guard down, let the gaps between her plates of armour show. Maybe she thought the darkness covered her. Maybe she didn't care if Loki saw her like this. Maybe she had a reason for showing her softness.

He didn't know what to say, so instead, he pointed to the table. "Can I help? With... whatever you're doing."

"Rigging a new trick."

"You mean you don't use *actual* magic to contact *actual* spirits?"

She rolled her eyes. "What a waste of my precious life. Come here, I'll show you." She pulled a couple of the chairs up to the table, and he sat in one obediently. "Now," she said, sitting down in the other. "Pretend there's someone you want to contact. Someone who has died and you're desperate to tell them one last thing."

"All right."

She reached under the table and withdrew a bell on a stand. She placed it in the centre, over the painted alphabet. "Sometimes I like to do a bit of theatrics – going into a trance and spiritual tremors and all that." She did a half-hearted demonstration, and he laughed. "That proves your spirit is here."

"There were no such theatrics last night."

"Yes, well. I was too distracted for a proper trance." Her eyes flicked downwards, mouth curling in a small smile. "So we call to the spirit of whomever it is you're wanting to talk to, and I see if they're here." She rapped her knuckles on the table, then looked around the room as though searching for a face in the dark crowd, her arms raised. "Spirit, if you are here, make yourself known!"

A pause. The silence of the theatre suddenly felt vast. In the club above them, Loki heard the tinkle of a glass breaking.

Then the bell on the table rang once. Twice. Three times.

Loki jumped, though he had expected it. Even knowing it was her operating it, a chill still went through him. Amora bit her lip, suppressing a laugh. "Do you want to ask the spirit a question?"

"Spirit, how did you do that?" Loki asked. He looked from the bell to her hands, still raised, trying to find the string or the mechanism in her fingers.

She pulled back the tablecloth and he saw the foot pedal beneath her chair, the rod leading up to the bar on which the bell was suspended. When she pumped the pedal, the bell rang.

Loki laughed. "That's quite clever."

"If it's clever enough to fool you, the humans will be dumbstruck."

"What else is down here?" he asked, starting to drop off his chair, but she held up a hand.

"Don't look, you'll spoil it! Let me show off for you a bit." She fished in her pocket and came up with the planchette, then placed it over the top of the letter A on the talking board. The letter was magnified through the hole in the centre.

Amora ducked under the table, then crooked a finger at Loki to follow. The tablecloth dropped around them, suffocating and thick. Amora slithered onto her back, motioning for him to lie down beside her, staring up at the bottom of the table, where the mirror image of the board on top was painted. Amora reached into her pocket again, this time coming up with a magnet, which she pressed against the board atop the letter A. "Usually one of the stagehands is under the table for the show, if we use the board. He got kicked in the face once by one of the customers, and his nose was bleeding all down his front for the whole show."

"So you mean to tell me last night I was having an intimate conversation with a stranger under a table?" Loki demanded with false indignation.

"I make exceptions. There are some people worth wasting your magic for." She winked at him, and he laughed. "So the person asks a question and then..." She slid the magnet across the underside of the table, and over their heads, he heard the scrape of the planchette's wheels against the table grain, spelling out *HELLOLOKI*.

He smiled. "Hello to you too."

"Here, go sit at the table and try it."

He slid out obediently and took his seat again. Her legs were jutting out from under the table, and she clicked her heels together as she called "You first must greet the spirits."

"All right." He placed his hands flat on the table. "Um, good morning, spirits."

The planchette slid across the board with a low scraping sound and landed upon the word *HELLO*. A few select words surrounded the letters, simplifying the answers of the spirits.

"They're not as formal as a good morning," Amora called. "It takes too long to spell."

He laughed again, and he felt the muscles in his shoulders unclench. Had he felt this relaxed since he arrived in Midgard? Had he felt this relaxed in years? How much tension had he been carrying in his body without realising it until it floated away? It felt like the past few years had lifted; like he was with Amora, in court, before the Godseye Mirror had written his future for him.

"Now you ask your question," she prompted.

He pressed his fingers together against his lips, not sure how much of this was a game and how much was her baiting him. "What shall I have for breakfast?"

The planchette shuddered for a moment, and it felt suddenly eerie, though he knew it was her controlling it below him. Then it slid across the board in slow formation, spelling out the answer. *BLOOD OF YOUR ENEMIES*.

"A good suggestion," he replied frankly. "How much longer will it rain?"

The planchette spun this time before landing on the first letter of *FOREVER*.

"I fear you're right again." He fished with his foot under the table until he found the softness of Amora's stomach and poked his toe into it. She laughed, and the planchette lurched. "What wise spirits you are."

"Ask them a real question," she called. "Something they can tell you about your future."

He paused. He could always tell when Amora was trying to manipulate him, but he'd never been able to resist it. She would open her arms, and he would step into them every time, whether or not there was a knife in her hand.

"Will I be king of Asgard?" he asked.

The planchette scrabbled back and forth, like it couldn't make up its mind, flying from one corner to the other and back. Then, at last, it spelt out:

MAYBE.

"Sometimes they must be vague," she said, sliding out from under the table. Her hair was speckled with clumps of fuzzy dust. "Simply to avoid being wrong." She smiled. When he didn't return it, hers faded. "Come here." She patted the ground beside her. He slid to her side, and she pushed herself back under the table and he followed so that they were lying side by side. Above them, the white letters of the alphabet on the talking board seemed to glow, fireflies against the black wood.

"I wish I could help you," he said.

"Help me?" She snorted, reaching up to trace the alphabet with her fingertips. "With what? I think I've done quite fine on my own, princeling."

"I wish I was king and could bring you out of banishment and back to Asgard."

"To practise simple spells and be a docile queen, like your mother?"

"To be a sorceress," he said. "The most powerful sorceress in the Nine Realms. To never have to hide your strength."

"I wish I had any strength left to hide."

"How long can you last?" he asked. "Without taking anyone's life force?"

"It depends," she replied. "Though it's becoming less and less." She let out a laugh laced with bitterness. "I don't even have the strength to be strong."

"If you could hold out, just for a bit," he said. "Let everything die down. Let the SHARP Society think it's all over. If I can find something else to blame it on and convince them it's all been cleared up so long as no one is finding bodies. I can pretend to find some other reason no one else is dying, the murders stop long enough for father to bring me home, and then..." He trailed off.

"And then I stay here until either you are made king or I die?" she finished for him.

He reached out and let his fingers brush her wrist. He couldn't lose her, now that they had tumbled back together. It had to be more than just luck or chance. "We just need some time."

"Time until what?"

Loki bit his lip, weighing his next words carefully. "Just trust me," he finally said, though it sounded sillier when it left him than it had in his head. "I won't let you die."

"I don't think you'll have much say in the matter, Your Majesty."

"I'll take you somewhere else. Somewhere safer. We'll find a way to restore your power without the humans." She didn't say anything. "What's the matter?"

"I just wish you thought bigger." She pressed her forehead into his shoulder. "Promise you'll raise me along with your living-dead army when you conquer Asgard, won't you? I would hate to miss the fun."

She said it lightly, but he felt the sting of it, of all the years since that feast day when Odin had looked at him with distrust, every time he had favoured Thor, every time he had overlooked Loki because he was too afraid of what he and his power could do.

"Maybe there's a reason people fear us," Loki said.

"They should fear us," Amora replied. "Because we're strong."

"Not because we're dangerous?"

"What's wrong with being dangerous? Odin is dangerous. That's why he rules the Nine Realms. I'd rather be deadly than dead." She rolled over on her side, pillowing her head upon her hands, and though he didn't look at her, he could feel her gaze hot upon his face. "You can't save everyone, darling. Best to think of this as goodbye and good luck."

"No. You're here because of me."

"It was my choice."

"It was my fault."

"Let's not waste any more time on the past."

"Then what is there to dwell upon? The future, me as a second son and you turned to dust?"

"Why not the present?"

He rolled over so he was looking at her, and suddenly he realised how close their faces were, how beautiful her hair looked, puddled around her fair skin, how long he'd wanted to know what her mouth felt like to be pressed against his – not in a way that was accidental or quick. He'd never truly kissed her – not even when they spent every moment together in Asgard, when he'd thought of it as often as breathing. He'd never been brave enough. Never thought she would say yes. He still wasn't sure she would.

"Any final questions you want to ask the spirits?" she said, and her eyes flicked to his mouth.

How long had he missed her? How long had he wanted her? How long had he been certain she was the only person who knew him, the only person who would ever know him or understand him? The only person with the same fire in their blood, but hers buoyed by a current of certainty that they were made of gemstones and light, made to shine brighter than others? As he looked at her shadowed face in the pale glow of the gaslights, he almost believed it too, all the things that had made him feel strange and outcast turned to gold by the strange alchemy of being near her again.

"May I kiss you?" he asked.

She leant forwards and closed the space between their mouths, still and gentle for a moment before her lips parted against his.

She was intoxicating, like sweet wine. He'd be drunk before he realised she'd refilled his glass. Had it always been like this? Even when they were children? Had he truly never noticed, or was it easier to ignore because she was the only person who made him feel like he was worth noticing? Any sort of attention had become water in the desert after being so long neglected by his father.

This, he thought, and released a deep breath against her mouth. As his heartbeat swelled, the stage lights flickered and died.

Chapter Twenty-Four

The next days passed in quiet deathlessness.

Amora had promised to preserve her strength and buy Loki as much time as possible to leave the realm. He mostly stayed near the SHARP Society, walking to the British Museum with Theo during the lunch hour to look at the artefacts of Midgardians past. On the days it rained, Loki used a spell to keep them protected from the wind and the mud, and though he knew it was an unnecessary waste of his precious reserves of magic, he enjoyed the way Theo's eyes widened every time a carriage passed over a rancid puddle and the water bounced from the air before it struck them, like they were encased in a bell jar.

In spite of himself, Loki was starting to enjoy being around Theo. In Asgard, he always preferred his own company to that of anyone else, aside from Amora, and he had hardly expected that a human, of all creatures, would be the one to snare him. But Theo had a quick wit, laughed at his own jokes, read too many books and knew too much about everything. He chewed loudly but ate slowly, wore his hats low so that his curly hair was smashed into his eyes and didn't like walking on the outside of the pavement where the carriages passed. Loki wasn't sure why he didn't mind any of these things.

He'd even started to enjoy Mrs S, in moderation, over dinner after her day at the museum ended and she joined Theo and him at the offices. Gem sometimes came as well, when he wasn't on patrol, and would finish two plates before any of them had finished their first. Midgardian food was mostly lacking and tasteless, but Loki found himself growing attached to the thick, warm chocolate that could be purchased from coffee shop windows, and which Mrs S even brewed on their little crooked stove in the office. It was dark and bitter enough for him, and it may have been the only thing about Midgard he'd miss.

Mrs S told him stories of her work with her husband, both before and after Odin had employed them. Her exploits made some of the Asgardian warriors look like trainees sparring with wooden sticks. She told them about sucking poison from her husband's forearm after he was bitten by a venomous snake in the Amazon and then carrying him seven miles to civilisation on her back. About jungle fevers they had survived, cursed tombs they had raided, caves whose entrances had fallen in behind them, so they had continued walking through them in the dark, not sure if they would die or find light first. She told them about the dog sledge teams they had run to collapse on the tip of Norway, where they had first found the artefacts that belonged to Loki's father, how she had dug them out of the snow as her bare fingers turned blue, afraid that if she left to retrieve her gloves, the snow would cover them again and they'd be lost.

"Why don't you travel any more?" Loki asked her one night, as they sat in the back office waiting for Theo to join them.

"It's much harder to be a professional adventurer as a woman alone," she replied. "My husband had to secure all the funding and make our travel arrangements and publish any of the papers we wrote after we returned."

"That's hardly fair."

"So little is. Including losing him." She twisted her

wedding ring with a sad smile, and Loki noticed the edges of the band were worn silver and smooth from the repetition of the gesture.

Loki looked down into the dregs of the thick chocolate at the bottom of his mug. "My father should have done more," he said suddenly. When they all looked at him, he added, "To protect your husband. To protect all of you. It's not risk-less work you do for him."

"Nothing in life is without risk, my dear," Mrs S replied. "My husband was never one for safety. We preferred excitement."

"But he shouldn't have died," Loki said. "If you hadn't been employed by my father—"

"You'll waste your life on what could and should and would have been," Mrs S interrupted. "What if we had never met your father? What if I had never met Mr Sharp? What if my parents had shipped me off to India when I was a child and married me to a sultan with a menagerie of tigers? What if I had made coffee instead of chocolate tonight? You'll drive yourself mad considering it all." She took a sip of her drink, then added, "We knew our job was dangerous. It's always been dangerous. But it was important as well. That's the way Mr Sharp liked it. Dangerous and important."

Loki wanted to tell her that their work couldn't have mattered less to his father. Not to be cruel – simply because he felt they had the right to know. A right to know they could put down their knives now and walk away from a fight that could cost them their lives. Already had.

But instead, he finished his drink and said nothing.

The bell over the front door rang, and a moment later, Theo pushed through the velvet curtain. His shoulders were dark with rain, and he threw himself at the stove, pressing his bare hands as close to the heat as he could without burning himself. "Flippin' cold out there."

"Did Gem have anything new for you?" Mrs S asked.

Theo shook his head. A few stray raindrops slid from the brim of his hat. "No new bodies."

"What about the autopsy?"

"Rachel Bowman paid the wife a call, and she suddenly withdrew her permission and has gone to Cornwall to stay with her parents."

Mrs S let out a frustrated sigh through her nose. "Dammit."

"Who's Rachel Bowman?" Loki asked.

"The head witch with the anti-burial lot," Mrs S replied, then added, "No offence to any actual witches present."

"She's the one who's rallied all the protests at Southwark

Morgue," Theo added. "Gem said that any time the police get close to convincing a family to grant permission for an autopsy, Rachel suddenly appears on their doorstep with a bunch of flowers and a very convincing argument about why their dearly departed is probably not departed at all, but rather just waiting to be revived."

Loki tipped his chair back on two legs and arched his neck. He had been waiting for an opportunity to introduce the idea he and Amora had concocted to cover her tracks. Or rather, he had concocted and Amora had grumbled and sniped at him about. He had a sense she would have continued guiltlessly sucking humans dry of their life force if he hadn't come along. The only thing that had tempted her into cooperation was the promise of leaving Midgard with him, though where they'd go, Loki still didn't know. He was taking this plan one step at a time.

"I have been doing some investigating on my own," he said, his tone light. "And I have a theory as to why you haven't caught your murderer yet."

Both Mrs S and Theo turned to him. Theo was still caved round the stove.

"Do you wish to enlighten us further upon it, or are you simply stating a fact?" Mrs S asked.

Loki let his chair fall forwards, the legs clattering

against the wood floor. "You haven't caught a murderer because there isn't one to catch," he said. "You don't have a killer, you have a virus."

"A what?" Theo asked.

"A disease," he clarified. "Whatever this spell is that's striking these people down, it's not being cast upon them by some rogue sorcerer. It's spreading like any other plague in London. You don't have a magical murderer, you have an epidemic."

"Does magic spread in that manner?" Theo asked.

"It can," Loki replied. "Several years ago, one of Asgard's provinces had a plague of magic. It bubbled up from the ground – unlikely here because of the lack of magic present in the atmosphere – but it caused those who caught it to claw their own eyes out. Anyone who came into contact with them or tried to stop them was struck with the same affliction."

He was, of course, lying. He'd never heard of a magical plague. But Theo looked suitably horrified.

"So if that is the cause, what can we do to stop it?" he asked.

"You cut out the cancer," Loki replied. "You locate the source and remove it."

"So how are people catching this magical plague?" Mrs S

asked. She looked less convinced than Theo. Her eyes were narrowed at Loki, her face unreadable.

"Most likely it passes from the already infected corpses. Those bodies in Southwark need to be taken from the city. They need to be buried."

"That won't do us any good if the source of this magical virus is still present in London," Mrs S said. "How do we find that?"

Loki took a breath. "I think I found it." Mrs S raised an eyebrow. *Stay calm*, he chided himself. Lying is easy. Lying is natural. Lying is a native tongue. "The Enchantress, at the Inferno Club." At the stove, Theo raised his head. Loki didn't look at him as he went on. "She was a sorceress on Asgard once, but here I think her magic may have turned toxic from too long on Midgard. She told me she used her sorcery to read cards for that chimney sweep who died – the one we found last week. That's why he had her card."

"So she uses her powers at the club to mimic spiritualism?" Mrs S asked. "And that poisons anyone who comes into contact with her?" When Loki nodded, she asked, "Have you told her? Since you two have been chumming it up and you never felt the need to mention it to any of us."

"I told you I was going to the club."

"And you reported very little after," she countered. "And told none of us you'd gone back."

Theo looked down at his hands but stayed silent.

"We were friends," Loki said, meeting Mrs S's beady gaze. "She trusts me. If I had involved any of you, she might not have. I couldn't risk it."

"You could have kept us informed."

Loki shrugged. "I don't work for you, Mrs Sharp. I work for my father, and I did what I thought was best for his investigation here. The Enchantress likely doesn't know she's poisoning the humans she's using her magic upon."

"So we tell your father, return her to Asgard and see if the deaths stop," Mrs S said. "Simple."

"She isn't allowed to return to Asgard," Loki said. "She and my father have quarrelled. But I could take her elsewhere. I know her. She wouldn't want to hurt humans. If we tell her, I know she'll help us stop it."

Mrs S swiped a finger over the corner of her lips, thinking. "That still doesn't solve the issue of how to get the bodies in the ground."

"Organise some sort of rally – or a seance." He congratulated himself on what an excellent job he was doing at pretending this was something that was just occurring to him, rather than a story he had been carefully fabricating over the last several days. "We ask the Enchantress to contact the souls and confirm they *are* well and truly dead and can't move on without burial." Loki leant forwards on the table, doing his best imitation of excitement over a realisation he had just had. "When I went to her show, there was a couple there whose daughter had died. They wanted exactly that – confirmation from the Enchantress that their daughter had moved on from this world. We could find them – once they have the confirmation that their daughter has passed on, they may give permission for the autopsy. Then the bodies can all be declared dead, and buried."

"And we are sure they're dead?" Mrs S asked.

"Of course they are," Loki replied. "No heartbeat – isn't that what you humans generally look for?"

"What about the chimney sweep you reanimated?" Theo asked quietly.

His facade slipped for the first time. He had almost let himself forget that strange moment that the dead man had moved beneath his hand. "That wasn't life," he said, and tried to sound certain.

"How do we know your theory is correct?" Mrs S asked.

"Why would I lie to you?"

"I can think of a few reasons," Mrs S replied. "Not the least of which being that when you arrived, your singular focus was getting home. How do we know this isn't a ploy to accelerate that process?"

"I suppose you'll have to trust me," Loki replied. "But that's what you brought me here for, isn't it? To advise you. Consider yourselves advised." He leant back in his chair. "Do with it what you want."

Mrs S stared at him, fingers steepled against her mouth. She glanced at Theo, then said, "Come away from the stove before you singe your eyebrows off." Theo dropped into the chair between Loki and Mrs S, stretching his leg out under the table. "What do you think?" Loki started to speak, but Mrs S held up one finger. "Not you." She nodded at Theo. "What do *you* think of this?"

Theo's throat bobbed as he swallowed hard. He looked from Mrs S to Loki, then back again. Loki felt, for the first time since he'd laid out this carefully woven theory, a twinge of apprehension. Theo knew he'd gone to the club more than once. He had told him more than was likely wise about his relationship with Amora. How had he let himself tell Theo so much, about himself and Asgard and all of it? He'd let his guard down without meaning to.

Theo chewed his lip, then said, "I think we should listen to him. He knows more about this than we do."

Loki bit back a sigh of relief as he looked to Mrs S. Her face was still frustratingly unreadable. But then she nodded once and said, "Fine. Let's go find the Enchantress."

Chapter Twenty-Five

The only liar better than Loki was Amora.

When Mrs S explained their theory to her in her dressing room at the Inferno, she burst into tears. Actual, real, running-down-her-cheeks tears. Loki was impressed – he wasn't sure he could have managed that.

"I didn't know!" she sobbed. "I didn't... I didn't mean to hurt anyone."

Theo passed her his handkerchief. "You couldn't have known," he said kindly. "It isn't your fault."

Mrs S, leaning against one of the dressing room counters, added, "Oh, it's most certainly her fault. Ignorance isn't synonymous with blamelessness."

Amora raised her face from Theo's handkerchief and looked at Mrs S, her eyes shining. "Please—please," she stammered, interlacing her fingers before her, "I beg you, forgive me! I never meant to hurt anyone."

"We're not sure you did," Loki added quickly. "It's only a theory."

"However," Mrs S added. "There is a way you can make some penance."

"Anything," Amora cried, then gave a fantastic sniffle. "I'll do anything to make this right."

Mrs S glanced at Loki, then nodded to Amora. Loki sighed. "We need the police to grant permission for the bodies of the dead to be buried," he explained, like the two of them hadn't already reviewed all of this. Get the bodies buried, then get her out of the realm and the deaths would stop. The SHARP Society didn't need to know what was truly responsible, and neither did Odin. "We were hoping that, through your spiritualism, you would convince one of the families of the victims to allow for an autopsy and the pronouncement of death."

"The prince will then take you somewhere in the cosmos where your powers will be less destructive," Mrs S added. "Whether intentionally or otherwise."

"Of course. Of course, I'll do anything." Amora sniffed

again, another fat tear rolling down her cheek. She swiped it away with the back of her hand. "I can't believe…"

"Don't be so hard on yourself," Loki said, crouching down before her and taking her hand. He had almost begun to fall for her performance, but then she shifted so that her fingers were pressed against his palm, tracing the lines on his skin with a gentle touch that made him light-headed. "Do you remember the couple that came to the show the same night I did?" he asked. "The ones looking for the spirit of their daughter, to see if she had passed on. Do you think you could find them again?" Amora nodded. "If we can get them to agree, all you need to do is tell them their daughter has moved on to the spirit world—"

"Without using any of your actual magic," Mrs S added. "Lest you render all your good intentions moot."

Amora let out another sob. Loki shot Mrs S a disparaging look. She was entirely unmoved. "Then tell them she can only truly find peace in the afterlife when her body is buried. That way, with all the bodies buried, the source of the plague is removed from London and it will stop spreading. Can you do that for us?"

Amora blew her nose into Theo's handkerchief, then offered it back to him. Theo wrinkled his nose. "You can keep it."

"Amora," Loki prompted. "Will you help us?"

"Of course," she said, clutching his hand in both of hers and looking between the three of them. "Anything. Anything to make right the mess I've made."

As they left, Loki offered Amora a comforting embrace that was mostly an excuse to murmur in her ear, "That was an impressive performance."

"I don't know what you mean," she replied, then she let out a large snuffle onto his shoulder. "I'm clearly distraught."

*M*rs S filled Gem in on the details, and he volunteered to find the Matulises. He located them through Southwark Morgue, and Amora paid them a call, accompanied by Mrs S. In the end, they needed very little convincing, and the date for the seance was set.

"That *horrible woman*," Amora raged to Loki in her dressing room that night.

"Who?"

"Sharp." She stabbed her cheek with one of the cosmetic brushes, leaving an inelegant splash of rouge. "All the snide remarks and little comments she thinks are so clever. How do you stand her?"

"Mrs S isn't so bad."

"Mrs S," Amora snorted, throwing her brush onto the counter and scrubbing at her cheeks with her palms to blend the powders. "She probably thinks that makes her sound like some sort of vigilante."

"She does good work for this planet," Loki replied.

Amora laughed. "Believe me, her work has much less impact than she'd like you to believe." She surveyed him in the mirror, her eyes narrowing. "Don't tell me you've grown fond of her."

"Of course not," Loki replied, then he changed the subject.

The Inferno Club was thrilled with the idea of a seance to contact the living dead and deliver a judgement about which of those two things they actually were – they prepared an entire night themed for the occasion, collecting newspapers with headlines about the spate of deaths and papering the club interior with them. Someone managed to procure crime-scene photos from several of the deaths, which could be viewed in a stereoscope for sixpence. A special drink was even added to the menu in honour of the occasion – Draught of the Living Dead, with a small note chalked on the board beneath it: *Served Warm.*

With the date set, posters went up around the city. The narrow streets of Southwark were so thick with them they obscured the dirty bricks. Theo and Loki went to the morgue daily to spread the word about the event among the crowd that seemed always assembled outside, waiting to see the bodies on display.

The protesters were there relentlessly, mostly the same faces day after day. Loki caught a few of them eyeing him and Theo and whispering to one another. A dark-haired woman, whom he recognised from the first day they had visited the morgue, was particularly prone to glaring at them each time they came. One morning, Loki caught her eye and gave her a small nod, which he meant to be more of a warning to stay away, but she took it instead as an invitation to approach.

"Excuse me, sir?" she called to him, her gait hobbled by the wooden signs strapped over her shoulders clomping against her shins. The front read LIFE IS PRECIOUS AND MUST BE PRESERVED. On the other side, NOT ALIVE IS NOT THE SAME AS DEAD.

Loki gritted his teeth and offered her his most unwelcoming smile. "Can I help you?"

"I thought it high time we met properly, as I've seen you around here so often. I'm Rachel Bowman." She held out a hand for him to shake. He didn't take it.

"I'm not interested."

"It seems like you and your companion are making quite the preparations." She glanced across the crowd, and Loki followed her gaze to where Theo was talking to a group of girls about his own age. He appeared to be trying to explain the seance to them, and they appeared to be flirting in return. He looked rather panicked. "Do you work for the Inferno Club?" Rachel Bowman demanded, and Loki turned back to her.

"Why does it matter?"

"I suppose it doesn't, unless the people you are trying to bury are actually alive."

"Who says we're trying to bury them?" Loki retorted.

Rachel scowled. "I know what you're planning. The Inferno Club is being paid off by the police to convince the families to allow their loved ones to be buried so they can wash their hands of this crime."

Loki burst out laughing. "Now, that's a theory I hadn't heard. Congratulations, you're certainly very creative and skilled at jumping to conclusions."

She extended a leaflet to him. "Perhaps you should educate yourself before you mock me."

"You already got me," he replied. "It's riveting reading, really. I've been up all night dying to see what happens next."

He started to walk away, but Rachel Bowman jumped in

front of him. Her signs bounced with the sudden movement, slapping him in the kneecaps, and he winced. "If you put these people in the ground," she said, her voice trembling with the effort of keeping it low, "you will be complicit in murder."

Loki folded his arms. "Last time I checked, they already had been murdered. That's why they're all laid out in a morgue."

"Have you seen them?" she jammed a finger towards the doorway. "I mean, have you actually looked into their faces? Have you touched their skin and felt its heat?"

"No," Loki replied. "As there's glass in the way."

"Well, I have." She seized him by the arm, her grip surprisingly tight. "I have seen them move. I saw one lift his hand."

Loki struggled to keep his face blank. Had she been there that day, somewhere in the crowd? He'd been so distracted it would have been easy to miss her. "I doubt that."

"That is not death, sir," she hissed. "Not earthly death. If you let this happen, I hope it haunts you. I hope you some day feel the weight of all you've done. I hope it crushes you."

"With all due respect, madam," Loki replied, prising her fingers from their grip on his jacket. "You have no idea what you're talking about."

Chapter Twenty-Six

The night of the seance, the Inferno Club was packed.

People had been queueing to get into the show since dawn, the line leading from the mouth of the tunnel growing at such an alarming rate that it spilt into the street, blocking traffic. The police had to be summoned when a carriage driver and a man waiting for admission got in a shouting match over his standing in the road that seemed likely to come to blows. When the club opened, the tunnel flooded, the crowd so thick and moving so fast that several of the plaster demons along the walls had their extremities broken off.

Theo waited backstage, while Mrs S was out in the

theatre and Amora finished dressing. Loki had volunteered to be Amora's lone chaperone for the evening, but Mrs S had maddeningly sent Theo along with him – like walking the Enchantress from her dressing room to the stage, then watching the stage to be certain nothing unplanned happened required a pair. Particularly when one-half of that pair had limited mobility that made walking anyone anywhere a less-than-ideal job.

"You know, I'm perfectly capable of handling things back here on my own," Loki said to Theo as they stood between the shafts of curtains, both of them shadows in the darkness. Beyond the edges of the stage, he could hear the rumble of the crowd, their excitement somehow rendering them unable to speak at a reasonable volume, for it seemed everyone was shouting. When Theo didn't respond, Loki nudged him with his elbow. "You should go watch the show."

Theo shifted his grip on his cane, his shoulders hunched. "I'd rather stay back here. I'm too easy to trample if I'm knocked down."

Loki stared at Theo, trying to get him to turn by the strength of his gaze alone. "You don't trust me," he said at last.

Theo made a soft humming noise with his lips.

"Still?" Loki demanded. "After all this time?"

Theo shot him a sideways look. "It's been a week."

"That's not an insignificant amount of time," Loki protested. Theo rolled his eyes. "Why don't you trust me? You follow me everywhere. You took my magic when I first arrived because you assumed I was going to put some sort of violent hex on you."

"In our defence, you did try."

"In *my* defence, you put me in a box, rather than just inviting me to walk downstairs with you, as you would with someone you trust. What did my father tell you about me, exactly?"

Theo was still staring determinedly out onto the empty stage. The lights were low, and his face was mostly in shadow. "Your father didn't say anything."

"Then why are you so suspicious?"

"Call it caution."

"I call it aggravating." Theo laughed. Loki wasn't sure how much of his own words was play-acting and how much was sincere – for some reason he couldn't fathom, it mattered to him that Theo didn't trust him. That none of them seemed to. Particularly since he was actively deceiving them and had done nothing to earn that trust. "I brought you here," he said, stepping in front of Theo so he was forced to look up at him. "I helped you. If I were scheming with Amora, why would I bring you straight to her doorstep? I have lit the stove every morning this week so you didn't have to waste matches. And I held the door to the stage for you, didn't I?"

"Yes, that's called *manners*. There's a difference between being sneaky and being well behaved. I'm sure Genghis Khan was very polite at a dinner table."

"I don't know who that is."

"He's sort of like your Rajmagarfen." Loki gave Theo a playful shove, and Theo laughed.

"Nearly time to start," Theo said, glancing at his pocket watch.

Loki offered a bow of mock supplication. "My dear chaperone, may I go fetch Amora alone, or do you need to accompany me down the hall, because who knows what magical trouble I may get up to on the way there? You know, my mother used to tell me if I rolled my eyes like that, they'd roll straight out of my head."

"That must be an anatomical folly on the part of the Asgardians," Theo replied. "As far as I know, there are no documented cases of humans rolling their eyes out of their heads. Observe." He did it again, even more dramatically this time, with his whole head. "I suppose you may travel unaccompanied."

"Ha. See, you trust me."

"Don't test me."

Loki knocked twice on Amora's dressing room door before he pushed it open. She was sitting at the dressing table, staring at herself in the mirror with her fingers pressed into her cheeks like she was making certain she was still there. "All right?" Loki asked her. "We're nearly ready for you."

She met his eyes in the mirror, and he was shocked to see tears there. Not the enormous pearls she had pulled out for Mrs S to prove how sorry she was, but a shine in her eyes she seemed to be desperately trying to fight.

Loki sank onto the stool beside her and took her hands. Somehow she felt more delicate than she had the last time he'd touched her, her skin thinner and her bones brittle beneath. She felt, for the first time in his memory, fragile. "What's the matter?"

"Where will you take me when this is finished?" she asked, and her voice wobbled.

"Somewhere else."

"Where?" she repeated, and her voice broke. "Is there anywhere else in this galaxy that will restore me to who I used to be? No matter what we do, I'll never be whole again. I'll never be *myself* again. I'm so tired. Loki, I'm so weak, I have so little left. I can't survive like this much longer."

Her voice was rising in panic, and he pressed her fingers to his lips gently. Her hands were shaking. "We'll find somewhere. I promise, I won't let you lose yourself."

She turned to him suddenly, and in the darkness, the paint on her face made her look ghoulish, cheekbones sunken and eyes rimmed in dark smoke. "You could take me back to Asgard with you."

"I wish I could."

"Why can't you?"

"How would we make it past the Bifrost?" he asked. "My father would never allow you back in his borders, let alone in his court. Neither will Karnilla."

"But if you had control over both of them?" she said.

His hands slackened round hers. "I don't understand."

"If you were king, you could bring me back to Asgard."

Anger rose inside him. "You know I can't do anything about that."

"You could—"

"No."

"But you won't." Now it was her turn to press his hands between hers. A tear slid down her cheek, and she let it fall. "You've given up. You're so determined to continue to cast yourself as the least-favoured son that you've surrendered any choice you have in the matter."

"Choice?" he repeated, his tone rising. "I don't have a choice if my father names me his heir or not."

She was standing now, wringing his hands between hers, then climbed onto his lap. Their faces were a breath apart. "If you love me – if you have ever cared for me – you would do *everything* you could to bring me home. To restore both our birthrights. Loki, I'm suffocating here. I'm dying. I never know which breath will be my last. I'm on the run because I sacrificed my life for yours. This should be you here in banishment – it could have been, but I gave myself for you."

He looked away. "Don't—"

She took his face in her hands and pulled him to her. "Please. I just want to go home. Is that so much to ask?"

"I'm not king—"

"But you could be. You should be. For you, and for me, and for Asgard. And if your father will not give it, you should take it."

He shook his head. "I don't want to take the kingdom."

"Why not?"

"I want to earn it. I want it given freely."

"Freely by a fool." She let her hands fall away from his face as she stood, stalking away from him and snatching her veil from the counter. "If there's no other way because your father is too small-minded, what choice do you have?"

"That's very villainous logic."

"So maybe we're villains." She whirled on him, her veil fluttering at her side like she had grown wings. "Maybe there's a reason people fear us."

Loki mashed his fingers to his forehead. "I don't want to have this conversation now. You have to do the show."

"Of course. The show." She swept her veil over her shoulder and pressed the comb into her hair, watching him. "The two of you are adorable, by the way."

Loki raised his head. "What?"

"What happened to not growing fond?"

"I don't know what you're talking about."

She gave him a withering smile. "Please."

"If I've grown anything, it's bored," he snapped. "And weary of this place."

"But not weary of Mr Bell."

"We get on. Why does that matter to you? Are you jealous?"

"And what do you think he thinks of you?"

"I don't think he's *fond*, if that's what you're asking."

"What do you think any of them think about you? Why do they follow you and doubt you? Why did they put you in chains when you first arrived? Have you looked at what your Mr Bell is reading?"

"Why does it matter what he's reading?" Loki asked.

"Believe me, darling. It matters." She pressed herself against his chest, letting her fingers trail along his jawline. The tears that had been shining in her eyes when he'd arrived were gone, vanished so completely he wondered if they'd ever been there at all. "I'd have a look before you cut your heart from your chest and offer it to the humans. You are no more a hero to them than you are in Asgard. You never will be. It was written in their mythology long before they met you."

"What are you talking about?" he asked, his voice hoarse.

"You're already the villain in everyone's stories, Loki," she replied, dropping her veil over her face. "Why not start playing your part?"

Chapter Twenty-Seven

*A*n eerie hush fell over the theatre as Amora took to the stage, a quiet too absolute for such a large crowd. From the wings, Loki felt a shiver pass over him as he watched her cross the stage with slow, purposeful strides that seemed to take too much effort. Beside him, Theo fidgeted, flipping the lid of his pocket watch open and closed.

Amora gave the same speech she had when Loki came to her show. The same instructions about the thin veil between worlds, the admonition to the audience to open their hearts and invite the spirits to join them.

Loki was hardly listening. He was trying not to stare at Theo, trying not to interpret the distance between them, or the lack of it, or feel his skin quiver every time Theo shifted. He was not fond. Theo was certainly not fond of him. Amora was goading him. She was jealous – that must be it. He had found companionship on Earth in a week, while she had been banished here for years and seemed to have found nothing but loneliness. She was doing what she did best. And he would not be manipulated by her.

"Here we go," Theo said softly, and Loki watched as Žydre Matulis took the stage alongside Amora. The set-up was different this time. Simpler. Just two straight-backed chairs facing each other – Amora in one, Žydre in the other and a small table between them for the talking board. Amora had rigged a mirror above the table so that the letters could be seen by the audience. Even from a distance, Loki could see Žydre's hands shaking as she reached into her coat pocket and withdrew a ring.

"This belonged to your daughter?" Amora asked.

"Yes," Žydre said quietly.

"And she is one of the bodies in Southwark Morgue, correct?"

"Yes."

"Not living, not dead."

"We want to know what's happened to her," Žydre said. "Where she's gone. If she's gone. And if she can move on."

Amora put the ring on the table and began to light the candles, digging into her speech again about her abilities to contact spirits who had passed from this life.

"Do you believe in any of this?" Loki asked Theo suddenly.

"Are you asking me if I'm a spiritualist, or if I believe in magic while I am literally standing next to an other-worldly god?"

"I thought I was an alien. That's what your name implies."

"Like I said," Theo replied, his eyes still on the stage. "We started with the acronym and worked backwards."

"I've been thinking about what you could call yourselves," Loki said. "Instead of the SHARP Society, which may have sentimental value but I maintain is completely daft."

"Who says we're changing it?" Theo asked.

"What about the SWORD Society?"

"What does that stand for?"

Loki waved a hand. "You come up with that part – you started with SHARP and worked backwards. I assume you'd be capable of such mental gymnastics again."

Theo shook his head. "It's sort of violent, don't you think?"

"What about something protective then? What about SHIELD?"

"SHIELD?" Theo repeated. "You think SHARP is daft and you're suggesting SHIELD?"

"I like SHIELD, because there's an *L* in there, so you can work *Loki* into it."

"Is that right?" Theo glanced at Loki, his lips twitching. "This society is now all about you, is it?"

"Of course," Loki replied. "It may have only been a week, but believe me, you'll never be the same now that we've met."

"I don't doubt that," Theo said, turning back to the stage to hide his smile. Loki felt his heart stall, and he almost stepped away from Theo without knowing why.

"What do you wish to ask her?" he heard Amora say onstage.

Loki glanced through the curtains. Žydrė and Amora both had their hands on the planchette, over the talking board. In the reflection in the mirror, he could see it was resting on the word *HELLO*.

Žydrė was crying silently, the tears on her cheeks turning her skin to porcelain in the stage lights. "Is it really you?" she choked. "Molly Rose, is it you?"

The planchette jerked across the board to the opposite

corner. Žydre gasped, her hands dragged with it as it landed over the word YES.

Žydre was quiet for a long time, her throat pulsing with the effort of holding back sobs. The whole theatre was silent. Beside him, Loki heard Theo catch his breath.

"Does this…" Žydre said at last. "Does this mean you… Are you dead?"

The planchette did not move. Loki could see Amora's shoulders were tight. She was using a spell to move the planchette around the board, but it seemed to be taking more out of her than he had thought it would. How weak had she become these last few days without human energy?

YES.

"Can you be returned to us?" Žydre asked, her voice pitching with desperation. She was half standing now, her fingers pressed against the planchette with such force her knuckles were white. Loki feared it might snap beneath her.

The planchette moved again.

NO.

"Are you at peace?" Žydre whispered.

A pause. Then, YES.

Žydre's head dropped, her shoulders shaking. "I'm sorry we sent you out to the market alone. I should have walked with you. I should have given you a warmer coat. I should have mended the holes in your boots long ago and let you wear your hair in curls to that dance—"

"It must be a question," Amora interrupted.

Žydrė nodded, her whole body swaying. "Do you forgive me?" she said quietly.

The planchette did a slow circle round the board. Then settled back on top of YES.

"Liars!" someone shouted from the audience. Loki peered out from behind the curtain, Theo at his side.

"Oh God," Theo muttered. "It's her."

Rachel Bowman was in the crowd, on her feet and screaming, partly at Amora and Žydrė, partly at the rest of the assembled audience. "She's a fraud with no real power! She's trying to make you a murderer! You'll murder your own daughter!"

"Fraud?" Amora stood up and stalked to the edge of the stage. Loki felt his stomach drop. *Let it go*, he thought desperately, wishing she could hear him. *Ignore her, it doesn't matter.* But it was too late. "You think I have no power?" Amora called.

"You're a cheat like the rest of them!" Rachel shouted, then she turned to the assembled audience. "She's asking you to kill your children! Your families! Your husbands and wives! Just so this city can be rid of them!"

"Let me show you power, you foolish human." Amora moved forwards, but Loki dashed onto the stage, seizing her by the arm and pulling her back. "It doesn't matter."

Something flew through the air and smashed across the stage at their feet, splattering them both. Someone had thrown a rotten cabbage and it was now oozing over the boards. Amora's face hardened, and she kicked the cabbage back at the audience. The front rows flinched with a scream as it burst against her boot. "How dare you!"

The audience was in disarray now, half trying to get to the doors, the other half being trampled by those trying to exit. Policemen were fighting their way down the aisles, trying to find Rachel Bowman in the chaos, but the crowd had swallowed her. Theo was escorting the now-sobbing Žydrė offstage, one arm round her shoulders.

Loki felt Amora test his strength, but he held firm. "Let it go. It's finished, you did what we needed."

"Powerless," Amora spat, trying to rip her arm from his grip. "She thinks I'm powerless. Let me show her what power looks like."

"Amora, stop." He yanked her into him, pulling her against his chest. "She's no one," he said quietly. "She doesn't know anything."

He felt Amora's muscles tense, and he thought she might try and tear herself away from him again. But then she relaxed, sinking against him so that he wasn't sure if he was holding her or holding her up.

"You're right," she said, her voice breathy. "She's no one."

Chapter Twenty-Eight

The police cleared the club and shut it down for the evening, but the patrons still roamed the street outside like restless ghosts. Žydrė had been given an escort home by Detective Ashford, and Amora was in her dressing room with Gem guarding the door to prevent any protesters from harassing her, or other distraught families begging for help.

"That didn't go quite as expected," Theo said as he and Loki sat in the deserted bar area, waiting for Mrs S as she tried to talk sense into the club owner, who was furious that the place had been emptied while so many patrons still had open bar tabs. "Do you have any idea how much that flamin' living-dead draught costs us?" Loki heard him shout.

"Did you speak to Žydrė before she left?" he asked Theo.

Theo shook his head. "But Mrs S mentioned the autopsy to her. I don't know what she'll decide about it. If she says no, we find some other way to get the bodies out of the city and stop this plague, I suppose." He sighed, his breath ruffling the curls hanging low on his forehead. "Are you going to take Amora away tonight?"

"I think Mrs S will want us to stay until the bodies are in the ground," Loki said. "And it may take some time to contact my father."

"What about the water?" Theo asked. "He gave us a way to find him when we needed help."

Loki considered, for a moment, telling him that Odin clearly didn't care whether or not he missed messages from the SHARP Society delivered via the washbasin, but he didn't have the heart. How could he tell Theo how little they mattered to Odin when they had given their lives in service to him?

"He's likely still away from the court," Loki said.

"Ah, yes." Theo folded his hands on the bar. "Looking for the lost amplifiers. Perhaps you'll have to wake Heimdall from his nap, then." When Loki didn't reply, Theo prompted, "Where will you take her?"

"There are a lot of places in the Nine Realms where she can't do any damage. Any accidental damage," he added.

"I believe the word you're looking for is *collateral.*"

He glanced over at Theo, and Theo smiled. Even in the bare light of the empty bar area, his eyes were bright, dancing with sharp curiosity. This world had given him a thousand reasons to walk away from it, but he had stayed. He had stayed because there was work to be done.

Amora's words rang in Loki's ears. *What happened to not growing fond?* The way she had said it made it feel like a weakness, like she was chiding him for missing a shot on the archery range or forgetting the sequence of the Asgardian kings.

He hadn't grown fond. Had he?

Theo was still watching him, and Loki couldn't let those bright eyes take any more of him than he'd already given them. He stood up, nearly knocking over his stool in his haste. "I'm going to go talk to Amora."

Theo reached for his cane hanging off the bar. "Let me come."

"No!" Loki said too quickly, and Theo froze. Loki took a deep breath, trying to loosen the sudden tightness in his chest. "I'm not plotting the destruction of the Earth with her," he said, trying to infuse his voice with light sincerity.

"I just want to see if she needs anything. Food or a drink. And make certain she's all right. It was a difficult night."

Theo stared at him, teeth working over his lip. His hand was still resting on the top of his cane.

"I'll be right back," Loki said. "Tell Mrs S if she asks."

Theo nodded. "All right."

Gem was still standing guard at the door to Amora's dressing room, but when Loki reached for the handle he said, "She's gone out."

Loki stopped. "What?"

"Said she needed some air. Put on her coat and left."

He had no idea where she would have gone. Or why. There was no reason for her to leave. And he'd told her to wait for him. He'd asked her to stay. "Which way did she go?" he demanded.

Gem shrugged. "Not sure. The road behind the theatre goes down to the water, though. She may be there. You never said not to let her out," he said indignantly. "Just to keep people away."

"Yes, well, I assumed you capable of picking up implications." Gem looked like he was about to ask for the definition of *implications*, but Loki cut him off. "If you see Mrs S or Theo, don't tell them Amora's gone."

Gem scratched his head. "I don't think I'm supposed to—"

"Just do it," Loki said, then stalked off into the night. As soon the theatre door had shut behind him, he broke into a run, not sure where he was going but certain what he was looking for. Somewhere dark, somewhere out of sight, somewhere hidden and secluded. This city was made up of crevices and shadows. There were so many choices.

But he found her down an empty street lined with brick-built flats, their chimneys belching smoke. She had someone else with her, someone pressed up against one of the walls. Amora held their mouths close together and breathed deeply, like she was inhaling incense. Loki swore he saw a shimmer in the air like he had through Theo's green-lensed glasses, saw the soul pass from one to the other.

"Amora!" he called.

Amora stepped backwards in surprise, and Rachel Bowman's body collapsed onto the cobbled street at her feet, her limbs puddled like an unstrung marionette. Living dead.

"Oh, it's you," she said as he approached her.

"What are you doing?" he demanded, seizing her by the wrist. He was shaking, furious she had gone back on her word and risked compromising all the work they'd done.

In contrast, Amora looked startlingly calm. "You were right," she said, nudging Rachel's body with the toe of her boot. "She was no one."

"Come away from her." Loki tried to drag her back from Rachel's body, but Amora stood her ground. She seemed to be savouring the scene, breathing deeply through her nose with her head tipped back to the sky. "Amora," he snapped, and when she didn't reply, he grabbed her by the shoulders, spinning her to face him. "You think this won't betray us? The SHARP Society has spent weeks thinking it's a murderer, and then as soon as we start to convince them otherwise, you go and suck dry the only person in that theatre who made a fool of you."

"She made a fool of herself," Amora murmured.

"It doesn't matter!" He wanted to scream at her, to shake her until she understood. How could she not understand what she'd done? How could her word to him have meant so little? "You've given it away."

Amora crossed her arms. "You're being hysterical."

"I am not being hysterical," Loki snapped. "You're being reckless and stupid. You want out of this realm? Because you won't get out of here if you keep doing *this*."

"Do *you*?" she challenged, her voice savage. "Or are you having too much fun luxuriating here with your human friends?"

He turned from her, his hands balling into fists at his sides, and returned to where Rachel was lying. "We have to cover this up. Help me carry her to the water. We'll throw her in the Thames. When she washes up it may look like she drowned."

"Whatever you say, Your Majesty," she said, but she didn't move. She stayed in the shadows, watching him hoist Rachel's body into his arms, with her arms folded.

"What's the matter with you?"

"I'm just not certain who it is you're loyal to," she replied coolly. "And I'd rather not take my chances."

"You." He let Rachel's body slip back to the cobblestones as he straightened to face her. "I'm here, aren't I? I'm covering up your mistake. This was all for you."

She didn't say anything. Loki bent down and seized Rachel Bowman's body again, this time hefting her arm over his shoulder. "Help me."

He thought for a moment she'd refuse, but then she grabbed the other side and they pulled up Rachel between them. The path to the water was steep and slick, but almost empty. The few people they passed hardly glanced at them. The neighbourhood was thick with bars, and it was not a strange sight to see two friends carrying a drunken third home over their shoulders.

Together, they carried Rachel Bowman down to the banks and dropped her body into the black water of the

Thames. As the gentle current carried her away, Amora turned and stalked back up the path towards the club.

"If this is how you want it to be," Loki called to her, "I'm done. I won't help you any more."

She waved to him over her shoulder, wiggling her fingers. "You'll come back to me."

"I'm done, Amora."

She spun on her heel and blew him a kiss. "Check those books. You've got so much still to learn, Trickster."

Loki turned away as she disappeared. He stayed on the banks, watching Rachel's body float farther and farther away until it was out of sight, another thing dumped into the water in the hopes it would be forgotten.

Chapter Twenty-Nine

When Mrs Sharp burst into the Society office three mornings later waving a newspaper, Loki felt his blood run cold, certain Rachel Bowman's body had been found and his plan exposed. He hadn't spoken to Amora since they had parted on the banks of the Thames. He didn't know how many more bodies she had left littering the London streets, or if she'd kept herself locked in her dressing room, starving herself of magic, or something in between, though she had always been one to go to extremes.

Either way, he was expecting to see her handiwork in the headlines.

But instead, in bold letters across the top of the

newspaper Mrs S dropped on the table where he, Gem and Theo were eating breakfast: AUTOPSY ORDERED ON LIVING DEAD; CAUSE UNDETERMINED, BUT DEATH CONFIRMED.

"They're dead!" Mrs S said, clapping her hands together in a merry bout of delight that didn't at all fit the morbidity of the statement. "Žydrė Matulis and her husband let them autopsy their darling girl, and the living dead have been confirmed as actual official corpses. They'll be taken from London to Brookwood on Sunday on the Necropolis Rail."

Theo picked up the paper, his eyes scanning the article. "It worked."

"It did indeed." Mrs S wrapped her arms around Loki's neck from behind. "I apologise for putting you in that box and keeping you magic-less when we first met – did I ever tell you that? Oh God, this is such fantastic news. We're celebrating. I'm going out for Chelsea buns. Do you want one? I'll get a box – you might think you don't, but you will once you smell them."

Loki sat in silence for a moment after she left. Theo was still reading the paper. "Did you know about this?" he asked suddenly, turning the page to face Loki. A small piece, overshadowed in the corner by the lead story, was about Rachel Bowman's body being dragged from the Thames.

"No," Loki replied. "Why would I know about it?"

"She's the woman who was at the show," he said. "We saw her at the morgue. I thought she introduced herself to you."

"She must have been drunk, interrupting the show like that," Loki said. "Then she tipped into the Thames on her way home and drowned."

"Perhaps." Theo turned the paper back to himself, fiddling with the corner. "You were with the Enchantress that night, weren't you?"

"Yes," Loki said. "In her dressing room. Weren't we, Gem?"

Gem looked up from his food, then between them. "He came to see her," he said to Theo, and Loki was impressed by what a careful sidestep of a statement it was. Not a truth, not a lie. He didn't think Gem had it in him.

---

*I*t took three tries to catch the attention of someone in Asgard through the magical connection to the arena's washbasins. It was a servant boy, who was more than a bit alarmed by the talking washbasin, and was still bug-eyed when Loki sent him off to fetch Thor.

"Welcome back," he said as he saw Thor's silhouette approaching. His brother's face dipped over the basin, long strands of hair tumbling over his shoulders and rippling the surface of the water. The disruption was reflected on Loki's end. "Did you find the Norn Stones?"

"Not yet," Thor replied, a raw note of frustration cracking his voice. "How goes the work on Midgard?"

"I think I've achieved what I set out to do here."

"That's brilliant. I'll tell father. He's just returned home."

"Don't – not yet. I have—"

Behind him, he heard the flump of the curtains and turned as Theo stuck his head through. "I'm going out and thought you might— Oh, sorry, am I interrupting?"

"I'm speaking to my brother."

"Are you really?" Theo's cheeks went pink. "Your brother, Thor?"

"That's the one."

"Tell him I said hello."

"I'm sure he'll be thrilled." He turned back to his brother's reflection in the water basin. "Theo says hello."

Thor frowned. "Who?"

Loki glanced over his shoulder at Theo. "He says hello back and that I'm both the better looking and more talented of the pair of us, all hail Asgard."

From the door, Theo gave him a salute as Thor cried, "I did not say that! Loki, tell this Theo I did not say that."

Loki heard the bell jangle in the shop. "What a shame, he just left."

"Who is he?"

"Someone I've been working with here. A Midgardian."

Thor's face broke into a wide and maddeningly sincere smile. "You've made friends."

"I have not," Loki replied crossly.

"I didn't mean it as an insult," Thor replied, then added, "Most people wouldn't have taken it as such."

"You learn to tolerate people when you spend so much time in proximity to them. That's what growing up with you taught me."

"Why are you getting defensive?"

"Because I haven't grown… I haven't made friends." He ran a hand through his hair, pushing it off his face. Behind Thor's head, shadows passed on the ceiling, and a voice that sounded like Sif's called for him to follow.

"Just a moment!" Thor called, then turned back to Loki. "What is it you've summoned me here for?"

Loki took a deep breath. "Brother, I need your assistance."

"Sorry, what?" Thor leant closer to the surface of the water. "What was that? I can't hear you."

"I need your assistance."

"Once more." Loki might have fallen for the trick had Thor not done a theatrical cupping of his hand round one ear to punctuate it.

Loki rolled his eyes. "You really are the worst, brother."

Thor, still committed to his cupped hand, accidentally leant too low and splashed the surface of the water. "Did I hear correctly? *You* need *my* assistance?"

"Don't make me say it again," Loki grumbled. "I'll turn to stone."

*T*heo hadn't returned when Loki poured the water back into the pitcher and set it in its place on the office shelves. He looked around at the cramped space and was horrified to realise he would miss it. What was happening to him?

Loki left the shop, the hanging sign clattering against its chains as it swung in the breeze, and began to walk, not certain where he was going until he found himself outside the door to Theo's flat. He'd been staying there since the first night Theo had invited him. He'd been staying there and had never looked at the books. Why had Amora told him to?

Ignore her, he told himself as he opened the door to the

flat. *She was jealous. She was goading you. She was afraid. She was lashing out.*

Everything was the same as they had left it that morning. A pair of Theo's socks were crumpled on the end of the bed, and his towel had slid off the rail of the washstand. Loki picked it up, folding it neatly before replacing it and trying not to look at the books. Which was difficult, since there were more books in the room than anything else.

Feeling watched, even though the room was too small for anyone to hide in, Loki crossed to one of the stacks and began to peruse the titles. It only took him a few minutes to find the volume Theo had been reading when Loki had found him waiting at the Inferno Club. When Theo had followed him there. The script along the spine was small, but he recognised the blood-red binding and lifted it off the top of one of the piles. *Tales from the North.* He hadn't thought anything of it then. He crouched down and tipped the cover open.

The first page was the title, *Tales from the North*, followed by *A Dictionary of the Myth, Lore and Legends of the Old Norse.* On the page opposite, there was an illustration of a ship. Loki froze. It was familiar to him in the same way the items in the museum were. The shape of the sail, the engravings along the mast, the curling head of the bow.

The ship was breaking over an icy wave, and on its deck were illustrations of what looked like Asgardian warriors.

These were the tales the humans had of Asgard.

He vaguely remembered one of his cultural tutors mentioning this – that in past generations, some humans had had an awareness of Asgard, and had worshipped the Asgardians as gods. They had written their stories, and used Loki's family as an example to teach their children not to be vain or prideful, to be brave and true, not to seek mischief. And now he held a collection of those stories, tales of what may be humanity's past but perhaps were Asgard's future. Time did not always take a straight path forwards. He certainly hadn't lived any epic-worthy poems yet.

But Theo had known him, before they ever met.

His fingers hovered over the next page. There would be no going back. There was no way to know if he was in this book, or what weight these words might hold. *You cannot live to fulfil or avoid what may come to pass*, his mother had told him on the day he had broken the Godseye Mirror. He couldn't know if these stories even were the future, or just inventions of human minds.

He turned the page.

Images flashed across his vision as he skimmed the book. Ships. Swords. Dragons. Some of the same stories of

Asgard's glorious past that he'd been raised on. He stopped, his fingers hovering over an illustration of a man with dark hair and an overstressed pointed chin, his lips spread in a leering, wicked grin. A hard, unflattering portrait of a man with a sharp smile and a cruel stare, beneath the title *Loki, the Trickster. God of Chaos.* A few words and phrases jumped out at him.

Vain.

Shallow.

Manipulative.

A cruel predator.

The father of lies.

He cheats.

He steals.

Murderer.

Villainous.

Villain.

Was this a description of him? Was this what he was, or what he would become? If the humans knew these stories, did that mean they had already happened? Time, he knew, was a slippery, changeable thing. But *villain*? Is that what he was destined to be? Was there even any point in trying to do the right thing if his future was already written in the myths, if he was the antagonist of everyone else's stories?

The floorboards creaked, and Loki looked up. Theo was standing in the doorway of the bedroom – Loki hadn't bothered to close it. "What are you doing?" Theo asked, but it sounded less like a question and more like he already knew.

Loki slammed the book shut as he pushed himself to his feet. "Just some light reading to pass the time."

He wasn't certain if he imagined it, but Theo seemed to lean away from him. His grip on his cane shifted. "I wanted to tell you."

"Tell me what?" Loki said. "That before I even arrived, you all had made up your minds about me? You had decided I was not to be trusted, that I was slippery and cruel and wily, because of a lot of old stories you had read about me? How disappointed you must have been when it was me who showed up instead of my brother with sunshine spurting out of his backside. I'm sure this book" – he flung the volume onto the ground between them – "has some very flattering things to say about him. Because he's the hero, isn't he? He was always going to be the hero. And I'm not. I could descend from the heavens surrounded in angelic light and give everyone in your realm cheese sandwiches and a unicorn, and you would all still know me only as the villain from the stories."

"I didn't know what else to think!" Theo replied. "It's all we have. These stories don't come from nowhere, do they? They're rooted in something. They told us who you are."

"No one gave me much of a say in who I am. You think my father and my brother are so wonderful and brave because some book told you so? Here's the truth: Odin doesn't give a damn about your little society. He doesn't give you a thought. Mrs Sharp's husband died because you humans don't matter to him. He didn't care enough to send help, or even consider it. I'm here because he's punishing me – you're my punishment. You are all wasting your time – wasting your lives – thinking you matter to the ruler of the known universe or that you're doing something to keep the Nine Realms in balance. You're nothing – not to Odin, and not to me."

He didn't wait for Theo to reply. He pushed past him, out the door and into the hallway. He heard Theo call after him, but he didn't turn. His father had taught him that only the weakest of warriors looked behind at their home. They kept their eyes forwards, knowing the points of the swords landed where their eyes rested.

*A*mora was in her dressing room when Loki opened the door without knocking. She was curled in a chair beside the fire, a steaming cup of tea on the table next to her, and her fingers tangled in her long hair, working it from its knots as she skimmed the newspaper on her lap.

She looked up as he entered. "What are you doing here?"

Loki didn't reply. Instead, he pulled a stool up beside her, reached into his coat and withdrew a pouch that he dropped onto the table with a hollow clatter. The drawstring was loose, and the leather slipped back to reveal the glittering shine of the five stolen Norn Stones.

"All right," he said. "Let's be villains."

Chapter Thirty

*A*mora reached out and touched a finger to the surface of one of the Stones. It sparked gold where her skin met it. "Where did you get these?"

"I stole them."

"From who?"

"Who do you think?" he snapped. He felt frayed and skittish, still raw from what he'd read in Theo's book. "From Karnilla."

"You're the thief your father has been looking for." She plucked one from the rough material of the pouch, holding it up to examine. The Stones were each slightly smaller than her palm, angular and translucent. Colourless. "And what exactly were you planning to do with them?"

He didn't want to tell her that he had grown weary of Thor's glorious successes and decided to stage one of his own. A priceless object had been stolen, and he would be the one to find it. Something no one else could locate but him. It felt silly and childish to say *so my father would notice me.* He couldn't find a true opportunity for heroism, so he had had to invent one by stealing. Perhaps Odin was right. Theo was right. All the books were right.

"The better question is," he said, "what are *we* going to do with them?"

Amora looked up slowly. He could see the spots along her jaw where she hadn't quite wiped away the greasepaint from her stage show. "These are the most powerful magical amplifiers in the Nine Realms," she said. "The two of us, with these Stones – we could level planets."

"Raise armies."

"Form mountains with our bare hands."

"Conquer cities."

"Conquer Asgard." She kept her head down, examining the stone, but her eyes flicked to his face, studying him for a reaction through her dark lashes.

"Come now," she prompted when he didn't reply. "There's no chance you stole these without the thought crossing your mind."

It had. Briefly. That his father had had a vision of Loki leading an army against his own people, an army of the dead that could only be raised by power like those the Norn Stones contained. But he had convinced himself his actions were noble. Noble adjacent. Noble in that he was operating within a system rigged against him, so why not rig it in return?

He cheats. He remembered the phrase suddenly from the book.

"How would we do it?" he asked.

"Your father laid it out for you," she replied. "You saw it in the Mirror."

"An army?"

"An army of the dead. Humans would never stand against Asgardians, but the dead raised and endowed with the power of the Norn Stones would. You have a train full of the dead, dead I have preserved perfectly, dead who will make fine soldiers for you. All moving this Sunday on a train that will cross one of the points where Midgard and Asgard are connected. You could open the Bifrost yourself with the Stones."

Loki suddenly remembered touching the dead chimney sweep with magic at his fingers. It wasn't a spell he could have done on his own – reanimation – but with the Norn Stones, he had already done it.

"What about all the human passengers?" he asked.

"We uncouple the carriages," Amora replied. "Take only what we need."

"And you'd come with me?"

"I'm never leaving your side again."

He felt light-headed. This close, he could smell her perfume, something with citrus and spice. It wafted over him as her head canted to the side. "Think of it, Loki," she said, and she fell to her knees before him, clutching at his trousers. "Think of it, my king." She climbed from the ground to his lap, her arms round his neck, the touch feather-light upon his shoulders. Her fingers stroked his hair. "It could be ours, all of it. Everything we deserve. Everything Odin and Karnilla have denied us. We could take it back."

He had considered it. He had thought of it for years. Him on the throne. Amora at his side. Magic restored to the realm, venerated in the way it should be.

But he had not planned on returning to Asgard with an army.

He had a sense it was a gesture his father would have a hard time overlooking if this plan did not play out in their favour. But he'd take a life in the dungeon in chains before he'd settle for one of lock-jawed smiles, pretending he was happy to be the second choice. If fate had dealt him a poor hand, he would stack the deck. Or cut the cards and deal his own. He would win.

"Yes," he said, and he leant forwards and kissed her. "Let's lead an army to Asgard."

*T*he Necropolis Railway station was attached to the terminal at Waterloo Bridge, with its back to the Thames, where barges bobbed in the dark water. The facade was dark red stone, with an iron gate where the lettering he'd seen them polishing the night before – the words CEMETERY STATION – sat in a curve above it. The station crest – a skull and bones with an hourglass – was engraved above the office door. As he crossed the threshold, Loki glanced up at the inscription: *mortuis quies, vivis salus.*

The Allspeak translated for him, shifting the words before his eyes: *A good life, a peaceful death.*

A bell over the door jingled as they entered the office, empty but for the assistant behind the ticket desk. He looked up as they entered and gave them a smile that felt far too cheery considering he was charged with monitoring a death train. "Can I help you?"

"Yes, sir." Amora threaded her arm with Loki's and led him up to the desk. "My husband and I need to book passage for Sunday."

"Very good." The assistant licked the tip of his pen and flipped open the ledger book on the counter in front of him. "And what is the name of the deceased you'll be accompanying?"

Amora's smile faltered. "Do you need that information?"

"For Sunday we do, as we're moving all the living dead from the city to Brookwood. The seats are reserved for family. Trying to discourage tourists and onlookers, you understand."

"Of course."

"So the name of the—"

"How long is the ride?" Amora blurted, though Loki sensed she was looking less for the information and more for a way to stall.

"Just shy of an hour," the assistant replied. "Sometimes we have to stop to take water, but we nearly always come in under." He pointed to a map pressed underneath the glass worktop and traced the pathway with his pen. "Trains leave daily at half eleven, and the scenery along the route is very comforting. Starts here in Waterloo and goes out to Brookwood in Surrey. Lovely cemetery, Brookwood. Largest in England. Not so crowded and dirty like the ones here. Worth the expense, if you ask me."

"Now, aren't you just paid to say that?" Amora asked him with a flirtatious smile.

The assistant's ears went red. "Well, yes, ma'am, but I'd be saying it either way. Has your service been booked yet?"

"Not yet."

The assistant tipped his ledger shut and reached for a small pamphlet, which he slid across the counter towards Loki and Amora, then began pointing out the different options with the tip of his pen. "We offer first-, second- and third-class funerals, which correspond with the mourners positions in the train as well. A first-class funeral allows you to select the graves and a permanent memorial. The prices vary with the plot size. Second-class funerals cost a quid, and the erection of a permanent memorial is an additional ten shillings. Should you not opt for that, we reserve the right to reuse the grave at a future date. Third-class funerals are buried at parish expense in the section of the cemetery designated for that congregation. No permanent memorials can be erected, but you can upgrade your ticket later. Services can be held at the station – we've got chapels for the Anglicans – and we can provide ham sandwiches and fairy cakes, for an additional fee. Are you an Anglican or a nonconformist?"

Loki did not understand the question, so he decided not to respond to it. "How many bodies will you be taking on Sunday?"

"We expect the train to be full to capacity, and each carriage holds up to thirty bodies, and we've got ten hearse carriages on regular rotation, though we expect to be adding a few more for Sunday. We're still waiting on final numbers from Scotland Yard. Now" – he took up his pen again – "I really must insist on the name."

Amora glanced at Loki, and he replied, "Rachel Bowman."

The assistant consulted his list, then nodded. "Very good." He withdrew two blank tickets from his desk drawer and dipped his pen again. "May I have your names?"

"Sylvie and Jack Lushton," Amora said, without hesitation.

The assistant inked the names, stamped the tickets then traded them with Amora for shillings. "Do try to arrive at least a half of an hour before the train departs," he said.

"It's such an awful business, isn't it?" Amora said. "All those dead people."

"It is awful," the assistant agreed grimly. "Some of the worst this city's seen. And I lost both my parents to the cholera."

"Whoever's done it must be vile," she said. Loki ground his foot into hers, a gesture he hoped would convey not to get carried away. Amora ignored him.

"I heard it was a disease," the assistant replied.

"I heard it was a serial killer," she said, leaning in confidentially.

"Blimey." The assistant turned white. "Do you really think?"

"We should go," Loki said, taking Amora firmly by the arm.

"Of course. So sorry for your loss," he said with a gentle smile. "I do hope you have a pleasant journey."

Amora dealt him a devastating smile in return. "Oh, I'm sure we will."

They left the station arm in arm, but Amora stopped them on the edge of the platform, looking out along the tracks that disappeared into the dark corridors of the city. Amora's grip shifted from Loki's arm to his hand.

"Stop gloating," Loki said, unable to keep the annoyance from his voice.

"I'm not gloating."

"You were, just now to that assistant."

"Oh, him?" She waved a hand. "He's no one."

"Until he goes to the police."

"And tells them what? Two strangers in his station were gossiping? Who cares about the police?" She spun round so she was standing in front of him, swinging their linked hands between them. "We leave Midgard in two days, and we are in possession of the most powerful magical amplifiers in the galaxy. Let me revel in my handiwork a bit."

"We need a better plan before we board the train," he said. "An hour isn't long to raise an army."

She stopped, her hand falling from his. "We have the Norn Stones."

"They won't change the spells. We'll have to crack open every coffin and wake each of them individually and then tell them to stay put while we go wake their fellows."

"Did your mother ever teach you runic magic?" Loki shook his head, and Amora clicked her tongue. "Frigga, I'm so disappointed. Runes are the way Karnilla does her work across the Nine Realms without leaving her perch in Nornheim. She has runes placed in all your father's outposts, then channels magic through them. It also makes it possible to perform spells you have nothing but energy to lend to."

"That's how the Mirror worked," Loki said, remembering suddenly the staves carved on each side.

"Precisely. The rune directs the magical energy." She crouched down and retrieved a handful of stones from around the tracks, then began to lay them out. "If we overlay the *kaun*, which is the symbol for death..." She laid the stones in two lines to form one half of an X. "... with the *bjarkan*, which means liberation..." Two triangles joined with the lines, one atop the other. "... we have a spell for liberation from death. All we then need to do is infuse it with energy."

"So where do we place the runes?" he asked.

A wind rose suddenly, tugging a chunk of her hair free from its arrangement. It tumbled over her shoulder. "One on the train, and one on each of the bodies."

"And who controls the spell?"

"We both do." She nudged one of the stones, rearranging the shapes slightly. "We'll work together once we're on the train. We board with all the living humans, then make our way through. You take one of the Stones, I'll take the rest."

"Why do you need the rest?" he asked.

"I'm not as strong as you, remember?" She stood, shoving her hair from her face. "Not all of us have been luxuriating in Asgard building up reserves of power." She looked tired, her skin grey and her gaze swampy and as dark as this city. Her eyebrows were pressed together, and her thumb was skimming her lips. "Do you have them?"

"The Stones? Of course."

"Let me see them."

He withdrew the pouch from his coat and pulled the drawstring open, revealing a glance of the shining gems. She reached for them, but he pulled them away, shoving them back into his coat pocket. "We have to wait. Karnilla can sense when they're used. She'd catch us."

"It's hard."

"I know."

"I'm so tired." She leant forwards, pressing her cheek to his chest, and he let his arms fold round her, holding her to him. "I want to be home."

"So do I."

"I want to be with you." She tipped her face up to his, and he felt himself pulled to her mouth, almost beyond his will.

"Soon," he said, then again as she leant up and kissed him so the word was lost in her mouth. *Soon.*

Chapter Thirty-One

They went to Southwark Morgue under the cover of darkness.

The morgue was closed, the moon just starting to drop below the smoky clouds along the horizon, but the red-roofed pub in the alley was still bursting and loud, off-key songs rising from inside and patrons spilling out into the street. A few of them were standing at the morgue windows, their hands cupped over the dark glass, trying to see in. There was a policeman guarding the front door, his hands folded and a truncheon hanging from one fist. A drunk from one of the pubs was poking him in the arm, asking over and over again to be let inside, only to be ignored.

Loki recognised the officer suddenly – it was Gem.

"I can handle this," Loki said to Amora as they approached. "Stay here."

Gem didn't look at him as Loki approached. He was too busy growling at the drunk man, "Shove off or I'll have you in irons."

"Gem," Loki called as the drunk stumbled off, muttering to himself.

Gem looked his way and gave a small nod. "Evening, ma'am."

He wasn't sure how good his impersonation of Mrs S was. Good enough to pass in the darkness, he hoped, but the lights from the pub were brighter than he would have liked. He should have conjured a hat, though he'd never seen her wear one. "Can you let me in?" he called.

"In?" Gem repeated.

"Inside the morgue. I have the Enchantress, and we need to get inside before they take the bodies away."

"You and..." Gem's brow creased. "Her?"

"We need to test a few things," Loki said, with a vague wave of his hand. "Just to make certain the deaths will stop when she leaves Midgard. Earth. London." He mentally cursed himself for the slip-up but tried not to let it show in his face.

The creases in Gem's brow deepened. "I thought you said..." he started, but trailed off.

Loki folded his arms, alarmed by just how thin these arms were. Mrs S was remarkably small. "What did I say, Gem?" he demanded.

Gem's eyes darted down the street, like someone might be watching. "I can't be seen with you," he said quietly. "Or officially helping you. You said I can't lose my job."

"Well, listen to what I'm saying to you now," Loki said. "We won't do any harm. Come, Gem, don't you trust me?"

Gem took off his cap and rubbed a hand over his head, then replaced it with a nod.

Loki smiled. "Good boy."

He turned back to where Amora was waiting at the end of the alley, but then Gem called, "Did you find him?"

Loki stopped. "Find whom?"

"Him," Gem replied. "The God of Mischief."

"Oh. Him. He's gone back to Asgard."

"And is Bell all right?"

"Theo?" Loki asked, his voice pitching in spite of himself. "What's the matter with Theo?"

"I dunno. You said *affair of the heart* when I asked." Gem shrugged. "Dunno what that was supposed to mean."

He should have left. He should have turned and walked

back to Amora and not said another word that could jeopardise this disguise. But doing what he *should* had never been his strongest suit. "What did you think of him, Gem?" he asked. "Loki. The God of Mischief."

Gem shrugged, swinging his truncheon in a wide circle that reminded Loki of Thor with Mjolnir. "Seemed like a surly chap. Bit tense, though I suppose I would be too in a strange place."

"Do you believe all the stories about him?" Loki asked. "The ones Theo had in his flat?"

"Stories is just that, aren't they?" Gem replied. "Not worth putting much stock in. I'd rather know a man myself before I judge his character. Why? What did you think of him, Mrs S?"

"He seemed like a bit of a scoundrel to me," Loki replied.

"Yeah, well, so are you." Gem smiled. "I think that's why you liked him."

He had to stop. Any more of this and he'd want to turn round and run back to the offices at number 3½, or back to Theo's flat. Throw open the door and demand to know what 'affair of the heart' he was engaged in, though Loki already knew. He needed to hear Theo say it.

Instead, he swallowed. "Are you going to let me inside now?"

Gem dug a pocket watch from his coat and glanced at the face. "I got relief coming in twenty minutes. You'll have to be out by then."

"We'll be finished."

"I'll meet you round the back."

"Here, give me the keys so you needn't leave your post. I'll bring them back when we're finished."

Gem looked reluctant, but he surrendered his set. As Loki took them from him, he frowned. "Oh, you're not…"

Loki froze. "What?"

"Nothing," Gem said quickly, ducking his head. "Twenty minutes, all right?"

"I'll count each one."

The morgue was dark, the glass separating the hallways from the bodies on display looked opaque and glossy. The humans laid out on the tables looked ghostly in the faint glow through the windows, their skin luminescent, like the pale glow of the moon behind a cloud.

"Do you have your knives?" Amora asked, and Loki slid them both from his sleeves. "Here, let me have one." She held out a hand, and he hesitated only a moment before he handed one to her. "Don't forget." She took his hand

and carved the rune into his palm. His blood bubbled to the surface, then shrank back into his skin, leaving just a very faint impression and the sting. "They all have to be precisely the same for it to work."

"I'll get it right."

"You start here," she said, tipping her head towards the end of the hallway nearest them. "I'll go to the other side. We'll meet in the middle."

As Amora retreated, Loki approached the first corpse. A middle-aged man with dark hair salted with grey, and a neatly clipped beard. His eyes seemed closed so lightly that Loki almost expected that when he touched him, he'd wake. But he didn't have the Norn Stones on him this time. Somehow, these living dead were eerier in the dark, and alone, in the morgue with a hallway full of them.

Loki took the man by the chin and prised his mouth open. He and Amora had discussed where they might put the rune – nowhere that would be visible when the corpses were re-dressed and packed into their coffins. There had seemed only one option, but Loki felt his skin crawl more than he had expected when he reached into the man's mouth and prised his tongue from it. He had a strong inclination to pull his hand away – like he was afraid the man might bite him – but instead, on the tip of the man's tongue, he carved a delicate imitation of the rune on his palm. Blood bubbled up to the surface, and Loki doubted suddenly whether he was right – perhaps these people weren't dead after all. Perhaps their souls still existed somewhere. The dead didn't bleed, did they?

But this was what he'd chosen. Too late to start feeling empathy now.

He dabbed the blood from the man's mouth with the inside of his sleeve, then moved down the row to the next body.

He worked quickly and methodically, trying not to think about the warm flesh beneath his hands, how alive these people still felt to him. What Gem had said. He was in the second hallway, prising apart the jaws of a woman whose rotted teeth splintered from the force, when he heard the door at the end open – not the door to the hallway, but the one the public used. He ducked behind the table, crouching out of sight. Heeled footsteps echoed through the hallway. Not Gem – his boots wouldn't click so loudly.

Then Loki heard, through the darkness, his own name. "Loki."

A shadow blotted the glass, accompanied by a long beam of golden light that bobbed across the floor.

He stood, and the light stopped. "Mrs Sharp."

They met on either side of the glass. The beam of the lantern she unveiled turned it veined and gold as she held up a hand, tracing the shape of him, still glamoured in her form, against the pane. "Well, that certainly is eerie. Particularly with the glass here." She rapped one knuckle against it and it rang. "It's like looking in a mirror that has gone rogue on you.

"How did you know I was here?" Loki asked.

"Gem alerted me," Mrs S replied. "Though he said you did quite an impression."

As she raised the lantern, Loki realised what it was that had tipped Gem off to who he was – on Mrs Sharp's left hand, the gleam of her wedding band. He'd forgotten it.

"What do you want?" Loki asked, trying to paper over any cracks in his voice with the strength of it, but he didn't feel strong.

"Looking for you," she replied. "We've been worried."

"For me or the rest of the world?"

"Theo told me what happened."

"What do you mean *what happened?*" he demanded. "That I learnt my own story?"

The beam of the lantern guttered, then flared. Mrs S sucked in her cheeks. "I didn't know how much you knew."

"None of it," he said. "But it's already been written. It's

been told and retold. You humans know everything about me, so what choice do I have?"

"Everything's a choice," she replied, her breath fogging the glass between them as she leant in. "There's always a choice."

"Then I choose to be what you all think of me."

She smiled sadly. "That's disappointing."

"Are you surprised?"

"No," she replied. "But I wish it could be different. I wish so many things could be different. For all of us."

He saw Amora before Mrs S did, moving silently through the darkness like a shadow with her knife raised. A warning itched at the back of his throat as Mrs S touched the tips of her fingers to the glass, her lips parting to say more.

But then she caught the reflection in the dark glass and gasped, just as Amora struck her in the back of the head with the hilt of her dagger. Mrs S collapsed, the lantern tumbling from her hand and cracking against the tiles. Amora caught her, forcing her to her knees and pressing the blade to her throat.

She looked at Loki. So did Mrs S. Through the darkness, he felt their eyes upon him. He felt his fingers brush the glass, then fall. He did not know what he wanted. He did not know who he was. Everyone knew but him.

Amora buried the knife in Mrs Sharp's throat, then pulled it across, severing her neck. The blood was bright and jewelled through the darkness. It coursed down her front in thick rivulets that shimmered in the beam of her lantern, the candle still stubbornly burning. Through the glass, he heard the rush of air as it left her throat. Her body spasmed, and Amora released her, letting her body fall, still thrashing, to the ground. The glass between him and Amora was speckled with blood.

Amora could have stolen Mrs S's energy. She could have drained her and left her here in the morgue with the other dead, carved a rune on her tongue and raised her as a soldier, one more to join their ranks. But instead she had buried Loki's knife in her throat and let her blood stain the floor. If she hadn't thought herself a murderer before, in spite of the hallways of humans laid out at her hand, she couldn't have hidden from it now.

Everything was a choice. Amora had made hers.

And Loki had let it happen.

He dropped his hand from where his fingers had pressed to the window, half expecting to see the blood there too.

Chapter Thirty-Two

On Sunday morning, the train station was packed. Not just with mourners in their black crepe and veils, but with men and women from every class in London who had come to gawk at the Necropolis Railway full of the living dead, like they'd never seen a train before and hadn't been staring at the bodies on display in Southwark Morgue for weeks. The coffins were lined up on a barge with its back to the station, bobbing in the black water of the Thames. The day was appropriately grey, with heavy swirls of clouds so low they masked out the industrial smoke.

Loki and Amora stood on the platform with the queue of passengers waiting to board. They were both dressed in black, high-collared jackets and donned dark glasses in spite of the overcast day. No one looked twice at them. The mood on the platform was making Loki jumpy. With a crowd gathered round to witness a grizzly spectacle yet again, there was the same mismatched jumble of emotions as outside the morgue. The same merchants who had been hawking their wares at the morgue were here, offering bags of toasted chestnuts and postcards for sale. A group of children were running wild between the passengers waiting to board, their shrieks of laughter drowned by a bell from the station. He didn't like the mix. He wanted one feeling, one emotion, one face for him to read.

The policemen milling around seemed to share his discomfort. They had their truncheons out, or one hand resting upon them on their waists, prowling the crowd unsure of what trouble they'd have to quell. Loki shifted his weight on his flat shoes. He missed his heeled boots. He missed his black nails and his tunics, and he missed Asgard, he realised. He missed his home.

The line edged forwards, and as Loki moved with it, someone knocked into his shoulder, hard enough that he stumbled. On instinct, he grabbed the man, keeping them both upright, and felt the hard tip of a cane smash into his toe.

"Sorry," the man said, and they both looked up.

It was Theo.

His eyes widened when he saw Loki, and then he let out an astonished laugh. "You."

"Theo—" He reached out, not knowing what a consoling touch could offer, but Theo batted his hand out of the air.

"You are flippin' relentless, aren't you?"

"What are you doing here?" Loki asked.

"Mourning," Theo replied, and his voice cracked.

Loki glanced at the barge, still heavy with coffins. "Is Mrs S..." he started, but the words died in his throat as Theo's eyes narrowed.

"How did you know she died?" he asked, but it didn't sound like a question. It sounded like he already knew what Amora had done. What Loki had done.

"I..." Loki started, but a sharp whistle from the conductor cut the air. "They're boarding." He went to step past Theo and join Amora on the platform, but Theo stepped into his path, slapping his shins with his cane. Loki stopped, startled.

"Did you kill her?" Theo asked, and he sounded so tired. "Please, tell me you didn't..."

"I didn't," he said. His heart was twisting like a rag

wrung dry, but he snapped before he could stop himself, "Though I don't suppose you believe me, do you? What was it your book called me, *father of lies?*"

Amora appeared suddenly at Loki's side, taking him by the arm. "Come on."

Theo let out an astonished laugh. "Oh, good, you're here, too? What a pair you are."

"Stay out of this, Mr Bell," Amora said, her voice quiet. "This is not your concern."

"I'm not letting either of you on this train." Theo grabbed Loki, yanking him away from Amora, then reached suddenly into the pocket of his coat and drew out his wallet. He thrust it at Loki and, perhaps out of surprise or confusion, Loki took it. "Help! Police!" Theo shrieked, and Loki started. "I'm being robbed."

"Theo, wait—"

"Help!" Theo shouted again, loud enough that the crowd around them seemed to shrink away in unison, creating an unmistakable perimeter. "Help! I'm being robbed!"

Loki tried to pull away and dropped the wallet, but Theo grabbed him by the front of the shirt, pinning him in place against him. His cane fell between them with a clatter like a gunshot, and several people jumped in surprise at the sound.

Amora was melting into the crowd, her head tipped down so that the brim of her bonnet obscured her features. "Don't—" Theo started to shout after her, but Loki called over the top of him, "Get on, I'll find you."

A police officer shoved his way through the crowd towards them, a middle-aged man with sagging jowls and a thudding step. "Is there a problem, gentlemen?" he asked, pushing up his hat with the end of his truncheon.

"This man just reached into my coat and tried to grab my wallet!" Theo said, shoving Loki away from him and pointing an accusatory finger.

Loki quickly decided the best way to extract himself from this situation was to appear to be the far more rational and less hysterical of the two of them, so he pinned on his best approximation of a warm smile for the officer, though he had very little warmth left in his heart. "Sir, allow me to explain."

But Theo pressed on, limping up to the officer and grabbing his arm. "You can't let him on the train, he'll probably rob everyone on board blind. Can you imagine what sort of wickedness it takes to rob mourners?"

This was becoming a scene. The line was stalled behind them, and people were craning their necks to see what was happening. Several women nearby clutched their purses against their chests, like Loki might suddenly snatch them.

The policeman shook Theo off his arm, then held out a hand to Loki, gesturing him back towards the train station. When Loki didn't move, the officer seized him by the shoulder and dragged him down the platform, away from the train. "All right, there, mister, let's you and I go for a walk."

"Please, there's been a mistake—"

The officer didn't let him go. "Well, then, this shouldn't take long."

Panic rose in Loki's throat. The clock above the rail station struck quarter to eleven. Fifteen minutes until the train departed. He looked round for Theo, but the crowd had already funnelled back into the space they had created around them and he was gone.

The officer dragged Loki into the station and shoved him into one of the chairs near the ticket desk. Curious, the ticket assistant looked up.

"All right then, friend," the officer said, holding out a hand. "Let's see your ticket."

Loki handed over the boarding card, and the officer examined it carefully, then held it up to the light. "Want to explain what happened back there?" he asked, still squinting at the ticket like he was searching for a flaw.

"Just a misunderstanding," Loki said, already half standing in preparation for bolting towards the exit. "I wasn't watching where I was going and I bumped into that, uh, young man and he misinterpreted my intentions as malicious. That's all." Out on the platform, he heard the train whistle. He could still make it.

"And his wallet?" the officer asked. "If you just knocked shoulders, how did it end up in your hands?"

"It wasn't in my hands," Loki replied. "If you'd been observing the actual scene and not just the hysteria of it, you would have seen it on the pavement between us. He must have dropped it."

"Let's just make sure it didn't happen to fall into your jacket, shall we?" The policeman reached for Loki's pockets to pat him down, but Loki slapped the policeman's hand out of the air hard, grabbed his other wrist then dealt him a sharp uppercut to the chin. The policeman reeled backwards, a thin dribble of blood trickling from his nose. Behind the counter, the ticket assistant let out a little shriek, and when Loki looked at him, he fumbled a door open at the back of the booth and disappeared.

The officer shook his head a few times, then pressed two fingers to his nose. He swore, eyes darting back to Loki. Loki leapt for the door, but the officer grabbed him by the collar of his coat, dragging him backwards in a sharp, unexpected tug. Loki lost his footing and crashed into the officer, sending them both tumbling to the ground.

The officer was fumbling for a silver whistle hanging about his neck. Loki swatted for it, but the policeman dodged and gave it a sharp blow. A single high, piercing scream straight in Loki's ear. Loki drew a knife from his sleeve, then rolled off the officer and to his feet. The officer was clambering up too, his boots clomping heavily on the tiles. Standard issue, probably given to him with the rest of his uniform. They looked too big for him, judging by his size and the sloppy gait.

Loki aimed and threw the knife, one precise blow into the toe of the man's boot. The man cried out – not in pain, but surprise – as the toe of his boot was skewered to the ground, pinning him in place. He tried to yank it from the floor, but the Asgardian steel stuck fast. He reached for his whistle again, but Loki grabbed the chain before the officer could and ripped it from his neck, then tucked it into his own pocket.

There were more police on the platform. They would have been alerted by the noise of the whistle. The assistant at the ticket window had disappeared as well, likely to call for help. The knife wouldn't hold this man for long – the blade would stay embedded in the soft tiles, but the officer would likely think to take off his boot after a few more minutes of that hard tugging, once his panic had quieted. Loki wasn't sure where his train ticket had disappeared to, and he wasn't going to hang around to find out. He took off towards the back of the station building. There had to be a door, something for staff, somewhere people could exit discreetly if needed.

He picked a hallway at random, trying to find windows and follow the sallow light. When he finally located a back door, it opened onto the dock behind the station, where the barges brought coffins in from the city to be buried. There were still a few dozen waiting to be loaded onto the train, a handful of dockers lifting each coffin between them and hauling it up the steep stairs leading up the riverbank and to the platform where the train was waiting.

How cruelly ironic, he thought as he ducked behind a shipping container and waited for the next gap in the workers. He'd be leaving Earth the same way he'd arrived: in a box.

Chapter Thirty-Three

The bodies of the living dead may not have stunk, but the coffin did. Curled beneath the lid, cuddled up with one of those warm bodies, Loki tried not to retch as his throat was flooded with the smell of rot and mould. He felt the coffin rise as he was lifted into the train. "Heavy one, this," a worker said, the words muffled by the wood. Loki felt the sharp incline when they took the stairs, and his head banged sharply against the end of the coffin. He closed his eyes. It was already dark enough that he could hardly see, but the symbolism of the gesture helped.

There was a lurch, and then the coffin stopped moving and everything was still. Loki waited, trying to decide if he was on the train yet or not. Then another lift, this one at an incline as though he were being hoisted, then he heard the scrape of the wood as the box was slid into a slot like he was being buried in a vault. He lay still, listening to the scrapes of the other coffins being loaded, then the roll of the grating as the carriage doors were dragged shut and locked.

He waited until he heard the first screech of the train wheels on the track, felt the carriage heave forwards. The coffin listed with it, testing its tethers. As the train began to pick up speed, Loki wiggled his legs free and kicked at the lid. It took three sharp hits before it burst off, knocking the coffin stacked on top askew as well, and his coffin tipped, the lid cracking when it hit the ground. Loki clambered out, stumbling as he struggled to find his footing on the rocking train. He had to get to the front.

The compartment door was locked, but he knocked it open with a spell and stepped out onto the small platform at the front of the carriage. The wind immediately ripped at him, tearing his hat from his head and tossing it into the passing countryside. They were still in the city, but the houses had become cleaner and farther apart. A few chickens wandered along the tracks, pecking at weeds springing up between the stones.

He couldn't tell how many carriages were between him and the passenger carriages. His and Amora's plan had been to discreetly make their way to the centre of the train and spread their spell outwards, then uncouple the carriages holding the live humans from those with the dead. He needed to find her. He grabbed hold of the ladder beside the door and hauled himself up onto the roof of the train.

The wind was worse here, and the beams were slick underfoot. From this vantage point, he counted eight carriages ahead of him, plus the engine billowing thick black smoke. The first three would be for passengers – one for Anglicans, one for nonconformists and one for those who were too poor to be either. Then two for the Anglican first-class dead, three more for the nonconformists then the rest for the poor behind him.

Loki moved forwards, careful step by careful step, heel to toe as he tried to stay on the centre beam of the roof, where it was the flattest and easiest to balance. He missed his Asgardian boots, with their thick treads that would have gripped this metal like the bottoms were coated with glue. He leapt to the next carriage, repeated his careful wire walk then leapt again. His feet faltered when he landed, and he almost fell, but managed to fall forwards instead of back, his knees connecting painfully with the boards.

Ahead of him, there was a latched panel in the roof, and he crawled forwards, groping for the handle. It was stiff with disuse, and his hands burnt against the metal as he wrenched it open, then dropped down into the carriage, landing in a crouch.

The carriage was empty – he had feared there would be policemen, but there was no one, just coffins in their slings bobbing gently with the movement of the train. They rattled against each other, their tops scraping grooves into their neighbours. The air smelt like new straw and freshly cut cedar. Clearly these coffins were more expensive than the one he had ridden in.

He dropped to his knees and slid his knife from his sleeve, glancing down at the faint reminder of the rune on his palm before he began to carve its likeness in the floor of the train. The wood was newly varnished, and it splintered in crystal chunks beneath the blade. He was only two strokes in when he heard the door slide open and felt the rush of wind. He raised his head.

Amora was standing in the doorway, her skirt swirling round her knees like a cyclone until she shoved the door shut. Loki stood, tucking his knife back into his sleeve.

"You made it," she said, and she sounded relieved.

"Did you doubt me?"

"Never." She held out a hand. "Give me the Stones. I'm going to faint without some sustenance. You have no idea how much self-control it took not to bleed the conductor dry."

Loki didn't move. "You didn't take Mrs S."

Amora's smile didn't falter. "What?"

"You killed Mrs Sharp, but you left her soul," he said. "That would have restored you."

"It doesn't matter, does it? Let me have my Stones."

"*Your* Stones?" he repeated. "I thought this was a shared spell."

Her still-extended hand closed into a fist. "Give me the Stones, Loki," she said.

"Here's the thing." Loki stood, tucking both hands behind his back. "No."

Amora laughed, but it was a single, startled burst. In the dusty light, her face had gone pale. "What are you talking about?"

"No, don't waste your theatre on this," Loki said, holding up a hand. He couldn't resist shaking his head as well, the picture of a disappointed parent. Odin had given him so much material to draw from. "It won't do you any good. I worked it out a while ago."

Amora had gone eerily still, like a rabbit at the sound of a twig snapping under a hunter's boot. "Worked what out?"

"That you were going to betray me."

She didn't laugh this time. She hardly blinked. For a moment, he doubted himself, doubted the web he was certain he'd been unravelling. "You think I'd betray you?" she said, her tone flat.

"Oh, I'm almost certain that's what's about to happen," he replied. "Though it took me longer to catch on to it than I care to admit. Love truly does make you blind, but fortunately for me I'm not much for sentiment. It's so very" – he flicked his fingers in disdain, like he was brushing a bug from the air – "human."

"I don't know what you're talking about," she said, and he had to admit, it was admirable how committed she was to this feigned ignorance. "Why would I betray you?"

"I wondered that too, at first. But then I started to think, why does Amora need me for any of this? What purpose do I serve here? I'll be helpful in raising an army of the dead, but the only *real* reason you would need me here was so that you could take the Stones for yourself and then kill me, leaving your own way to the throne clear. And you had that whole plan about invasion and raising an army ready so quickly. Too quickly, if I'm being honest."

"I would not inherit the throne," she replied. "What about your father and your brother?"

Loki waved a hand. "Odin and Thor are nothing to you. Warriors you can obliterate in your sleep once your power is restored. If you want the throne of Asgard, it will be yours. Except I'm the only one who would give you a fight you couldn't win. You and I, we fight a different kind of battle than the rest of our people. I'm the only one who can match you. And you knew that. And you knew I would fight you for the throne."

She crossed her arms. "Who says I want the throne?"

"Well, you certainly wouldn't be content living out your days as my royal sorceress. You've never been the right-hand type. You saw Karnilla leashed for too long to want that position. You want to rule Asgard. And there's truly only one person who would stand in your way of that."

Her tongue darted out between her teeth, wetting her dry lips. "This is insane."

He held up a finger. "Hold on, let me finish. It really gets good from here. So I suppose your first mistake would be that you bet on my love for you. Which, sorry, won't hold up. There are so many things I love more than you – for example, those high-heeled boots you gave me when we were younger. I miss those boots, I shouldn't have left them at home. Also, Asgard itself, and I'm afraid you'd run it into the ground. Also, I've got some excellent ideas for government-funded theatre in the capital, and I just can't imagine you'd have a similar dedication to the expansion of the arts."

"So why are you here?" she demanded, her voice snapping like a whip. "If you worked all this out so long ago, why didn't you reveal me to be the murderer of all these dead humans and return with a whole host of Asgardian soldiers to arrest me and take me back to your precious homeland in chains?"

"Because I plan to do that myself," he replied. "Odin wants the Norn Stones returned to Asgard and I'm sure he'll be thrilled to see you in prison as well – you are their thief after all; at least that's what I'll tell him. And you're the murderer the SHARP Society was looking to eliminate. All wrapped up in one little treasonous package. Let's see Thor do that in a single trip to Midgard."

She didn't say anything. They surveyed each other through the darkness, the silence split suddenly by the low whistle of the train. "Well, then, are we going to play that out?" she asked at last. "Where you try to capture me and I overpower you?"

He shrugged. "If you'd like. Or you can surrender now."

"I'd rather not," she replied tersely.

"Well, I've never been fond of being overpowered." Loki shrugged. "So we find ourselves at a stalemate."

He raised his hand, ready to conjure chains, but Amora threw up her own hands and sent a blast of white-hot energy at him. Loki was caught off guard and it knocked him flat on his back, his head striking the corner of one of the hanging coffins with a *thump*. Before his head could clear, she was over the top of him suddenly, conjuring another spell, but he kicked out, sweeping her legs. She fell hard, her hair flying from its knot and flipping into her face. He staggered to his feet, gathered a bolt of hot energy between his hands, and blasted the door off its hinges, then swung himself out onto the ladder and pulled himself hand over hand up to the roof of the carriage.

The wind was vicious, and black smoke from the engine pricked his eyes. He started running along the top of the carriage towards the front of the train, as fast as he could on the slick metal bar that divided the centre of the roof. He leapt to the next carriage, landing just as the roof splintered below his feet. He managed to roll out of the way as Amora burst through the hole she'd just created and landed in a crouch on the centre beam of the roof.

Amora straightened and faced him. The wind caught her hair, and it seemed to flash from gold to white, electric ribbons twirling through the air. She gathered a ball of blue energy between her hands and shot it towards him, the movement so fast and graceful he didn't have time to process it. It struck Loki in the chest, knocked him flat on his back, and he felt himself starting to slide down the incline of the carriage roof. He flipped his knife from his sleeve and dug it hard into the beam, stopping himself from falling to the tracks, but now he was dangling, muscles shaking, struggling to find the strength to hold on, let alone pull himself up. His feet kicked at the air, searching for a foothold.

Amora flicked her hand, and another shot of energy, as hot as the bowl of a crucible, washed over him. He clung to his dagger, his boots slipping against the side of the carriage. "You think I'd bow to you?" she shouted over the wind. "You think any man will ever bow to you? You'll never be a king. It doesn't matter what you do. It doesn't matter if you bring me back to Odin trussed up like a Yule goose with the Norn Stones on a chain round my neck. You are a second son, Loki. He will never see you as anything more than a second choice. A snake waiting to strike. You will always be too dangerous to trust. And too foolish to take what's yours."

He managed to catch his foot on the edge of the roof

and haul himself back up to the beam. He'd never fought another magician before. In battles, he had always fought against soldiers without powers, who didn't expect the skinny Asgardian prince to manifest and disappear or to be nothing more than a figment their blades passed through while he stabbed them from behind.

Amora laughed at his knife, laughed at the way his muscles shook, the way the wild wind threatened to throw him backwards. "You want to fight?" She held out a hand, and some of the beams of the roof snapped away, the metal and wood re-forming themselves into a broadsword in her hand. "Let's fight."

Chapter Thirty-Four

*L*oki leapt, but Amora vanished. He spun round, and she had appeared behind him. He ducked as she swung, the sword crashing into the beam of the roof and cracking it. He could feel the supports groaning beneath them. She swung for him again, and he was able to dodge the blow, this time swiping forwards with his knife. But it shattered in his hand, breaking into dozens of sharp fragments that buried themselves in the beam.

Amora hurled another blast of heat energy at him, and before he even hit the ground she was behind him again, her boot connecting with the side of his face. Loki felt a shudder down his spine. He landed flat on his back, the wind knocked out of him and his bones feeling cracked and sharp. A few of the dagger shards in the roof broke his skin, and he could feel blood starting to pool underneath him.

Amora grasped her sword and re-formed it in her hands, changing it into long ribbons that clamped down upon Loki's limbs, pinning him to the top of the carriage. She held out a hand and his own dagger re-formed, the slivers pulling through his skin to get to her hand. The pain was sharp and hot, and tore a scream from him, his neck arching.

Amora advanced on him, spinning his dagger against her palm and catching it. He'd die at the end of his own blade. "How did you think…" she said, pressing a foot into his chest and grinding her heel in, driving all the breath from him. The bindings seemed to tighten with each press and he gasped. "… that you could ever be a king? How did you think that you" – she pressed harder, and he felt his bones protest – "pathetic, weak, cowardly you" – he felt her heel break his skin – "were ever a contender for the throne? How could you not see it every time you looked at your father? Every time you looked at your brother? I didn't need to look into the future to know it. Asgard needs a sorcerer at its helm, but that sorcerer would never have been you. Not in any universe, in any realm."

"Don't tire yourself," he said, his voice coming out in

more of a breathless rasp than he'd expected. "You haven't much strength to spare."

Her eyes flashed. "Give me the Stones, Loki."

"I haven't got them."

"Liar." He felt her free hand combing his coat, searching his pockets and the inside of his waistcoat and tearing at the buttons of his shirt. He let her paw, using the moment to lie still and catch his breath. She screamed in frustration, pushing hard enough against his throat that he felt the roof beneath him moan. "Where are they?!"

"How should I know?" he replied. "You're the one who stole them."

She staggered to her feet, his knife still in her hand and pointed at him. "I don't need the Stones," she said. "I can do it myself." She kicked in the door on the roof of the train and jumped through. Her spell broke, releasing him from his bonds, and he staggered to his feet. His skin felt bright and hot, and he could feel the blood soaking through his shirt, but he followed Amora, dropping into the carriage after her.

She was on her knees between the rows of coffins in their slings, driving the tip of the dagger into the wooden floor and carving the same symbol they had used to mark the bodies, then pressed her fist to the middle. Something thick and black began to fill the crude lines, half smoke, half tar, lethargically inching forwards and beginning to glow. The rune pulsed, the boards sucking it up and leaving a charred image behind.

Nothing happened.

Loki snorted, brushing off his sleeves for the theatre of it. "Well, that was a waste of—"

The end of the coffin beside him burst. He felt a hand – an unnaturally warm dead hand – claw at his face, covering his mouth and nose as the corpse tried to pull him backwards into the coffin with it. Its nails dug into his face, ripping at his skin. He shot a blast of magic over his shoulder and the corpse recoiled. Loki scrambled away, but more of the coffins were bursting open, the living dead climbing out and standing to attention before Amora. "Hold him," she snapped, and two of the corpses seized Loki, twisting his arms behind him and forcing him to the ground.

"You're not strong enough," Loki said, laughing in spite of the fact that his head was being forced towards the ground by a literal death grip. She had more strength than he expected, but he didn't show his surprise. "Not without the Stones. You could barely wake this carriage, let alone this whole train. And you can't take on the Asgardian army with a handful of soldiers. Some sorceress you are."

He felt her step closer to him, saw the shadow of her hand

still holding the knife. She wouldn't kill him. Not so long as she didn't know where the Stones were. She stood still for a moment, and he could feel her weighing her options. Then she kicked him hard in the face, knocking him backwards into the two corpses holding him. He felt warm blood spray over his face. "Lock him in the last carriage," she said to her soldiers. "Don't let him escape."

Loki was dragged to his feet, and pulled towards the back of the carriage as Amora went the other way. His heart stammered – she couldn't know. She couldn't be going to look for them.

The corpse soldiers threw him roughly onto the floor of the final carriage. It was a wagon with no corpses, just stored equipment and a few benches and a stove for any railway workers that rode there. Loki heard the door to the carriage slam behind him. He let himself lie still for a moment, then wiped a stream of blood from his eyes. The bones of his face were aching and he sat up slowly. His vision spotted, but he stayed conscious.

There was a shuffle behind him and he turned, wondering if one of the corpse soldiers had stayed and he hadn't noticed. But then, from behind a set of stacked crates, someone said, "Loki?"

His breath caught as Theo crawled out from his hiding

place, dragging his bad leg. "What are you doing here?" Loki asked.

"They wouldn't let me on the train." Theo scrubbed his hands over his face. He was breathing hard. "One of the officers recognised me and… I can't leave the city because of my history. Gem sneaked me on. For the funeral." He looked up and started when he saw Loki's face straight on. "You're bleeding."

"I know. Is it a lot?"

"It's" – Theo wrinkled his nose – "not a little." The train jolted suddenly, taking a hard corner and sending them both almost toppling over. Theo clapped a hand to his head, holding his hat in place. "What the hell is going on?"

Loki had nothing to lose with honesty any more, so he said, "Amora is raising the dead to make an army. She plans to take them to Asgard and use them to overthrow my father."

"How's she going to get back to Asgard?" Theo asked. "The fairy ring?"

Loki nodded. "With the Norn Stones, we can activate it from here without the help of Heimdall."

"The Norn Stones?" Theo repeated. "The things your father was looking for? They're here?"

"I stole them," he said, looking down at his hands.

Honesty was not his favourite. "Now Amora wants them so she can animate everyone she murdered."

"So she did knowingly kill all those people? You lied to us?" He laughed humourlessly. Loki hated the way Theo looked afraid. Afraid and angry. He liked the anger. That spark of defiance. But he found no strength in this fear. "Are we just cannon fodder in your wars?"

"You know who I am," Loki replied. "My story has existed for centuries. It's written in every book you've ever read, every myth you adore. I am the villain of your stories. That's all I ever will be."

"So write new stories," Theo said, the belligerence rising in his voice to match Loki's. "No one's destiny is written in the stars."

"I don't know if I have a choice," Loki said.

"There's always a choice," Theo replied. Loki heard Mrs S say it too. *There's always a choice.*

They looked at each other. Theo's eyes were shining.

"I wish I could make your world want you," Theo said.

"Yours too," Loki replied.

Theo pushed himself forwards, onto his hands and knees, then leant across the space between them and pressed his lips against Loki's. It was a soft kiss, chaste and closed-mouthed. When Loki didn't pull away, Theo's hand rose to cup his cheek.

"I hope you don't mind," he said softly, close enough that Loki could still feel his breath upon his lips.

Loki reached into Theo's pocket and pulled out the small pouch of Norn Stones. Theo stared at them. "Is that—?"

"Thank you for running into me on the platform," Loki said. "It was easier than finding you on the train."

The light off the Norn Stones reflected up onto Theo's face. His mouth was hanging open. "Why did you leave them with me?"

"Because I trust you."

Theo reached down and ran his finger along one of the edges of the Stones, the movement stuttered as he looked to Loki, like he might stop him. His hand closed round the pouch, the tips of his fingers brushing Loki's palm. "I don't know what you think you know about yourself," he said, "but none of it's true. You are the only one who gets to decide what you become. Not your father or Thor or the ancient Viking poets or the stars or any of them. They don't know a thing about you." His grip tightened, holding Loki's hand with the Norn Stones pressed between them. "No one gets to decide who you are."

Loki stared down at their hands. He didn't know what

to say. He wasn't sure if he believed it. Wasn't sure he dared. "It's so much harder that way," he said at last.

"I know," Theo replied. "No one to blame but yourself when you betray me."

Loki looked up at him, just as the train carriage jerked sharply, throwing Theo backwards and Loki on top of him. "What was that?" Theo asked.

"Amora." Loki pulled himself to his feet, then reached out and offered Theo a hand up. Theo retrieved his cane from where he had stashed it, then took Loki's hand.

"Do you have a plan?" he asked as Loki pulled him to his feet.

"Fragments of one," Loki replied. "There's a bit more improvisation than I'd hoped. I mean, there's always some improvisation. But this is getting concerning."

"What will you do now?" Theo asked.

"Stop Amora," Loki replied.

"How?"

"Like I said. Improvisation." Loki stashed the Norn Stones in the pocket of his jacket, then asked Theo, "If I get you to the front of the train, can you uncouple the carriages? Separate the living from the dead?"

"If you take me back to Asgard with you," Theo replied.

Loki released a breath, long and feathery. Theo held his

gaze, his face etched with stubborn determination. That brilliant stubbornness that had kept him alive in a world that had cast him out. "I can't," Loki said quietly.

"Yes, you can!" Theo grabbed his hand, clinging to him with such desperate ferocity that his nails dug into Loki's knuckles. "Please, there's nothing left for me here. Mrs Sharp is dead, and I'm alone, and I've got nothing. This world doesn't want me, so give me one that does. Please, Loki."

Loki was never letting himself grow fond of anyone again, he decided. It was too much strain on the heart. "All right," he said.

Theo perked up like a cut flower in fresh water, but then he stepped backwards, peering hard at Loki's face like he was searching for the lie. "Really? You mean it?"

"I promise."

"I'm not sure I trust your promises any more," Theo said with a crumpled laugh.

"Trust this one. Let's go. I'll worry about Amora – all you need to do is get to the front of the train and make sure the humans are safe."

Loki grabbed a pair of railway spikes from a discarded tool kit and tucked them into the waistband of his trousers, then blasted a hole in the roof and leapt up through it, pulling Theo up behind him. He didn't dare go through the train carriages – if Amora was going to each, raising as many dead as she could muster, her soldiers would slow them down. He leapt to the next carriage, then held out a hand for Theo to join him. Theo looked shaky balanced on the end of the carriage, clutching his cane, and he closed his eyes for a moment before he braced himself and jumped. Loki felt their fingers connect, and then suddenly Theo was dragged sharply downwards, nearly pulling Loki off the roof. He landed hard, his chin smacking the edge of the carriage, but his hands were still wrapped round Theo's.

One of the corpses had grabbed Theo's leg mid-jump and was now using him to climb to the top. Loki summoned his strength and yanked Theo up after him. The corpse followed, clawing its way onto the roof, but Loki was ready. He didn't have his knife, but he yanked a spike from his waistband and buried it in the corpse's wrist. Hot, foul-smelling liquid gushed from the opened veins and coursed between them. Loki twisted, and the dead man's hand popped off like a cork, the bone splintering. The corpse, seemingly unaware that its hand had been severed, continued to paw at the air with the gushing stump. Loki spun and jammed one of the spikes into the dead man's throat. More of that black, tarry blood coursed over his hands, splashing onto the roof. The corpse staggered backwards, and Loki snatched one of the Norn Stones from his pocket, gathering a spell to blast the corpse apart. But before he could, Theo raised his cane and bashed the man in the side, sending him flying off the train.

"Thank you," Loki said. "But I had that covered."

"Sure you did." Theo pushed himself to his feet, legs shaking. "Let's go."

They were halfway along the next carriage when a hand burst up through the wooden roof between them. Loki and Theo both stumbled, and Loki felt a hand snatch at his ankle. Nails dug into his skin when he tried to pull free. He yanked his leg up, hard enough to drag the woman latched on through the roof and onto the beam next to him. He was shocked to recognise her – Rachel Bowman, her eyes milky and empty as she swung at him. He ducked, then dealt her a hard elbow to the face that knocked her off the top of the train, and the wind snatched her. Another pair of hands grabbed at him, and he could see more pawing up from the carriage ahead. Amora was raising the dead, carriage by carriage.

Behind him, Theo was using his cane to whack at the corpses clawing their way up onto the roof. One yanked at his bad leg, pulling him off his feet, but Loki sent an energy blast at the corpse. Thick black blood sprayed over them both.

With the Norn Stone still in his fist, Loki focused his spell and sent a blast of energy through the whole carriage. He expected the strength to knock the living dead off their feet, but channelled through the Norn Stones, the spell obliterated them, each one vaporised. Loki stared down at his hand, the small translucent stone clutched in his fist. He felt powerful, the same way he had years ago when he'd broken the Godseye Mirror. Illicit, delicious power that only seemed to come from destroying things.

Loki turned to the front of the train, his eyes watering as the smoke struck them, searching for more hands, more signs of Amora. Where was she? She would have felt the use of the Stones, her spell breaking apart. He'd called her to him.

The roof was collapsing under them. Loki grabbed Theo and jumped to the roof of the next carriage, landing with Theo on top of him and all the breath knocked out of him.

"Keep going," Loki said, and they started off again.

They were one carriage from the place where the living and the dead were separated when Amora appeared.

She was between them. Theo had fallen behind, and she had come up through the centre of the roof. She grabbed Theo, yanking her to him and pressing a knife to his throat. She could have stopped his heart with a spell, but this wasn't meant to be a quick death. This was meant to be a trade.

Loki stopped. Turned back to her. They stared at each other, both breathing heavily. She looked exhausted. Her skin was grey and withered, her posture sagging. Without the strength of the Stones, she had raised her army but killed herself in the process.

Theo let out a small whimper of fear. "Give me the Stones, Loki," Amora called.

"Or what?"

"Or I'll kill him." She pressed the knife harder. "I'm sorry, was that not clear?"

"You think I'd barter for the safety of my realm in exchange for one man?" he shouted in return. "One human man?"

"I think you're far more sentimental than you admit," she replied. "I think you're weak."

"I am not weak," Loki said. "I am not your villain, and I am not your fool. I am a protector of my homeland." He thrust his hand in the air. "For Asgard!"

Amora stared at him, her forehead puckered in confusion.

"Sorry," Theo murmured, his voice hoarse from where her hand was pressing into his windpipe.

"What are *you* sorry for?" Amora snapped at him.

"He's just got very into his character," Theo replied.

And Loki released the illusion. It usually wouldn't have been possible to use so much strength on Earth, but with the Stones, he felt like a concentrated beam of light. The air shimmered, and suddenly the Loki standing across the train roof from Amora was Theo, as he had always been. And the Theo in Amora's chokehold was suddenly Loki. He struck backwards, knocking the blade from her grasp and flipping it into his own palm, then driving it hard into her shoulder. In his other hand, the Norn Stone glowed, the same spell that had vaporised the corpses now channelling through his blade and into her.

Amora screamed in pain, her grip on him wavering. Her body was shrinking and curling in on itself, like watching a life lived on the fastest speed. Her flesh began to suction to her bones, her face suddenly more of a skull, her hair turning white and kinked and then falling from her head. She shrank and twisted, and, in spite of himself, in spite of everything, in spite of the fact that she would have let him wither into nothing if she was on the other end of this blade, Loki reached out, the Norn Stone still in his hand, and grabbed hers. Her aging reversed suddenly, and for a moment, she was herself again. Vibrant and young and the girl who had taught him to belong to himself.

"I can't!" she screamed. "I will not return to Asgard this way. I can't go back."

"Amora," he said, and felt the surge of strength between them. "Please."

But she let go of his hand.

The wind took her, whipping her off the top of the train and snatching her from his view. Loki shouted, but it was too late. The train barrelled forwards.

The ceiling beneath his feet buckled, and suddenly the dead army was pawing its way upwards. Amora's spell was still in place, even if she had gone.

He turned forwards, and used the power of the Stones to part the smoke so he could see ahead of them. In the distance, his vision sharpened with this new channelling of his power – he could see the fairy ring. They were close.

Theo had climbed down between the carriages, throwing his weight into the heavy switch that would uncouple them. Loki raced to the edge and dropped down onto the platform beside him. "Do it now!"

He put his hands over Theo's and together they shoved until there was a creak and the hinge split apart. The train with the living began to separate from the carriages carrying the dead, the gap growing.

Theo turned to Loki, the wind ripping its fingers through his reddish curls. "To Asgard?" he said.

"To Asgard," Loki replied, then grabbed Theo by the shoulders and threw him off the carriage. Theo landed on the platform of the opposite carriage, which held the living, the gap between them now too wide to jump. He staggered to his feet, pressing himself into the rail and staring at Loki, watching them separate. "You promised!" he shouted.

Loki turned away.

The engine and passenger carriages passed over the fairy ring, and Loki channelled the strength of the Stones as his end of the train approached. Above them, thunder rumbled and Loki thrust his head back, staring up as the sky knit and unknit itself in stunning strands of purple and silver, not quite clouds. The Bifrost was opening. He could feel the initial pull in the air.

He knew he would regret it, but still he turned to look at Theo one last time. The carriages were far apart now, the dead carriages were slowing with nothing to propel them forwards. Theo was still pressed against the rail, but the hurt on his face had turned to something else. Disappointment. There was no surprise. He hadn't expected Loki to keep his word.

Then the air around Loki shimmered, the Bifrost tugging the train into another realm. He didn't get another look at Theo before his half of the train was lifted through the portal and away from Midgard.

Chapter Thirty-Five

*L*oki knew what it looked like, showing up with an army and one of the galaxy's most powerful relics.

He knew Thor knew it too. When he had warned his brother they would be coming, he had said it would only be him and Amora with the recovered Norn Stones, and asked him to meet them at the observatory with a battalion of soldiers. Instead it was three train carriages of the risen dead ploughing into Asgard, skidding down the rainbow bridge, tearing up shards as it went. The dead soldiers were climbing from the carriages, still in the grip of Amora's magic.

It was his father's vision. It was the scene from the

Godseye Mirror, Loki realised as he clambered down from the train, and his knees buckled beneath him. He was at the head of an army of risen dead, facing Asgard. He could see it all, reflected back at him from the obsidian surface of the Mirror.

He was exactly what his father had always known he would become.

But then a shadow fell over him, and he looked up. Thor was standing before him, Mjolnir in one hand, his hair twirling in elegant ribbons when the wind caught it. He looked like a warrior. He looked like a king.

For a moment, Loki considered it. He had the Stones. He had an army. What would happen if he took over the spell, turned the dead to his side and marched on the capital right now? Demanded his father surrender the throne? Pushed his brother from the bridge? Took his rightful place?

Thor held out his hand.

Loki took it, and let his brother pull him to his feet.

"I suppose I should have expected a grand entrance from you, brother," Thor said, swinging Mjolnir against his palm.

"You know me," Loki replied. "I love a little panache."

"Are you armed?" Thor asked.

"Always."

"Are you hurt?"

Yes, he wanted to say. "I'm fine."

Thor nodded, then raised his hammer. He stood just a little in front of Loki, the first step any of these undead warriors would have to get through to reach him. His brother was protecting him from his own army. It crystallised in that moment the difference between them. He would never be his brother, and his brother was the hero. So where did that leave him? *What* did that leave him?

Thor raised Mjolnir as Loki took a stance beside him. Around them, the Einherjar raised their shields, spears at the ready. Thor charged forwards, and smashed Mjolnir into the skull of the first corpse that charged them, the Einherjar surging round them. But the corpses weren't just coming towards them – they were crossing the Rainbow Bridge towards Asgard. They were going to flood the city, an unsuspecting population weakened simply by not knowing they should be expecting an army of the undead. The Einherjar would overpower them, but not without casualties. Not without loss.

Loki looked down at the Norn Stones in his hand. He had failed to deliver Amora. He was returning with these stolen relics and no explanation of how they'd come into his hands. No Amora to blame their theft upon. He'd be explaining himself with no proof of his noble intentions that had caused him to seek her out. Maybe they never had been noble.

He had told himself that if, as he suspected would come to pass, Amora betrayed him and made her own power grab, luring him to her only to make sure he was out of the way, he'd execute the double cross of his own that was waiting in his back pocket. Capture her, reclaim the Stones. For Asgard.

For himself. How could he claim noble intentions when their backbone all along had been to eclipse his brother, win back his father's favour after the disaster on Alfheim and put himself back in a position to claim the throne?

He could keep the Stones hidden. Wait until he had another chance to stage finding them. He could still look like a hero. Or he could unveil his power now, pin the blame on himself.

Loki looked at his brother, splattered with the black blood of the dead, the ground beneath his feet turning slick. Thor wouldn't hesitate.

Loki gathered the magic around him, a spell forming on the tips of his fingers. After Midgard, Asgard felt like an oasis, the air thick and humid with power. It buzzed inside him, vibrating to the tips of his fingers where the Norn Stones were clutched.

How much he could do with these Stones.

He closed his fist round the five Stones, channelling all the strength he had through their angled surfaces. The Stones glowed, releasing a wave of energy that nearly knocked him off his feet. Beside him, Thor staggered. The ground beneath them cracked and splintered. There was an electric-blue flash, and one by one, the corpses fell, their knees buckling and snapping beneath them, as they collapsed across the bridge. Each of them still.

At the end of the bridge, Loki could make out more soldiers running towards them, though they all had stopped to throw up their hands against the force of his spell.

When he looked up, Thor nodded once, then threw Mjolnir in the air and caught it. "It's good to have you back," he said, but Loki wasn't sure if he meant it.

O din was alone in the throne room when Loki approached him. No soldiers. No Frigga. No Thor.

His father's face was set as he looked down at Loki from his throne. Loki stopped at the bottom of the stairs. There was no point in delaying the inevitable. He opened his palm, letting the five Stones fall onto the steps between them with a clatter like soft spring rain. If Odin was surprised to see the Norn Stones, it did not register upon his face. He sat, looking down, letting them stew in a silence so long it became unbearable.

So it was Loki who spoke first. "In my defence, I was left unsupervised."

Odin's face did not change. His features were like steel, as sharp as the edges of the Norn Stones at his feet. "I will not ask what you were thinking," he said. "Because it is clear that you were not."

Loki kept his head high, but shame rippled through him. How he must look, standing at his father's feet, covered in soot and blood and the black tar that had filled the veins of the reanimated corpses, a smoking path of destruction leading from his feet all the way back to Midgard. "I had a plan," he said. "It isn't my fault it didn't all work out. If I had been successful, I would have brought you Amora and the lost Norn Stones."

"And instead you bring me nothing but excuses," Odin replied. He wasn't shouting. Loki wanted him to shout. "Do you know what this looks like, my son? It looks like treason."

Treason was a generous word for it. To show up with an army and stolen amplifiers. Though destroying said army should have at least won him a few points back.

Odin still didn't stand. "I wish you could at least tell me that you were hypnotised or enchanted or that some of her magic had a hold on you. Tell me that my son, whom I raised from birth, did not choose to bring this destruction upon his home and his friends."

It was an out. An opportunity to lie. To save face. But more than that, it felt like a trap. Like both he and his father knew the answer to this question, and if he said anything other than that, they'd both know it was a lie. Odin wanted to know he was a liar. He wanted to know his son was what he suspected – a trickster, a liar, the God of Chaos.

So that's what Loki gave him. "I was not hypnotised," he replied. "I was not enchanted, or bewitched. All the choices I made were my own, and not Amora's. Not anyone else's."

"Why?"

That was a trickier question, for he hardly knew himself. Because he wanted to be king? How could he say that when his father had not named an heir? It would sound foolish, another voiced truth that both of them knew in their hearts but neither expected the other to say aloud.

So instead, he said, "Because I wanted to."

"That is not an answer."

"I wanted to play with fire. I wanted to make bad

choices. I wanted to defy you." It didn't matter what he said, no matter how noble his heart had been – or at least, somewhat noble. At certain times. His father had seen him in the Mirror and assigned him his role long ago. Loki could have brought him all of Asgard's enemies knocked out cold in a giant cage, and Odin still wouldn't have believed his heart. "What do you want me to say?!"

"The only truth with which you need concern yourself," Odin said, "is that any man who sticks his hand into a fire will be burnt. You have disappointed me greatly today, my son."

"As opposed to what, exactly?" The vehemence of his own voice surprised him. Before he knew what he was doing, before he had truly considered it, he mounted the stairs and walked up to the throne, uninvited, and faced his father. "You have never given me a reason to believe you were anything but disappointed with me since the day I was born."

Odin shook his head. "You do not give me reason to show you anything but that."

"I have done terrible things, but you let me be nothing but those things. Tell me, Father, do you think me evil? Do you think me monstrous?" He spread his arms. "Did you need a villain and I was available? Someone to make Thor look prettier than he is so that when you give him the throne, everyone will be willing to overlook the thousands he's slaughtered in the name of peace and Asgard?"

"Enough!" Odin roared, flying to his feet, and Loki fought the urge to step back, that primal fear that Odin inspired in so many gripping him. But he didn't. He faced his father with nothing but stubborn defiance.

This, he thought, and he almost glanced at the Norn Stones discarded on the steps. *This is power.*

Odin's knuckles were white on his spear. "I could banish you," he said, as quiet as Loki had been loud. "I could send you to the darkest corner of the Nine Realms and strip you of your powers, or back to Midgard and let whatever is left of your Enchantress decide the best punishment for your treachery." He paused. Loki held his breath. "But I am a merciful king. Which you will never be."

Merciful? he thought, but Odin continued. "You are not fit to be a king, my son. You never have been, and no tutelage I offer can choke the darkness from your soul." He turned from Loki and began to descend the stairs to retrieve the discarded Stones. As he bent slowly, he said, "At the Solstice, I will name Thor the heir to the throne of Asgard."

Loki closed his eyes. Amora had been right. The deep, shadowed fear that lived inside him had always been right. He would not be king. Not only that, but Odin had never considered him a contender for the throne. Would never see him the way he saw Thor, a young, reckless creature whose rough edges could be sanded off with time and patience and lies. Loki was all rough edges to his father. All jagged and sharp and too difficult to touch without cutting yourself.

"Do you understand this?" Odin asked.

"Yes," Loki said, the word a quiet knife between his ribs.

"Do you accept this?"

"Do I have a choice?" he asked, the bite unmistakable this time.

"There is always a choice."

Theo's face flashed suddenly in his mind, the look in his eyes as he had split the train carriages, split them apart, as his chance to go to Asgard with Loki was ripped away from him.

There's always a choice.

He would never be king. He'd never be his brother. He'd never be a hero. He would never be Theo, cast aside and still strong without being brittle. He'd never be Amora either. He had proved that when he'd tried to stop their army.

What else was left?

He could be the witch. He could be the villain. He could be the trickster, the schemer, the self-serving God of Chaos, prove the mythology books right. Prove them all right in what they had all thought, that he was rotten from the start. He would serve no man but himself, no heart but his own. That would be his choice.

He could be the witch.

Be the witch, and know everything.